TWILA MASON

Piece by Piece

DESPERATE HEARTS BOOK 1

---

1. http://StreetlightGraphics.com

To Mom, for always saying "yes" to more books

Chapter 1

Aria

The weathered board creaked under Aria Sutton's feet as she pulled her keys from her threadbare jacket pocket. She shivered under the onslaught of Chicago's winter wind whipping her chestnut hair around her face and slicing through her to her bones. She blew hot air onto her stiff red fingers and slipped the key into the lock. Her body ached, and she longed for refuge as she flipped on the switch inside her half of the dilapidated duplex. Instead of relief, the sight before her sent her heart plummeting to the matted carpet, the flickering light illuminating an empty living room. Nothing. Pulse thundering in her ears, she sprinted to the bedrooms. Empty. Aria swallowed against the bile rising in her throat and backed toward the door, scanning the vacant space for clues. Everything was gone, but worse—everyone.

The blood drained from her face as she spun on her heels, colliding with a formidable mass blocking the exit. She pushed against it and regained her balance. The landlord, Vick, filled the doorway.

"What's going on?" she asked, hating the shrillness in her voice.

"I figured it was pretty clear, baby girl. You've been evicted." Vick sneered, baring his yellow teeth.

"But why? How? I paid the rent." Her stomach churned when she saw no signs of her brother. A twelve-year-old was too young to be alone on the streets in their treacherous neighborhood, especially at midnight.

"I guess Tasha didn't tell you about our little deal, huh? She asked me for a loan. Said she'd double the rent to pay me back. That was two months ago, and I still ain't seen a dime. Sorry, baby girl. It's business." He rubbed his thumb across his fingertips as he towered over her petite frame, his sick pleasure at the situation apparent in his wild eyes.

Of course her mother was behind this. "But… I didn't know. Give us another chance. Please. We don't have anywhere else to go. I can't pay double, but I could do a little each month." And not eat, she continued in her mind. She detested her pathetic begging, but she didn't know what else to do. She inspected the room again for any sign of her brother but found nothing.

Vick leaned against the door frame, eyeing Aria's slender body from head to toe and licking his lips. "Them jeans fittin' you good. Ya know, we could work out a little deal, me and you. I bet you'd be fun to do business with."

Her skin crawled as his eyes swept over her again. "No, thank you," she said, not bothering in the slightest to hide the disgust dripping from her voice.

Vick shrugged as he hauled himself away from the doorframe. "Suit yourself. Enjoy being homeless, baby girl. I'll be here waiting for you when you come crawling back. I'm always ready and willing to negotiate a deal." He winked and adjusted his pants as he stepped aside.

Aria's stomach heaved as she shoved past him, her nose burning from the assault of his body odor. Once outside, she gulped fresh air and squinted, willing her eyes to adjust to the darkness. Movement at the corner of the house drew her attention. Her instincts screamed at her to run away, but the need to find Ben overpowered everything. She clutched the Mace that lived in her pocket, finger ready on the trigger, and inched closer toward the movement. Relief washed over her as she took in the outline of Ben asleep among a pile of trash bags. She dropped to her knees, sending out a silent thank-you to the universe. Her brother was safe. For now.

A moan came from beside her, and she saw the shadow of somebody leaning against the house.

Aria flinched, but as her eyes adjusted further, her numb hands balled into fists of rage. "Mom? What the hell is going on?"

Tasha mumbled incoherent nonsense as her bony arm attempted to move, her eyes flittering open and closed again.

"I paid the rent. Why did you go behind my back like that? And why'd you borrow money from Vick, of all people?" Aria's face burned red-hot as her body trembled.

Tasha moaned again as her head bobbed forward then jerked upward, sending her dull blond curls flopping haphazardly until her eyes stayed open at last. "Aria... I'm sick. You know that. I needed the money... for my health."

"No, Mom. The only medical issues you have are being selfish and a druggie," Aria hissed through clenched teeth. She dug her nails into her palms, clenching her hands to keep from slapping the infuriating woman before her.

"Hey. You can't talk to me like that. I'm your mother." Tasha's head bobbed as she hurled the slurred words at Aria.

Aria scoffed. "My mother? When have you ever acted like a mother? Look at you. You can barely keep your head up long enough to talk to me. It's pathetic. That's why I work myself to the bone every day. I'm determined to be nothing like you. All we've ever gotten from you is your name on a shitty roof over our heads, and now we don't even get that. You didn't even have to pay for it. This is a new low, even for you." Aria stopped to catch her breath, the controlled effort of whisper screaming leaving her winded and with a pounding head. "Can't you go have sex with someone for rent? Or are drugs the only thing worth that kind of sacrifice? What are we supposed to do now? Where are we supposed to sleep? It's freezing out here. What about Ben?"

Tasha grunted as her eyes rolled back in her head. Useless. Aria's eyes darted around, desperate and seeking, as if the answers to her myriad of problems lay hidden in the dark. The hairs on her arms stood as she became hyperaware of people watching them, lurking in the shadows, waiting for her to fall asleep so they could steal their belongings—or worse. The same people she dodged every night on her way home from work. The lurkers using the cover of darkness to take whatever they wanted from the world.

She had to do something. Fast. A shiver rushed down her spine, as much from terror as from the ever-dropping temperatures. Resisting the urge to tuck her face down and huddle against the onslaught of wind, she tugged her thin jacket hood tight and kept her head high, her eyes making constant sweeps of their surroundings.

A passing car's headlights illuminated a graffitied pay phone across the street, a literal beacon in the dark. Digging through her backpack, she scrounged up enough change for three calls. Clutching the money, she scurried to the phone and angled herself so she could still see Ben's silhouette.

With trembling hands, she dropped some coins in the slot and held her breath as she dialed the number for Emily, her best friend throughout school. They hadn't talked very much since Aria started college, but surely all thirteen years of school had to count for something.

Four rings, and Emily answered. "Hello?"

Music and garbled voices permeated through the line. No doubt Emily was having a party and hadn't invited Aria. Again. Sure, Aria never would've been able to go, but being left out yet again still stung. She swallowed her pride, focusing on the matter at hand. "Hey, it's me, Aria."

"Oh. Aria." Shock rang loud in Emily's voice. "Hey, girl. It's been a while. Whatcha up to?"

"Yeah, sorry... This is kind of random, and I know it's super late, but do you think me and Ben could crash at your place tonight?" Aria chewed her lip as she waited for an answer. *Please say yes,* she chanted to herself.

The pause stretched on so long, Aria would've thought the line had disconnected if not for the party noise. When Emily finally spoke, her voice oozed fake sincerity. "Sorry, Aria, but I'm at my mom's, and she won't let me have anyone over right now. Total bummer, right? So sorry. I gotta go, though. Talk to you later, 'kay?"

Click. Aria gaped at the phone. So much for thirteen years of friendship.

She sent out a silent plea to the universe before dialing the next number.

Her second-best friend from high school, Marina, answered on the third ring. "Hello?"

"Hey, Marina. It's Aria."

"Oh, hey. How ya doing?" At least Marina's tone was warm.

"Well, uh, not so hot really. Can me and Ben crash with you for tonight?"

"Hang on. Let me ask my mom." Several agonizing moments passed before she came back on the line. "Hey, my mom said you can come over but not Ben. No boys allowed for sleepovers. Lame. I told her he's only twelve, but she won't listen. One pregnancy scare, and now suddenly I'm not trustworthy ever, I guess. Whatever. I tried to tell her I'm not a kid anymore, but she shoves the whole thing in my face about me still living in her house and blah, blah, blah."

Marina's rambling faded into background noise as Aria peered toward what used to be her house. She strained to make out the shape of her brother's slight frame among the trash bags. She refused to leave him to fend for himself on the streets. No way. Their poor excuse for a mother would never protect him. Tasha would sooner sell him for drugs than care for him.

"Thanks, but I need a place for Ben too. Sorry, but I have to go. Talk to you later." *Click.*

She stared at the remaining coins, shifting them around in her hand. One last call. It had to work. She reached into her backpack for her notebook and flipped to the page with phone numbers. Any other time, being so poor she couldn't afford a cell phone would've embarrassed her, but she didn't have time for shame. Name after name, a knot formed in her stomach as she realized how short her list of friends had become. Her breath caught as her finger stopped on Luke Hardin, the literal boy next door for the first fifteen years of her life. She couldn't ask him for help. Not after all these years. She ran through the remaining names, hoping to find someone, anyone, other than Luke. Nothing.

Her fingers trembled as she slid the change in the slot and dialed his number, praying he hadn't gotten a new one. She hung her head, ashamed at her new low. How pathetic. Her only hope was a guy she hadn't seen or spoken to in six years.

"Windy City Party Buses. Luke speaking. How may I help you?"

Aria froze, her throat closing up as her brain short-circuited from the sound of Luke's voice.

"Hello? Is anyone there?" Luke's deep voice blared through the phone.

Aria gripped the phone and forced her mouth to form words, for Ben's sake. "Hi, Luke. This is, uh... I don't know if you remember me, but this is Aria Sutton."

The line fell silent for a beat. "Aria? Hey. I'm surprised to hear from you. Of course I remember you. I'm not senile. How are you doing? Do you need to book a bus or...?"

She bit her lip and stared up into the night sky, wishing for an easy way to say what she needed to say. "Um, not exactly. I, uh... This is going to sound crazy and totally random, and feel free to say no, but... I was wondering if you know somewhere me and Ben could crash tonight. I'm kind of running out of options."

"Oh." Luke's initial cheerful attitude vanished. "Your mom hasn't changed much, huh?"

"Unfortunately," was all Aria could manage as she glared at her mom through the darkness.

"I can't come right this second—"

"That's okay. I understand. I'll figure something out," Aria interrupted.

"No, wait. I'm not saying no. It's just that I'm finishing up a job as we speak, but I can swing by and pick you guys up on my way home. It'll be another thirty minutes or so, though."

The apologetic tone in his voice stirred something inside Aria, something she'd fought hard to suppress for years. She moved her attention back to Ben and ensuring his safety. "Really? Are you sure? It's not too much trouble?"

"Yes, really. It's no trouble at all."

She straightened her spine, an ounce of the weight she carried on her shoulders being lifted by his words. "That would be great. Thank you so much. I'll pay you back somehow. I promise."

"Hey, no problem. I hightailed it out of there eight years ago for a reason. I remember how it is. Will you guys be okay until I get there?"

Aria's eyes burned hot with tears upon hearing the concern in his voice. "Yeah, we'll be okay. We're hunkered down beside the duplex. Same one we've been in for years." She hoped her voice alluded to more confidence than she possessed in the current situation. "Thank you."

As she sprinted back to her brother, pride and relief buoyed her spirits. She'd pulled through for him, yet again. As she watched him sleeping peacefully among the trash bags, his soft blond curls a wild mane around his head, her heart grappled with the torrent of emotions rushing through her. Pride at doing what their mom failed to do battled with resentment that she had to carry the burden in the first place. Relief that they had a place to go for the night sparred with guilt and shame for relying on others. In the end, she vowed to do everything in her power to keep Ben safe, her pride be damned.

Thirty minutes. That gave her enough time to sort through their meager belongings. One bag each would have to do. She tugged a trash bag from the pile, sending her mom tumbling to the ground.

"Huh? What's going on? Aria? What are you doing?" Tasha propped herself up on a wobbly elbow.

"I'm sorting through our stuff. I don't want to leave behind any-thing that's mine or Ben's."

"What do you mean?" Her speech was slurred.

"I found a place for us to stay tonight." Aria's jaw clenched as she shoved her mom's clothes into a separate bag.

"Oh. Good girl. Where are we going?" She reached a hand out-ward, patting the air a foot from Aria as if she were patting her on the back.

"Sorry, Mom. You can't come this time. It's only for me and Ben." Aria avoided eye contact, her tone as frigid as the weather.

"But... what am I gonna do? You're leaving me? Don't you love me?" Tasha employed her usual high-pitched whine akin to a tod-dler's, a tone that grated on Aria's last nerve.

Aria faced Tasha, fire in her eyes and ice in her heart. She gritted her teeth so hard she thought they might shatter. "How dare you try to guilt me," she said. "I've taken care of you since the day Dad shot himself. For twelve years, Mom. Twelve. I've tried so hard to do it all, but I can't anymore. But you wouldn't understand because you've never taken care of anyone. Not even yourself. Well, buckle up, but-tercup, because now you have to. And I'm taking Ben. I'm going to keep working my ass off to take care of him, but I've babysat you long enough. You didn't have to do anything but be a name on a paper, and you couldn't even manage that. This was the final straw."

"How can you do this to me?" Her mom wailed, grasping at the ground.

Aria's mouth fell open. "Seriously? You're seriously asking me that question? Are you insane? How could you go behind my back and leave us homeless? You put your kids out on the street to freeze to death. We could get molested or murdered out here, and you'd be too high to notice. If I take you with us, it'll be the same story. You'll do the same thing over and over. No, I refuse to let you shame me for this. You pushed me to this point. I have to take care of Ben." Aria shoved the last of her mother's things into the bag with so much force her hand pushed through the side. She huffed, tied off the ripped bag, and tossed it at her mom's feet.

She lifted Ben off the last bag, rubbing his arm to warm him. "Ben, wake up. I found us a place to stay. He'll be here in a little while."

"He? Of course it's a guy. I always knew you were a little whore," Tasha spat.

"You should know all about that," Aria shot back, glaring at her mother, whose eyes were rolling back in her head yet again. Finished sorting the last bag, Aria eased down next to a drowsy Ben, wrapping her arms around him, wishing she could secure him a protective cocoon. "We'll be warm soon. I promise I'll take care of you, Ben. Don't worry."

Chapter 2

Aria

Aria dragged her hand out of her pocket to check her watch. Again. With every passing minute, her desperation climbed higher and higher. She shivered against the plummeting temperature and tucked the blanket tighter around Ben. She blew hot air into her hands before shoving them back into her pockets.

Perhaps Luke wised up and decided he'd rather not take in two charity cases. Maybe he feared they would be leeches, taking a mile if he gave them an inch. Either way, she couldn't say she blamed him. She groaned, loathing herself and the charity case leech that life had forced her to become. Luke was smart to opt out of the veritable shit show she called life.

Headlights shimmered in the distance, growing brighter until they shone a path to her house. Aria's heart leapt. He came. Her beacon of hope had arrived in the form of a party bus.

Luke hopped out of the bus, and his loud whisper cut through the night. "Aria? Ben?"

Aria lumbered to her feet, pulling a sleepy Ben up with her. "Come on, Ben. Let's go get warm." She waved an arm to catch Luke's attention before grabbing the trash bags.

"Hey, sorry I'm late," Luke said. "The drop-off took longer than expected. One lady passed out drunk, and her friends left her lying in the seat. Thankfully, I do a walk-through after every drop-off, or she'd still be in there." Luke shook his head.

"You came. That's more than anyone else did. I seriously can't thank you enough." Aria shivered in the chilly air, her mind and body aching more than she ever thought possible.

Luke took the bags from her and cocked his head toward the bus door. "Let me get these for you. Go have a seat. I have the heater on blast. You can sit wherever."

"Hang on. There's something I need to do first." Aria studied her mom lying motionless on the ground next to what used to be her house. Through all the turmoil Tasha had caused, Aria couldn't extinguish her compassion. She knelt by the pile of remaining bags, hunting until she pulled out another blanket. Tucking the blanket around Tasha, she whispered, "Goodbye, Mom. Despite everything, I want you to know that I..." Aria blinked back unexpected tears and swallowed as emotion clogged her throat. "I wish it didn't have to be this way. I don't know what else to do. Good luck. Stay safe."

As she rose and walked toward the bus, her heart ached, wrestling with one of the hardest decisions she'd ever made. The glimmer of hope that she was walking away from her past and toward a better future served as her sole consolation.

"Okay, I'm ready." She gave Luke a nod, her heart too heavy for anything else.

Ben stumbled up the bus steps and collapsed on a bench seat with a thud. Within seconds, the low rumble of his snore filled the bus.

Aria lowered herself onto the bench across from Ben as her gaze traveled over the black leather seats and black walls. Blue rope lights outlined the walkway and ceiling contours. Green lights trimmed each window, which all had silver shades drawn shut. The back of the bus held what she assumed to be a minibar, also decked out in lights and silver. The pungent scent of alcohol hung thick in the air.

"Sleepy guy, huh?" Luke appeared beside her, his voice low.

"Yeah, he's a heavy sleeper. A good thing in our neighborhood. Sirens and lights don't faze him one bit. I'm not even sure he woke up enough to realize he got on this bus." As she watched her brother, she thanked the universe that she could protect him once again. She raised a hand to her mouth to stifle a yawn, the sudden warmth of the bus easing the tension from her body and beckoning her to sleep.

"How about we get home so we can all get some rest?" In two strides, Luke was at the front of the bus and buckling into the driver's seat.

Guilt gnawed at Aria as the bus rolled away from her house. Away from her mom. She chewed her lip as the blocks slipped past, taking her away from a life she'd always yearned to leave. Maybe she should've brought their mom along and given her another chance. But Tasha had a way of making the easiest things difficult, and eviction was far from an easy situation. With her mom tagging along, climbing out of the current pit of despair would be insurmountable. Aria had to keep her efforts concentrated on making sure Ben stayed safe at all costs, which meant leaving behind any extra complications. Add in the shame of begging for a handout from Luke, and the guilt ate her alive. She watched Luke as he drove, noticing he'd traded his long brown hair for a tidy cropped style, befitting a business owner. She found it odd how someone could seem so familiar yet unfamiliar at the same time.

She groaned and rubbed the tension at her temples. Unable to rein in her thoughts any longer, she made her way to the front of the bus and sat sideways on the top step, facing the dash.

Luke tossed a glance her way then in the mirror toward Ben, his dark eyes filling with concern. "Something wrong?"

"You mean other than the obvious? No, I just figured I'd come sit up here." As much as she tried to tamp down the guilt, it persisted like a severe case of heartburn. "Look, I... Thanks again, Luke. Really." Her voice trembled as visions flashed before her mind's eye of where she would've been if he'd said no. "You have no idea how much this means to me. To us."

"I grew up there, too, remember? I know exactly how much this means. That's why I'm doing it, honestly. And I know what it's like to be at rock bottom. It really sucks. I know you're in a horrible, rotten place emotionally right now. Trust me. But do you know the good thing about rock bottom? You can't go lower. All you can do is go up from here."

"Or you stay at rock bottom until you die." Aria's voice dripped with the bitterness that filled her aching heart as images of her mom filled her mind.

Luke drove in silence for a beat. "Yeah, I guess that's an option too. But it all depends on the person. On choices. You strike me as the type to make the better choices that will move you upward. People like your mom are the ones who make choices that keep them at rock bottom." He cringed as soon as the words left his mouth. "No offense."

Aria huffed, tucking one knee to her chest. "None taken. You can't say anything worse about her than what I've already thought. Trust me." Aria stared at her hands, her pulse quickening and her stomach lurching at the words forming in her mouth. "So, I, uh... I don't really have any extra money. I might need a day or two to figure out my next step for Ben and me. If you could let us crash with you until then, I'll find some way to pay you back. We could maybe... make some sort of deal. I'll do anything you want." Peeking up at him, she felt dirty and disgusted with herself, but she had to do everything possible to keep her brother off the streets. She couldn't let him down. If it came down to "doing anything" with someone, Luke was a million times better than sleazy Vick.

Luke shot a sidelong look at her she couldn't quite decipher, and she longed for a passing car or streetlight so she could see his face better.

When he spoke, his harsh tone told her everything she needed to know. "You don't have to 'do anything I want' to pay me back, okay?" He made quotation marks in the air with one hand and shook his head. "Is that the type of guy you take me for? Gee, thanks a lot."

Aria wasn't sure what colored her face the most, embarrassment or the heater blasting in her direction. She'd place her bet on shame. "Sorry, I don't... That's not what I think. I don't know. It's just... Why are you helping me? We haven't talked in six years, and we didn't exactly part on the best of terms. Sorry, but people don't help random people without wanting something back." She inhaled, her mind settling a smidgen from voicing the question that plagued her.

Luke's eyebrows knitted together in clear anger, and even in the dim lighting, his knuckles shone white as he gripped the steering wheel. "Random? You're not some random person. We grew up together. And yeah, okay, we haven't talked in a few years, but I've been busy busting my ass to rise above that place. You should understand that. Besides, if I'm such a bad guy who wouldn't help you unless it's for sex, why did you even call me?"

Aria hung her head, her spirit breaking under the weight of the truth. "Because no one else would help. My so-called best friends don't care if we're homeless. Everyone here has basically disowned me. My best friends never invite me to anything or even talk to me anymore. Emily told me they think I'm acting like I'm better than them by going to school and wanting to leave. They won't help me. But you left. I thought maybe you'd be the one person who wouldn't be so judgmental or mad at me. That maybe you'd have some compassion, even if we weren't really friends anymore." She sniffed, fighting to hold back her tears. "How pathetic, huh? The one person who helps me is the guy that stopped being my friend years ago."

"You're not pathetic. But everyone else in your life is for treating you that way." His voice softened, the hard edge of frustration gone. "And for the record, I still consider you a friend. Just because we didn't talk for a while, it doesn't mean I stopped being your friend. Honestly, there's been a few times over the years that I've thought about you and wished I could help you. I just never figured out how."

Her head jerked up, her heart somersaulting at the idea of him thinking about her. "You thought about me? Why?"

He shrugged, keeping his eyes on the road. "Because I knew you wanted out. I knew you had ambitions, same as me. You're the one who inspired me to be better, actually. I knew what your life was like, and you had no one else to help you. Your life was a lot harder than mine. Sure, my dad was an abusive alcoholic, but my mom at least halfway tried to take care of me. I didn't have a baby brother to support. My uncle let me work at the scrapyard to earn this bus. That gave me the leg up I needed. Compared to you, I was walking on easy street. I got out. I always felt like, with all the crappy hands life dealt you, you deserved to get out too. Maybe by helping you, I can give you the leg up you need."

Aria gazed up at him as the passing lights bounced off the hard lines of his face, giving her glimpses of the handsome man he'd become. His kind words reignited the fuse of her childhood crush, and the butterflies that fluttered when he had looked her way in their youth came to life yet again. Flustered, she scolded herself for behaving like a lovesick teenager. *He's only being nice because he feels sorry for you,* she reprimanded herself, dousing the spark and pulverizing the butterflies.

"So, what have you been up to these days?" Luke's chipper tone, an obvious attempt to lighten the mood, fell short of its goal.

Aria tapped her chin as if she had to think about her answer. "Let's see, work, work, school, and work. Stressing out. Trying to survive. Yep. That about sums it up."

"No time for any fun at all, huh?"

A sharp, bitter laugh escaped her lips as her mood plummeted. "Fun? What is this fabled fun you speak of? I don't even know what that word means. I can, however, tell you what is most definitely not fun. Fun sure isn't walking miles back and forth to college no matter the weather or the fact that you can't afford a coat, or umbrella, or gloves. It's no fun going to classes and working all day but also squeezing in time for homework and studying so you can keep the government grants that make the college classes possible. Fun isn't skipping lunch so you can feed your little brother. It sure as hell isn't fun coming home to find out your poor excuse of a deadbeat mom shot the rent money into her veins and now you have even more to figure out." She stopped, panting for breath, and realized she'd been yelling by the end of her rant. Craning her neck to see behind her, relief rushed through her upon finding Ben sound asleep. She braved a sheepish peek at Luke. "Sorry about that. Bet you didn't expect me to unload on you when you asked such a simple question. And I bet a pity party wasn't what you had in mind for your party bus, huh?"

Luke chuckled. "Feel better?"

She leaned her head back against the partition wall and closed her eyes, her mouth tugging upward at one corner. "I actually do feel a little better. I don't think I've ever said any of that out loud before. Of course, no one would've listened even if I had. It felt good to get it out."

Luke's hand settling on her shoulder made her eyes fly open. She sought his eyes, trying to read his expression, but only found a veil of shadows.

He gave her shoulder a little squeeze before returning his hand to the wheel. "Well, for what it's worth, I think the occasional pity party is perfectly acceptable, especially when you hit rock bottom. Let yourself feel all the crappy feelings so you can let them go. But from now on, if you need someone to listen, I'm your guy. I won't go AWOL this time or ghost you again. I promise."

Aria tucked her hair behind her ear, thankful he couldn't see the pink in her cheeks. "Careful. I might hold you to that."

A flicker of streetlight revealed the curve of his mouth. "Good."

Aria grinned like a fool into the darkness, her shoulder tingling where his warm hand had been.

Luke

The last thing Luke expected was having his old feelings spring back to life, but a slight touch on her shoulder had his teenage-boy heart rattling his rib cage. He gripped the wheel, trying to ignore the way his hand ached to touch her again. He imagined reaching over and taking her hand as she sat next to him, but his stupid bus only had one front seat. Catching glimpses of her sapphire-blue eyes in the passing streetlights sure didn't help him regain control.

Memories of the last time they had spoken flooded his mind, a most unwelcome guest. In an instant, he could smell the smoke and alcohol as they sat in a corner booth at the back of Tooley's Bar. She was only seventeen, and he was twenty, but no one cared to card people in their neighborhood. People casually broke laws every day with no one batting an eye. He could still taste the crappy beer he'd been drinking, his judgment getting cloudier by the minute.

Six Years Earlier

"I really am getting out of this place for good," Luke said. "I know people have this party-guy image of me. Sure, I do a little drinking maybe, but I've got to do something to get through living here. I made sure to never hit the drugs, though, because they hold you here. I can handle my alcohol fine. It's not holding me back. No matter how much they want it to. For the past two years, every time I come here, people get these smug looks on their faces like I'm proving them right. I can't stand it. Mark my words, I will leave here and not come back. I just need to drink sometimes to escape the pain. Is that so bad? It doesn't mean I'm failing."

Aria peeked at him through her lashes, the guilt written all over her face letting him know she'd thought the same about him. He watched her run her finger along the rim of her glass of soda. He'd always admired that she never had so much as a drop of alcohol or drugs, and he yearned for that caliber of strength.

She kept her eyes trained on her drink. "I get that. Everyone needs an escape. Mine sounds lame, but I read books. Every book is a new adventure. A new world to discover. The worlds better than mine give me something to hope for. Something to daydream about. A happy place to go when everything around me is going up in flames, which is basically all the time lately. The crappy worlds remind me I'm not alone. I'm not the only one with a sucky lot in life, and some even have it worse. Plus, you can get books for free, which is obviously a big deal for me. I've even toyed with the idea of writing my own a few times." Her cheeks flushed as she raised her eyes to his face. "See? I told you it was lame."

Luke studied her, watching her squirm under his stare. "I don't think it's lame. It's a lot better than my coping mechanism. A hell of a lot healthier, for sure."

"Yeah, I guess so." Her face lit up a bit.

He took a swig, further lowering his inhibitions. "You know, I never realized how mature you are. I figured you were like all the other girls and got obsessed with makeup trends and stupid crap while I've been out working."

Her face glowed under his praise. "Well, I haven't changed too much in the past few years. Just gotten older. Besides, I can't exactly play with makeup when every dime goes toward feeding Ben."

"Meh, you've never needed makeup anyway. You look better without it." He took another swig.

Aria scoffed. "Yeah, sure. That's why no one has ever so much as glanced my way."

"Ever stop to think it's because you're intimidating?"

"Me? Intimidating? How on earth did you come up with that? How many beers have you had?"

"No more than I can handle." He eyed her for a second. "You don't see it, do you? There are lots of ways to be intimidating. Size is one, but smarts is another. Everyone around here knows you're smart. We all go to the same school."

Aria folded her arms across her chest. "That sounds like a bunch of bull to make me feel better about no one ever being attracted to me."

He leaned back against the booth, his mind swirling. "Well, that's not entirely true."

She narrowed her eyes at him. "How is it not true?"

He shrugged, hoping he appeared nonchalant. His mind screamed for him to shut his mouth, yet the alcohol let it open. "I grew up living across from you. I was a boy with surging hormones watching my childhood best friend morph into a beautiful girl. You better believe I noticed you. A little too much, if I'm being honest. But I made myself walk away before I ruined both of our futures."

She gave a bitter grunt. "Yeah, sure. Nice try."

"It's true."

"Luke, I'm not blind. I've seen you notice plenty of girls over the years without once stopping to think about your future. Heck, I can see at least five right now." She made a point of scanning the bar and nodding toward a few women.

Luke leaned forward, elbows on the table, and locked eyes with her. "I know I have that reputation, too, but it's not as many as you think. At any rate, the difference is that those other girls didn't want a better life. They're fine with what they have here. No future to ruin, so it was safe. And believe me, I made sure there was no chance of an accidental kid. Despite my reputation, I don't sleep around, and I'm far from careless."

Aria raised a disbelieving eyebrow and pursed her lips. "Oh, really?"

"Scout's honor." He took another swig, and his gaze intensified as the alcohol carried his thoughts back to his teenage lust. "You know, I've always wanted to kiss you. It's too bad you're a little young for me now."

Her eyes shot up to his, at first full of surprise, but then something took over he'd never seen in her eyes before. "You say that like you're so much older than me. I'm seventeen. Besides, I won't tell if you won't."

He leaned forward, watching her close her eyes and swallow. Seeing her ready and willing emboldened him even more than the alcohol already did. He closed the distance between them. Just a couple more inches...

"Luke, my man." A voice boomed across the bar.

Luke twisted toward the sound as Aria's eyes flew open. He caught the hint of disappointment before she ducked her face back toward her drink. He pushed away the nag of guilt and disappointment, plastering a smile on his face as he greeted the boisterous man strutting toward them.

"Brandon. Long time, no see, man. How's it going?" Luke forced a casual tone as they clapped each other on the back.

"Long time for real. Dude, where've you been? You done abandoned all your friends. I heard you was living in a bus or something?" Brandon's voice carried a judgmental edge.

Luke dropped back to his seat and leaned back, heat traveling up his neck. "Oh, you know. I've been around. Doing a little of this, a little of that. Trying to stay afloat." Luke took a peep at Aria, whose eyes remained glued to her drink. All the alcohol in the world wouldn't make him admit he was a loser living in a party bus.

Brandon followed Luke's line of sight. "Oh, hey, man. Did I interrupt something here?" He jabbed his thumb at Aria.

Luke panicked, imagining Aria's reputation ruined by rumors and the legal ramifications of her being underage on the off chance anyone cared. "What? Oh, her? Nah. That's silly. She's just a kid, man." When Aria locked eyes with Luke, he winked, attempting to signal that he didn't actually mean those words. The hurt in her eyes, though, told him she didn't pick up the signal.

Aria stood, looking everywhere except at him. "And this kid is out past her bedtime. I better get home and check on Ben." She put a five-dollar bill on the table in front of Luke, which he knew she couldn't afford. "That should cover my drink. Nice chatting with you." She made eye contact then, the moisture in her eyes noticeable even in the dim lighting.

Luke opened his mouth to speak, but Aria spun around and squared her shoulders as she marched away. Luke's stomach knotted, and he wondered which culprit caused his nausea, the cheap beer or the fact that he had messed up things with Aria.

Chapter 3

Aria

Present Day

Aria studied Luke as he rubbed his temples. He'd been silent for a while, seeming to be preoccupied with something more than driving. She wracked her brain, trying to remember if she'd said something offensive, but came up empty.

He slowed to a stop and shifted the bus into park. "Well, this is home."

Aria scrambled to her feet and peered through the windshield. Even in the faint glow of the porch light, she could tell the house was nice. Nothing fancy but nice and orderly. Leaps and bounds better than anything she'd ever lived in. She peeked back at Ben, his light snoring rumbling to the front of the bus. "We can sleep in here tonight. I hate to wake him up again."

Luke crossed his arms over his chest. "Not on my watch. It'll get cold in here fast. Trust me, I know."

"It's still better than the streets," she countered.

"If you get the doors, I can get him in the house asleep." Luke dangled the house key in outstretched fingers.

"Are you sure? I know he's small for his age, but he's still pretty big."

"And I'm a lot bigger." Luke gave the keys a shake.

"Okay, if you say so." She grabbed the keys and shrugged at Luke's triumphant smirk.

The crisp night air slapped her skin as she stepped from the bus, forcing her to admit, to herself at least, that Luke was right about the cold. It wouldn't take long for the bus to be freezing. Walking to the front door, instinct took over as she scanned the area for threats and held the keys between her knuckles, ready to defend herself.

Luke trailed behind her, carrying a still-sleeping Ben with ease as if he were carrying a couple of pillows. As she unlocked the front door, Luke leaned in and whispered, "The lamp."

Aria stepped inside and switched on the lamp beside the door. The light illuminated enough of the house for her to see that the inside matched the outside, nice and tidy. Her nose welcomed the hint of lemon-scented cleaner clinging to the air.

Luke stepped past her, carrying Ben down a hallway off to the left. She followed him, averting her eyes from his broad shoulders.

She halted in the bedroom doorway, watching as Luke gently laid Ben on the bed and slipped off his shoes. Seeing someone else caring for Ben was a strange-yet-welcome sight that warmed her heart. She stood, watching the slow rise and fall of Ben's chest and listening to the gentle purr of his snore.

Luke's hand brushed her shoulder as he moved past her. He whispered, "He'll be okay. Let's let him sleep."

A shiver coursed through her body as Luke's whispered breath caressed her neck. She eased the door shut, careful to be quiet even though Ben could sleep through a police siren. He had. Several times. Aria wrapped her arms around herself, more for comfort than warmth, as she followed Luke back to the living room. Her eyes adjusted to the faint light, allowing her to see the kitchen along the far wall.

"It's not much, but I hope you like it." Luke waved an arm at the room.

"Seriously? It looks great, Luke. You've done well for yourself. And thanks again. Really. This means the world to me, to us. I don't know how I'll ever thank you enough."

Luke caught and held her gaze. "Look at me, Aria. It's no problem. Really. I promise. I meant it when I said I'm happy to help. Now, I'm going to go get your bags and lock the bus."

Before Aria could speak, he was out the door, reappearing a couple minutes later with their bags slung over his shoulder. In his clean house, the trash bags looked, well, trashy. Her cheeks burned with shame.

He set the trash bags down by the hallway. "The bathroom is the second door on the right, past Ben's room. Your bedroom is across the hall from the bathroom. I'll be in here if you need anything."

Aria held her hands up in front of her. "No, no, no. No way. You've done enough already. I'm not taking your bedroom. I can sleep on the couch. I don't mind. It'll be a lot more comfortable than the poor excuse for a bed at my house. Well, what used to be my house."

Luke plopped onto the navy-blue couch. "Nah, that's okay. I usually fall asleep on the couch anyway. I watch TV to unwind. There's no TV in the bedroom."

Aria bristled and crossed her arms over her chest. "Seriously, Luke. I don't want you to regret helping us. We're the beggars here. We will work around you. Not the other way around."

Luke grabbed the remote and wiggled farther into the cushions. "I don't regret it now, and I won't in the future. Don't worry about it. Why don't you get ready for bed? You look exhausted."

Aria put her hand on her hip. "Gee, thanks. I know I'm no looker, but you don't have to go complimenting me like that." Her voiced oozed with sarcasm, but inside his words stabbed her heart.

Luke kept his focus trained on the television, but his eyes filled with mischief. "I never said you weren't a looker. Just a tired one, is all. Now go get some rest."

With a huff, she grabbed her bag and headed for the bathroom.

Luke

Afer changing into pajamas, Luke lounged on the couch and flipped through the channels, settling on an old sci-fi movie. About fifteen minutes later, Aria walked into the living room, her shoulder-length brown hair slick from her shower. She reached up and tousled her hair, her shorts peeking out from under the oversized band T-shirt. With her arm down, his mind imagined her wearing nothing but the shirt, and his teenage hormones surged back to life.

She hesitated in the hallway, and he caught himself hoping she would curl up by his side and watch TV with him. Her soft body pressing against his...

Snap out of it, he chided, giving himself a mental slap.

She tiptoed forward, glancing back at Ben's door. "I wanted to let you know I actually don't have to work tomorrow. Well, today, since it's technically already Saturday. The gas station manager hired this other girl, and he's hoping to get in her pants, so I got fired. Who cares if a little boy goes hungry, right?" She shook her head with a scowl. "Anyway, I plan to do some job hunting. My job at the library doesn't pay much, so the gas station was my second job. I need something more reliable that pays better than the gas station, though. Maybe with less hours since I'm all Ben has now. Not that Mom's efforts amounted to much, but still. Do you get a newspaper?"

"Yeah, but I only get the Sunday paper for the comics and the coupons. I think the one from last week might still be in the kitchen. I have internet, though." He pointed to a computer to her right.

Her eyes followed his and widened. "Oh, wow. That's great. I'll search for some apartments too. This isn't forever. I don't intend to outstay our welcome. I needed you to know that before I could even think about sleeping."

Luke held back a chuckle. "Still a planner, I see. Honestly, I'm not worried about how long you'll stay. Promise. Now please, go get some sleep."

She studied him, and he wished more than anything that he could read her mind. He wondered if she was drowning in old memories and feelings, too, or if he was the only sappy fool. She took a step down the hallway but paused and spun back toward him, her mouth open.

"Just sleep in the dang bed. Please. It's fine," he blurted before she could get a word out. He must've guessed right because she huffed and stalked off to the bedroom. That was the Aria he remembered, full of sexy spunk that drove him crazy in the best of ways.

Chapter 4

Aria

Aria groaned as she forced her eyelids open. Sunlight streamed through the side of the curtain, and she winced as her pupils constricted. Wait. *Sunlight?* She never woke up to sunlight. She bolted upright, her head spinning as her eyes darted around the unfamiliar room.

A man's shirt hanging on the door jogged her memory, the events of the night before filling her mind. Being evicted wasn't a horrible nightmare but a harsh reality instead. As her chest tightened, she squeezed her eyes shut again, willing herself back to sleep so she could pretend she was living someone else's life.

With her eyes closed tight, she focused on her breathing to stave off the impending panic attack. The mattress and comforter enveloped her in a marshmallowy softness. She inhaled deeply as she sank farther under the comforter, the smell of Luke's earthy cologne filling her nose. Or maybe it was his shampoo. Either way, it smelled amazing and soothed her frayed nerves like nothing she'd ever experienced before. *A girl could get used to this.*

Laughter bounced down the hall, drawing her out of her dreamland. Reluctantly, she crawled out of her Luke-scented marshmallow cocoon and yawned as she shuffled to the door. Her hand flew to shield her squinting eyes against the brightness of the living room. Following the voices through the living room, she found Ben and Luke at a small table off the kitchen.

The instant Ben saw her, he set his orange juice down and beamed at her. "This place is amazing. You hit the jackpot when you called Luke."

"Thanks, but I couldn't have done it without Luke." Tears sprang to her eyes as gratitude filled her heart. "You know I'll always take care of you, right?"

"Yeah, I know." Ben's face scrunched. "But nothing this big has happened before. When Vick came and started throwing all our stuff outside and yelling, I didn't know what to do. Mom just lay on the couch and let him do it. He dragged her outside and then grabbed my arm and pulled me out there too. I didn't cry, though. Everyone was pointing at us and laughing. I picked up all our stuff off the ground and made a fort with the bags so I could hide. I thought I was going to puke." His pale-blue eyes darkened with tears.

Aria patted his blond curls. "I know that had to be traumatic for you. It was scary for me, too, when I got home. But I want you to know it's perfectly okay to cry. Crying doesn't make you weak. It's not bad. Okay?"

Ben nodded, wordless.

Raising her eyes, Aria found Luke watching them. She cringed inwardly at the sympathy seeping from his face, something she didn't want or need from anyone but especially not from Luke. She ruffled Ben's hair and plastered on a cheerful face. "Do I smell bacon?"

Ben's face brightened like the flip of a switch. "Yeah, it's so good. I think I ate a pound of it. Plus, Luke fried me, like, six eggs and made me four pieces of toast. He has so much food. I don't think I've ever been this full." He rubbed his belly and sighed with satisfaction.

Aria glued her eyes to the floor, her cheeks blazing with shame. Now Luke knew how bad their food situation had gotten, even with her working herself to the bone. "Whoa, there, bud. We don't need to be eating Luke out of house and home. Can you slow it down some?"

"But I was starving," Ben wailed, using his irritating whine that made Aria grind her teeth.

"I told him it was okay," Luke said. "And it is, I promise. I had extra made for you, but it looks like it vanished." He waved his arm over the table as he nodded at Ben. "No worries, though. I'll make some fresh. It would've gotten cold anyway."

As Luke sauntered toward the stove, Aria noticed the clock showed a little after eleven. "Oh, my gosh. I can't believe I slept that late. I don't think I've slept past six in... well, as long as I can remember. Sorry, I should've been up hours ago."

"Sorry? No need to apologize for anything. You mentioned you didn't have to work today, and I figured you needed the rest. Though keeping loudmouth here quiet was a challenge." Luke jutted his head toward Ben.

Aria looked at Ben, who snickered and beamed as if he'd won the lottery. The crack of an egg drew her attention back to Luke. She stepped up to the stove and hovered a hand over the skillet handle. "I can cook for myself. You've done enough. More than enough."

Luke cracked another egg. "Nonsense. You had a long, crappy day yesterday. Have a seat. I'll have you some food whipped up in no time." When she didn't move, he gave her a playful push. "Go. Sit. Rest."

Aria stalked over to the table and plopped down beside Ben, crossing her arms over her chest in mock annoyance. "Fine. I'll sit and eat your food, but I don't have to like it."

Luke guffawed. "You'll survive."

Aria contemplated that word, rolling it around in her brain. Survive. She supposed she would survive. She always had. Even if she'd barely hung on by a single dingy thread a few times, it still counted as survival. But she didn't want to just survive all the time. She wanted to chase her dreams and maybe even relax now and then—to start actually living.

Her thoughts traveled back to her words a minute ago, that she didn't "have to like it." While true, the thing that bothered her most was that she did like it. She loved waking up in a soft, warm bed instead of on a cold, lumpy couch. She enjoyed being in a clean house that smelled of lemon and bacon instead of a run-down duplex smelling like mildew and smoke. Her body appreciated not freezing. It was warm enough inside Luke's house that she could stay in her shorts during a cold snap in October. Her heart rejoiced in watching her brother do a crossword puzzle at the table with a full belly and not a care in the world. Deep down, buried under the guilt, she even liked the fact that Luke insisted on cooking for her. Being taken care of for once in her life was a welcome change. It was all so warm, so cozy, like a dream come true. Maybe a better life was finally shining as a tiny dot on the horizon.

Aria jumped back as a plate passed in front of her face.

Luke set down the plate and held up his hands with a chuckle. "Whoa, easy there. It's bacon and eggs, not a snake."

Aria tucked her hair behind her ear, her face burning again. "I guess I got a little lost in my thoughts."

"I'll give you a penny for them." Luke threw the words over his shoulder as he walked to the refrigerator.

Ben raised his eyes from his crossword puzzle. "Huh?"

Aria gave Ben a patient smile, grateful for a distraction from Luke's question. "It's an expression. A penny for your thoughts. It's a funny way of asking what someone is thinking." She squared her shoulders and planted a wry look on her face as she spoke to Luke. "I was thinking how any minute now you're going to realize what a huge mistake you've made by helping us. That we're taking advantage of you by taking over your house and eating all your food."

Luke smirked as he set a glass of orange juice in front of her. "Pretty sure it's impossible to take advantage of someone if you fight them every step of the way."

Aria gave him a smirk of her own. "Touché. I guess I'm not used to anyone being nice unless they want something in return."

Luke leaned back in his chair and laced his fingers behind his head. "Actually, I do want something in return."

Aria's blood ran cold. Just when she'd let her guard down. *How could I be so stupid?* Of course he wanted something. Everyone did. Fear surged through her as she set down her fork and attempted to appear casual. "Oh? And what's that?"

Luke's mouth twisted into an adorable, lopsided grin. "I want you to have a good life."

"What?" She gripped the table, her head spinning as she waited for him to continue.

Luke leaned forward and held her gaze. "I helped you because I want you to have a good life. That's it. No ulterior motives. Part of leaving that hellhole behind was leaving behind the mentality that went along with it. My philosophy is to only give if that's all you want to do. You give just to give, not to get." He paused, his eyes gaining a playful gleam as he nodded at her plate. "Now, you better eat before Ben gets your plate. I'm pretty sure his stomach is a black hole."

Laughter erupted from Aria, a pleasant surprise amid her crushing guilt. "Yeah, it appears he can definitely pack away the food. It seemed like we never had enough." She picked up her fork but paused. "Thanks again. I mean it. Literally, no one else I know would've done even half of what you have. Trust me, I called them."

"Gee, nice to know I'm your last resort." The glint of amusement in Luke's eyes let her know he was teasing.

Aria bit back a grin, their playful banter lightening her mood. "I already explained that." Aria took a bite of bacon, closing her eyes and savoring the explosion of flavor. "Oh man, it has been so long since I've had bacon. I forgot how amazing it is." She opened her eyes to find Luke watching her, heat in his chocolate eyes.

"I'll make sure I pick up some more, then."

Ben's head shot up. "Yes, please," he said then returned his attention to the crossword puzzle.

Aria opened her mouth to protest, but the smell and taste of bacon killed the words before they formed. "By the way, I know for a fact you lied about never using your bed."

Luke raised an eyebrow. "Oh yeah? And how do you know that?"

Aria pursed her lips with attitude. "Because it smells like you. Your bed wouldn't smell like you if you never used it." She didn't even try to hide the triumphant smugness on her face.

Luke leaned closer, his eyes teasing. "So what you're saying is, you paid attention to what I smell like?"

She stared slack-jawed like a deer in headlights. He'd caught her. She shoved a forkful of eggs in her mouth, hoping to distract from the color creeping up her neck. She wracked her brain for something witty, but alas, it turned to mush when she needed it most.

Ben nodded, seemingly oblivious to the real meaning behind Luke's comment. "Everything smells so good here. It's all so clean. No stains or holes anywhere. And there's no bugs. This place is amazing."

His words, though accurate, punctured Aria's heart and wrung it dry. She strained to maintain her composure as tears burned her eyes.

Luke cleared his throat. "I'm glad you like it, Ben. Hey, since you're done, you can go see what's on TV."

"Awesome." Ben jumped out of his chair and bounded into the living room, oblivious to Aria's devastation.

Once the television clicked on, Luke put a hand on Aria's shoulder. "It's okay."

Aria shook her head, a bitter tear rolling down her cheek. "No, it's not. How is any of this okay? Ben's benchmarks for a nice place is that it's not nasty, dilapidated, or full of bugs. He's twelve. He shouldn't be used to deplorable conditions, and he shouldn't be dealing with his sister taking him to a random house because his mom cares more about getting high than making sure her kids are safe."

Luke leaned forward with a sigh. "You're right. Nothing about any of that is okay. But you're okay now. You're here. He's here. Safe and fed. You guys can stay as long as you want. I promise. So take that worry off your plate."

She peeked at him through her tear-soaked lashes. "I'll try, but I'm not sure I know how to not worry about something, though. I've never had a worry taken away before, just always piled on deeper." She hated to admit it, but she felt an inkling of safety with Luke. Whether she could trust that feeling remained to be seen.

Ben shouted from the couch. "Aria, you have to come see this! He has, like, a hundred channels. That settles it. We have to stay here forever."

Aria laughed despite herself, her cheeks squeezing a stray tear from her eye. "Slow down there, Ben. Forever is a long time. Let's take it day by day, shall we?"

Luke shrugged as he reached for a magazine. "As long as you want."

Aria stole glances at Luke as she finished her food. He sat reading his business magazine so casually, as if every Saturday morning began with feeding a couple of homeless people who had invaded his house the night before. He seemed like a great guy, at least on the surface. She grappled to integrate Luke the hero with the vilified version of him in her mind. Years of writing him off as a jerk threatened to melt away and leave her defenseless against his charms.

Unable to fit any more food into her tiny stomach, she rose and began gathering the dishes. Luke reached out to stop her, taking hold of her hand. A tender warmth radiated from his skin through hers, so comforting. Intoxicating. Looking from their hands to his chocolate eyes, she saw a flash of something that made her wonder if he felt the same way. The electricity that coursed between their hands danced in their eyes as they stood, gazes locked.

Ben's raucous laughter snapped her out of her trance. She yanked her hand back as her eyes darted away from Luke and scanned the dirty dishes. "Come on, Luke. You paid for all this food plus cooked it all. At least let me do the dishes. At least let me contribute that much."

Luke pursed his lips in thought. "Okay, fine. I'll let you do the dishes. But only because I know you need that in order to ease your guilt."

While Aria waited for the sink to fill with water, Luke leaned his backside against the counter next to it. "Sorry there's no dishwasher. The kitchen is too small."

Aria sank the first dish into the hot, soapy water. "Luckily, I've never used a dishwasher, so I don't know what I'm missing. At least you have hot water. Washing dishes in cold water always chills me to the bone." She watched her hand swirl around on the plate and couldn't help but sigh. "I've actually always enjoyed doing dishes."

Luke cocked his head to the side. "Oh, really? Why's that?"

She shied away from him, regretting having opened her mouth. "It's kind of silly."

"I won't judge."

Aria squirmed. He had a knack for bringing out her raw honesty, which always left her questioning herself and feeling exposed. "I love the transformation. You take plates that have food smeared all over them. They're dirty and no good. Then you dunk them in the hot, soapy water and give them a little scrub. They come out shiny and clean. Brand-new. I always look at the dishes and wish that I could throw some soap and water onto my life. Maybe transform my stressful, bleak, and dirty life into one that's clean and full of happiness and light. Maybe I could dunk my mom in the sink and have her come out competent and sober." Aria and Luke both watched as she rinsed the plate and set it in the drying rack.

"That's beautiful. Tragic but beautiful." Luke moved his arm as if to give her a hug but stopped short, letting his arm fall back to his side. "I... I hope this is your time in the soapy water. I hope your life gets better from here. And I'm here to help."

Aria studied him, his deep-brown eyes holding hers with an intensity that caught her off guard. She hunted for clues to an ulterior motive. She searched for hints of lies or deceit but came up empty. Perhaps, just once, she could put a little faith and trust in someone other than herself. Perhaps, just this once, she could lean on someone for support. A tear slipped down her cheek as a wall around her heart cracked and crumbled away. "Thank you."

Luke

Every cell in Luke's body begged to sweep Aria into his arms and kiss the pain away. He couldn't remember ever seeing her so raw and emotional before. Her whispered "thank you" had barely reached his ears. He panicked, unsure of how to proceed. A hug seemed like the plausible thing to do... except it was a lot of physical connection. The tiniest of touches left him wanting more. Craving more. Holding her hand to stop her from gathering dishes had overwhelmed his senses to the point of losing his ability to think. *I'm officially going insane,* he thought. He'd touched plenty of women, more than he cared to admit, but he'd never experienced these sensations before. A simple touch of the hand sent electricity buzzing through him, short-circuiting his brain. His body refused to let go of the memory of her skin on his.

As his body screamed for more, so did his heart. Whenever she had a stray hair, he craved tucking it behind her ear for her. He wanted her to curl up against him on the couch as he watched his late-night movie. To wrap her in his arms and tell her it would be all right. But thinking about having his arms around her made him want to kiss her. Thinking about kissing her made him want to...

"Hey, Luke, come here! This is the show I was telling you about!" Ben yelled from the living room, much louder than necessary.

Luke started and cleared his throat, grateful no one could read his thoughts. "Be right there," he called back. He stood by Aria with his arms dangling by his sides like useless noodles, his awkwardness reaching higher levels than he thought possible. "Please, try to relax and let me help you. I promise I'm not a bad guy." He stepped away without touching her, no matter how much it hurt.

Sitting on the couch with Ben, Luke tried his best to pay attention to the bright bursts of anime characters on the television. Despite his best efforts, his mind kept wandering back to Aria like a lost, starving puppy sniffing for some food. No, he had to control himself. The last thing she needed was some guy to step in and muddle her plans. He refused to ruin anything for her. He was helping her for the sake of helping, not to get in her pants, and he was going to prove it. If he made any advances toward her, she might feel obligated to go along with it as some sort of twisted payment for his help. He would never forgive himself if that happened. She deserved better than that. So much better. He had to keep his hands to himself and let her live her life in peace, no matter what her presence was doing to him.

Ben laughed next to him as Aria cleaned up after the breakfast Luke had cooked. Teamwork. It all felt so... natural. An alien contentment unsettled him. His entire life had always revolved around striving for change. For a different life. Even as a small child, he knew he didn't want to be like his parents, and he had accomplished precisely that. He'd moved to a better neighborhood and made enough money to open a savings account. He thought he'd done well for himself, and seeing where he came from, he certainly had. But with

Aria and Ben, he felt content for the first time in his life. He felt comfortable. Happy, even. His house had life in it. Not even twenty-four hours had passed, yet it was enough to give him a glimpse of what a healthy family life could be. And it could all be gone in an instant. His stomach knotted at the thought. Aria could find a job and an apartment, and his house would be lifeless again in the blink of an eye.

Chapter 5

Aria

"A penny for your thoughts," Aria quipped, using his line against him.

Luke flinched as his head jerked up. "Huh? Oh. No penny necessary. Just going over tonight's work schedule in my head. Saturdays are my busiest days, working from four until whenever."

"Good, because I don't have a penny to give you."

"I wouldn't have taken it anyway," he retorted as he rose to his feet, stretching his arms overhead.

Aria stared, transfixed, as his muscles flexed and moved under his snug white shirt. *He definitely works out in his free time,* she thought. Her mind painted a picture of him stretching his arms over his head like that but lying in his bed. The one she slept in. She all but drooled at the imagery, her imagination running wild.

"Your cheeks are a little flushed. Do you have a fever?" Mischief twinkled in Luke's eyes as a smile played at the corner of his mouth.

Aria darted her eyes to the computer, tucking her hair behind her ear. She berated herself for acting like a lovesick teenager. "I'm fine. The dishwater made me warm. Anyway, I was wondering if I could use your computer. I was going to do a job search and work on some homework, if that's okay."

He studied her, unsuccessful at hiding his self-confident smirk. "Go ahead. What's mine is yours." He tipped his head toward the trash bags sitting behind her. "Actually, how about I take Ben and get out of here so you can concentrate better? I need to hit up the laundromat, and I can take your bags too."

"But this show just started," Ben whined in protest behind him.

Luke held up a finger to Aria. "And maybe we'll hit up the snack machine while we're there." He did a triumphant fist pump when Ben jumped up, ready to go.

Aria laughed at Ben's excitement for more food. "That's really nice, but—"

"No buts," Luke interrupted. "I'm not doing anything I don't want to do. Remember? Besides, it'll give Ben and me some guy time. Nothing but testosterone and food." He flashed her a cheesy salesman grin.

Aria tried to keep her expression neutral, but her curving lips betrayed her. As cheesy as it was, his salesman face was a clear winner. "Okay, fine, but don't let Ben use up all your change." She started toward the computer but stalled. "Are you sure it's okay if I use this? I'm fine with going to the computer lab on campus."

Luke hoisted the trash bags and flung them over his shoulder like Santa with his bag of toys. "Aria, seriously. It's okay. Stop worrying so much. If you cross a boundary, I'll tell you. I didn't get where I am now by being a pushover. Okay? If I say I'm okay with something, it's because I actually am. I promise."

Aria held up her hands in surrender. "All right. Got the message loud and clear. Just... thanks, again."

Luke headed for the door, motioning for Ben to follow. "Don't search for anything that'll get me in trouble with the feds."

Aria placed one hand on her heart and raised her other hand as if being sworn into testimony. "I solemnly swear to keep all searches at the PG level."

"See you when we get back." Luke stepped out but stuck his head back through the door. "And we'll be careful. Don't worry." He winked as he pulled the door shut.

"Time to get to work," she said aloud as she watched them leave. Dragging everything from her oversized backpack, she made a fortress of books and folders on the desk. A beautiful lake surrounded by trees with fall foliage lit up the computer screen. She sighed, imagining the calm serenity of such a place. The peace. Her mind trailed off, wondering about Luke's life in the eight years he'd been gone. Sure, she'd heard bits and pieces, like the rumors that he lived in his bus, but not enough to paint a full picture.

Before she could stop it, her mind transported her back to that night in the bar six years ago, the last time they'd seen each other. Her heart had pounded against her ribs as he leaned in for the kiss she'd been so beyond ready for. Instead of delivering her teenage dreams, he stopped short and called her a silly kid, thus shattering her lovesick heart. The words still stung years later. She hadn't felt at all like a kid back then, let alone silly. That phrase implied she had an actual childhood rather than having it stolen by her alcoholic, suicidal father and drug-addicted mother.

Maybe Ben still had a chance at a decent childhood, though he was already twelve. As much as she tried to shelter him from the realities of their life, their home and neighborhood made it impossible to shield him from everything. Maybe she could break the cycle.

The warm wetness of a teardrop on her arm startled her. She touched her fingertips to her cheeks and found them soaked. Alone and safe for the first time in her life, she allowed herself to break. As another wall around her heart crumbled to pieces, the tears held back for over a decade rushed out in a torrent. Tears for herself, for Ben, and even for her parents and their unfortunate choices in life. Dropping her head to the desk, she let the sorrow flow unhindered until the well ran dry.

Aria sighed, at once drained and relieved as she patted her face dry. Studying her red and puffy reflection in the bathroom mirror, she squared her shoulders.

"You can do this. You'll finish college, become a writer, and change the world with your words. You can keep guiding Ben through this world. You will be happy," she said, trying her hand at manifesting her destiny.

She gave one vigorous nod and marched back to the computer, back to her fight for a better future.

One and a half hours later, she shut the last textbook and marveled at the short time that had passed. Not having to walk miles for everything sure freed up a lot of time. She rubbed her eyes, which were achy from crying and staring at a computer, and she got up to explore her new surroundings.

Paying attention to the details for the first time, she was struck by the lack of personalization. The décor exuded utilitarian practicality, very ordered and simple. No pictures hung on the cream walls. The bathroom held nothing more than the essentials, with dark-blue towels coordinating with the pale-blue walls. The white subway tile shower shone and smelled of lemon and Luke's shampoo. Back in the bedroom where she'd slept, she found much the same. The only signs of personality were the shirt on the door hook and house shoes by the bed. She made the bed, smoothing out the sage-green comforter and closing her eyes as she breathed in Luke's comforting scent. The soft tan carpet caressed her feet as she made her way to the other bedroom. Ben had left his bed a mess, of course, so she set to work straightening the plain maroon bedding.

The bland basics filling the house surprised her, in stark juxtaposition to the Luke she knew. Her Luke had personality for days, and a "cool dude" style. Her Luke was far from basic and bland.

Her Luke. She chastised herself for taking ownership of him. He was not hers in any way, shape, or form. He never had been and never would be. The sooner she accepted that, the better.

Back in the living room, she explored the bookshelf, finding a tiny window into Luke's life at last. A crystal award on the top shelf caught her eye. Running her finger along the curved edges, she read, "Rising Star Award, presented to Windy City Party Tours by the Chicago Tourism Association." Impressive. Luke must be even more successful than she thought.

Perusing his books, she found over a dozen business strategy and financial planning titles, all well-worn. One shelf contained some old westerns and cheesy science fiction works. She selected one about an alien cat from outer space and made her way to the kitchen.

Her mouth hung agape at the well-stocked refrigerator, still full despite their giant breakfast. Luke obviously made enough money to not run out of food. She blinked back tears. She'd never seen a full refrigerator before. Clutching the book to her aching chest, she shut the door, her appetite having vanished. The aroma of coffee warming in the pot caught in her nose. Glorious coffee. Hunting for a mug proved easy in the well-organized cabinets full of plain, utilitarian dishes. Sunlight danced through the back door, beckoning her to try out the one area she had yet to explore.

She scanned over her T-shirt and shorts, a poor choice of apparel in a vicious cold snap. She plopped onto the couch, resigning herself to exploring the backyard later, once Luke and Ben returned with her clothes. Her brain had other ideas, refusing to pay any attention to the book as the urge to explore drew her thoughts to the back door. It wasn't every day she could be outside and enjoy it.

She tiptoed into Luke's room and eased open the bottom dresser drawer then ridiculed herself for her slow, sneaky movements with no one there to catch her. She took a pair of gray sweatpants from the drawer and pulled them on, tugging the drawstring as tight as it would go. Then she yanked on her boots and wrapped herself in the blanket from the couch. She grabbed the book and coffee on her way to the back door, giving in to her curiosity.

The air stung her face as she stepped onto the patio, but for once she found it invigorating, knowing she had a warm place to go back to. The small yard boasted one tree, whose pale-yellow leaves littered the ground. Sounds of the city trickled into the space, but in the absence of the constant cacophony of sirens and shouting, she could appreciate the chorus of life. She planted herself on the glider at the far end of the patio, the metal chilling her despite the blanket and clothes. She inhaled the scent of earth and sighed as she relaxed farther into the seat.

Strands of lights hung along the underside of the roof covering the patio. Of course the party bus guru had a party patio. Images of Luke hosting a party in his yard filled her imagination. She pictured Luke sitting on this very glider with a woman, charming her with the ambience of the twinkling lights and his dreamy eyes. She shivered, telling herself it had everything to do with the cold and nothing to do with imagining Luke with another woman. Sipping the warm coffee, she leaned back and opened the book, pushing visions of Luke into the far recesses of her mind.

Luke

Luke flung the door open, jokingly calling out, "Honey, we're home." Silence greeted him. His face fell. He eyed Ben, who frowned at the empty house. There was no way the Aria he knew would ever abandon her brother. "Aria? We're home. Where are you?"

He dropped the laundry on the couch and explored the bedrooms. "Aria?"

Ben followed on his heels. "Hey, sis? You here?"

Having searched everywhere else, Luke pulled open the back door and stuck his head out. "There you are."

Aria jumped, throwing a book in the air. "Oh my gosh, you almost gave me a heart attack." Nervous laughter bubbled out as she put her hand on her chest.

Luke tried to hide the massive amount of relief that flooded him upon finding her, his heart having seized in her brief, unexplained absence. It had been less than a day, and he was already too attached. He had to get a grip on his raging hormones. He pasted on a neutral expression, attempting to hide his inner turmoil. "Sorry about that. We were... Ben was worried when we couldn't find you."

Aria retrieved the book and grabbed her empty mug. "Sorry to make you guys worry."

Luke held the door open as she shuffled inside, clutching the blanket against her. "It's okay. And I'm glad you made yourself at home."

Aria tucked her hair behind her ear, something Luke noticed she did when she felt unsure of herself. "Sorry, I actually had free time for the first time in... well, ever, I guess. And I can never resist a bookshelf."

Luke chuckled as he shut the door behind them. "I remember that about you. But there's nothing to be sorry about. I really am glad you finally let yourself get comfortable. I wasn't being sarcastic."

"I shouldn't have gone through your bookshelf." She tossed the blanket on the couch, her cheeks blazing crimson as she revealed his sweatpants hanging on her hips. "And I shouldn't be wearing your clothes."

Luke gaped at her, the sight of her wearing his clothes doing funny things to his insides. His mind filled with thoughts of what it would be like to peel them off her. He cleared his throat as he dragged his eyes away from her, retrieving the laundry basket to distract himself and hide the effect she had on him. "Meh, I don't mind. Besides, we kind of had all your clothes. They look better on you than they do on me anyway." He handed her a laundry basket, eager to have something filling the space between them before temptation got the better of him. "Here's your stuff. All clean and folded."

As Aria examined the basket, her face flushed again.

Luke followed her line of vision to the bundle of underwear tucked beside a stack of shirts. "I had Ben fold your stuff, so if anything got wrinkled, it's his fault. It felt like an invasion of privacy if I did it."

Aria took the laundry basket, her features softening. "Thanks."

Ben returned from putting his basket in his room. "I'll take that for you." He took Aria's basket and headed down the hallway.

Aria stared after him, slack-jawed. "Okay, where is Ben, and what did you do with him?"

Luke sauntered to the couch and plopped down with a shrug. "Maybe I brought home the wrong kid."

A laugh trickled out as she took a few steps toward the couch. "Seriously, though. That's the first time he's ever done anything to help without me asking him to. Did you tell him to do that?"

"Nope. We talked about life and, you know, guy stuff."

"Well, something you said must've inspired him somehow. Getting him to help me has always been like pulling teeth. Not that I ever asked him to do much, but still." She crossed one arm over her stomach and grabbed her other arm, shrinking into herself.

"I'm glad I could have a positive influence on him." Luke willed her to look at him so she could see how much he meant it, how much he cared. "He's a great kid. I'd love to have more guy time with him, actually. He's fun to hang out with."

She eased down on the other end of the couch, a sparkle in her eyes that hadn't been there before. "That would be great, Luke. Really great."

Seeing how much such a tiny gesture meant to Aria, Luke's heart filled with pride.

Chapter 6

Aria

Aria exhaled and relaxed against the couch pillow, another piece of the wall around her heart chipping away. The way Luke interacted with Ben was a sight for sore eyes—and a sore heart, if she were honest. Ben had tried to latch on to other men in the neighborhood over the years, but they'd all treated him like an annoyance. None of them were the type of positive influence Aria wanted for Ben anyway. But Luke... Luke took Ben under his wing without batting an eye, and a few hours spent together had already resulted in a positive change in Ben's demeanor. Luke was exactly the type of man Ben needed in his life, a fact that made her want Luke in her life even more. She needed to find some terrible qualities in Luke pronto because her teenage crush clamored to reignite full force.

"So, did you find your place?" Luke motioned to the book on the coffee table.

Aria blinked, her brain taking a second to leave her musings and return to the real world. "Huh? Oh yeah. I only had a few pages left, so it was easy to find where I was."

Luke took a seat at the other end of the couch. "Wow, such a voracious reader."

Aria raised an eyebrow.

"What? Surprised I know big words? I'm more than muscles and a pretty face, you know." Luke feigned exaggerated offense.

Aria huffed, trying but failing to hide the smile tugging at her lips. She needed a change of subject to distract herself from thinking about those muscles and that pretty face. "I don't think I'll ever stop loving to read. Plus, reading helps with writing. If I want to be a successful writer, I'll need all the help I can get."

"So are you still wanting to write a book?"

Aria stared for a second, shocked he remembered her long-ago dreams. "Maybe someday, but I've switched gears a little. I'm studying journalism. The grand plan would be to shine a light on the hidden disparities in the world and effect societal change to give future generations of people like us more of a fighting chance."

Luke nodded his approval. "Wow, that's a big dream. And very honorable, I might add."

Aria shifted her focus to the coffee table. "That's what I wrote for the academic-planning seminar I had to attend. That would be a dream come true, don't get me wrong, but I'm keeping my actual expectations much more realistic. I'm hoping I can be a journalist and leave even the tiniest of marks on the world. To help at least one person and maybe leave some proof that my existence mattered."

"Look at me." Luke waited until Aria's eyes met his. "There's no doubt you'll do great things in the future, but your existence already matters. Even in ways you might never see. You matter, Aria."

Aria's eyes swam as she wrestled with her tangled emotions. Those words, the affirmation she'd sought her entire life, meant more to her than she could ever explain. "I..." she croaked. Nothing more came, no matter how much she willed her tongue to move.

Luke placed his hand on her knee and then rose, disappearing to the kitchen behind her.

Aria listened to the clink of glasses and running water, letting the sounds of ordinary life ground her. She took the glass Luke offered and sipped the refreshing ice water as he reclaimed his seat.

She sucked in a deep breath and cleared the emotion from her throat. "You know, while I was outside, I didn't hear any sirens. It was so peaceful. Like another planet. You have a pretty amazing neighborhood. Maybe I could find a place near here."

The bathroom door opened, and Ben's eyes danced as he strode up to the couch. "Did you ask her yet?"

Aria's eyes bounced from Ben to Luke. "Ask me what?" She frowned at their silence and being left in the dark. "All right, you guys. What are you up to? Ask me what?"

Luke rubbed the back of his head, and his eyes darted around the room at everything but Aria's face. "Well... while we were stuffing ourselves with junk food at the laundromat, we got to talking about you two not having a place to stay." Luke paused with his mouth agape, his eyes betraying his apprehension.

"I want to stay here with Luke." Ben's words burst out like air from a balloon.

Aria swiveled toward him, trying her best to keep her face compassionate while her patience wore thin. "Look, Ben, I know you've had fun today, but we can't stay here. We can't move ourselves in and impose upon Luke like that. He has his own life, and we can't come in here and mess it up because he was nice enough to help us for a couple of days."

"Actually, I don't," Luke interjected beside her.

"Don't what?" A dull ache began forming behind Aria's creased forehead.

"I don't really have a life to interrupt. I mean, I have my job, but that's pretty much it. Outside of work, life gets a little bland in the day to day. I can only rewatch old sci-fi movies so many times before it gets pathetic. It's pretty boring being alone all the time. My house even looks boring. I'm rambling." He paused, scrubbing a hand over his face. "Okay, so what I'm trying to say is, I think you guys should stay here. At least until you get your feet under you better. You don't have to rush off. You're not imposing. It's kind of fun." Luke inhaled a sharp breath and winced as if waiting for a slap.

Aria had never seen Luke nervous before and couldn't help but find it endearing. In fact, her mind obsessed over how cute Luke was being rather than the major issue being discussed. She sprang to her feet, hoping some distance from Luke would help her think better. "I don't know. We haven't spoken in six years, and now suddenly we'll be roommates? That's quite a leap. We can't swoop in and take advantage of you like that."

Luke stood, holding up his hands to stop her. "Let's get this straight and settled once and for all, shall we? You're not taking advantage of me. If I don't like something, I'll say it. I'm not a pushover. Never have been and never will be. Besides, it's not like I'm not getting anything out of the deal. I get someone to talk to when I'm home, and I get some help around the house because I know for a fact you'll clean even if I tell you not to. Plus, I'm sure you're much more meticulous than I am in everything you do, so whatever you do will be an improvement on the status quo. I might even get some personality in my house, which honestly I think it needs. All my creative efforts go into the party bus, and my house suffers for it. After living here for two years, you can't tell who I am at all. I'm sure you've noticed. Heck, I'll even let you chip in on the utilities and groceries, even though it's only because I know you'll go crazy otherwise."

Aria looked from Luke to Ben again, her head whirling. Ben's eyes held such hope and excitement, something she'd never seen before.

As if Luke could sense her defenses weakening, he reasoned some more. "Seriously, though, I won't do anything to jeopardize what I have here. I've busted my a—" He stopped himself from cussing and glanced at Ben. "I've busted my butt too much to be careless now. You guys staying here won't put any kind of financial burden on me. I know I can trust you, and you won't be frivolous. I'm pretty sure you don't know how. Just let me help you out with this. Please."

Aria's resolve melted like snow in the spring. Luke must've learned some negotiation tactics from all those books on his shelves. No wonder he was a good businessman. She massaged the creases in her forehead, attempting to ease the tension gathered there. "I don't know, Luke. It still feels wrong for us to barge in like this."

"You want to make a better life for you and Ben, right? Well, what's the best way for you to do that? It's going to college and doing the best you can, so then you can get a good job afterward. Then you can be on your way to your dream job as a world-saving journalist. You've been a real rock star already, especially with all you had on your plate. Seriously. It's amazing. But close your eyes for a minute and imagine all the things you could accomplish without all that other bullsh—crap weighing you down. If you push aside your pride and fear, you know I'm right."

Aria closed her eyes and envisioned the life he painted. She couldn't argue against his logic, as much as she hated to admit it. When she opened her eyes, the hope on Ben's face did her in. With a deep inhale of courage, she pushed her fears aside and allowed herself to take the leap. "Okay."

"What?" Ben and Luke spoke in unison.

"If it's what you want, Ben, and Luke is on board... we can stay."

Ben flung his arms around her and squeezed. "Yay! Thank you. I want to stay so bad. I love it here."

Aria kissed his temple and soaked in his affection, which hadn't been so readily doled out in quite a while. She found Luke's eyes shining at her. "Thank you, Luke. This means a lot to Ben. To us."

"It's my pleasure," Luke said.

Ben raised his head, his eyes moist with emotion. "Come here, Luke. I wanna hug you too."

Luke hesitated, uncertainty flitting across his face, then walked over and joined the group hug.

Aria tensed as Luke's right arm wrapped around her, his touch sending tingles all over her body. Ben let go of her with one arm to put it around Luke. Aria inched her left arm around Luke, completing the hug circle. Luke's warm, muscular arm on her shoulders evoked a foreign sense of protection and security, and the tension in her muscles melted away. Against her better judgment, she closed her eyes and allowed herself to absorb the feeling, a soothing balm on her aching heart.

Ben pulled back, breaking the hug and breaking Aria's trance. "I'm going to go put my clothes away in my new closet." A giggle trickled down the hall as he disappeared into his room.

Luke's eyes fell to his arm still draped around Aria. Clearing his throat, he lifted his arm away and stepped back. He shouted down the hall to Ben. "The dresser and closet in your room should be empty, but let me know if you find something. Feel free to make the room your own however you want."

Aria tucked her hair behind her ear and shifted her eyes to the floor to hide her swirl of emotions, especially how much she'd enjoyed his embrace. "Thank you again, Luke."

"It's no problem. I promise."

Her throat constricted, but she forced her next words out, her voice a strained whisper. "Please... Please don't make me regret it."

Luke put a gentle finger under her chin, raising her eyes to his. "I promise I won't make you regret it. I'm glad you let me help you. You're one of the few good people left from the old neighborhood, and you deserve better than that life."

Aria's pulse quickened as Luke's dark eyes held hers, the intensity and sincerity she found there taking her breath away. She could've sworn he just licked his lips and swallowed. No, that had to be her teenage fantasies playing themselves out in her mind. Then again, she remembered seeing that look on his face one other time. Six years ago, in the dim light of a sleazy bar. Maybe he still wanted her as much as she wanted him.

The thud of Ben's closet shutting ricocheted down the hallway.

Luke dropped his hand from her chin and took a step back. "So it's a deal, then?"

She extended her hand for a shake as her body ached for his arms around her. "It's a deal."

Luke shook her hand. "Let's put this laundry away and make it official." He grabbed his basket from beside the couch and motioned for Aria to follow him. In the bedroom, he opened his sock drawer. "My dresser is only half full, and the closet is about the same. If you need more room than that, let me know."

Aria snatched up her laundry basket. "No, absolutely not. If this is going to be a long-term thing, I refuse to kick you out of your room. I'll bunk with Ben, and you can have your room back. End of discussion." She headed for the door, but Luke shoved his socks in the drawer and held up a hand to stop her.

"Hold on. Let's think about this. The couch has a pullout bed I can sleep on."

"Then I'll sleep on the pullout bed. Not you. This is your house. And I'll put my stuff in Ben's room." She squared her shoulders and started for the door, pushing his hand away with the basket.

"Slow down a minute, will you? I work weird hours. I drive a party bus, remember? If you sleep in the living room, I'll wake you up when I come home. If I sleep in the living room, I get to come home and watch TV without worrying about waking anyone up. So you sleeping in here makes more sense. Your stuff being in here with you makes sense." Luke paused, lowering his voice as he eyed the hallway. "And, between you and me, Ben is at the age that any day now he is going to be needing more privacy for... for stuff teenage boys may or may not do as their bodies grow. I'm pretty sure you don't want to walk in on that."

Aria recoiled, taking a step back with her mouth in a grimace. "Eww, no. Ben's only twelve. He's not old enough..." Her eyes grew large as she realized he was, in fact, at that age. At once, his recent moodiness made complete sense. "Ugh. Okay, you're right. I don't want to bunk with him. I don't even want to think about it now that you brought that up."

Luke held his hands up in defense and snickered. "I hate being the bearer of bad news, but you needed to know. Now you see why sharing a room with him is a bad idea. He needs his space as a growing teen. And so do you, being the only female in the house."

Aria balanced the laundry basket on her hip and jutted a finger at him. "And so do you. It's your house, but you're the only one left with no space to call your own." She dropped her hand to her hip. "Tell me how that's fair."

Luke shut the last drawer and swept an arm over the room. "Because I've had the entire house as 'my space' for almost two years. I can survive sharing for a while. Now, are you going to put your clothes in here, finally? I can help."

Aria put her body between him and her basket. "Okay, fine. You win. I'll put my clothes away in here. I'll take over your room. But only temporarily. Any time you want it back, say the word, and I'm out. No hard feelings."

Luke gave a triumphant nod. "Deal. I'll be in the living room if you need me."

Aria watched him leave, her traitorous eyes darting to check out his backside before she could control herself. She resisted leaning her head into the hallway to watch him walk away, instead focusing her attention on her laundry basket. Her vision landed on the bundle of ratty underwear tucked beside her shirts. Her face flamed at the possibility that Luke saw the deplorable state of her poor excuse for lingerie. She ran through her catalogue of memories, concluding it must've been almost a decade since she'd bought new panties. They'd stretched out as she grew so they fit her womanly body even though she'd gotten them before puberty. Bras were another story, needing to be replaced occasionally as her breasts grew, but it had still been at least five years since she'd splurged on a new one. She could never bring herself to waste precious money on new underwear when the cabinets sat empty. It wasn't like anyone ever saw them anyway. Putting them away in the dresser, she concluded part of her next check would go toward new underwear as a treat to herself after years of neglect. No other reasons. No ulterior motives, especially none concerning Luke. At least, that was what she told herself.

Luke

As Aria walked into the living room, Luke clamored to restrain his utter joy that she'd agreed to stay. He also neglected any further introspection about why it made him so giddy. "Hey, roomie."

Aria threw herself onto the other end of the couch with a defeated groan. "I can't believe I let you two talk me into this."

Luke laughed, dispelling some of his pent-up glee. "Me neither, frankly. I figured you'd be too stubborn. Glad we finally wore you down."

"Worn down is right. I'm too exhausted to put up much of a fight. I think I could sleep for a week." She leaned her head back and closed her eyes.

"Not much of a fight? Dang, I would hate to see what you're like when you're really fighting," Luke joked.

A bitter laugh devoid of humor bubbled from Aria that sent a chill down his spine. "Oh, I have some stories. But that's for another time. Or never. Never sounds good."

Luke took advantage of her eyes being closed, his gaze traveling over the wounded woman before him. The pain etched all over her face stabbed his heart. She held the look of a girl who had been through more than her fair share of hell in life. He knew how hard it must be for her to trust someone, and he vowed to prove himself worthy of the trust she gave him.

Aria lifted her head and looked over at him. "I'm serious, though. I don't mind sleeping on the couch. It's ten times nicer than my bed back home."

Luke groaned and rubbed his eyes. "Back to that again? I'm serious too. You take the bedroom and let me watch TV until I fall asleep. End of discussion." A devilish grin began spreading despite himself. "If you try to sleep on the couch tonight while I'm gone, we'll end up sleeping on it together." Even as he teased, he couldn't help but think that didn't sound like a bad way to spend the night.

Aria pursed her lips, yet her eyes twinkled. "Well, I definitely don't want that."

For the first time in his life, Luke didn't want to go to work. Even the fact that Sunday was his second-busiest day of the week wasn't enticing enough. Because for the first time, he actually had something worth staying home for. And yet he pulled on his self-made uniform of a black shirt and dark-gray pants anyway. He found Ben watching television and Aria with a book. It took all Luke's strength to not plop down on the couch with them.

Aria set down her book, pink rising in her cheeks as her eyes flicked over him. Fairly certain he knew what that look meant, Luke squared his shoulders and puffed his chest a bit so his shirt pulled tighter over his muscles. "Well, I'm off to work, then."

"Bye, Luke," Ben said, keeping most of his attention on the television.

Aria joined Luke as he walked to the door. "Thanks again for letting us stay here."

"Eventually, you'll have to stop saying thank you every five minutes. You know that, right?" Luke gave her a playful smirk.

Her eyes dropped to the floor. "I'll try. I'm just so thankful."

"I know. And you're welcome." Luke slipped on his coat. "Now, I already ordered a pizza to be delivered in an hour, so don't freak out when you hear knocking at the door."

Aria's eyes shot to his face. "You didn't have to do that. I can cook. I—"

"It's already done and paid for," he interrupted. "Don't worry about it. I want you to have one whole day to relax. Okay? Enjoy." He grabbed his keys from the table by the door. "I'm not sure when I'll be back. The last bus is supposed to end at midnight, but we'll see." He put his hand on the doorknob, anchoring his body before it gave in to the overwhelming urge to give her a kiss goodbye. "Bottom line is, don't wait up. See you guys tomorrow."

Please be here tomorrow, he added to himself. The fear of coming home to an empty house gnawed away at him. If left alone with her worries, Aria might decide living with him was a mistake.

Aria bit her lip, making him wonder if she was struggling with saying goodbye as well. "Be safe."

"I will. Save me two slices." And with that, he stepped into the chilly evening air, counting down the minutes until he'd be back.

Chapter 7

Aria

Aria jolted awake at the creak of a door opening, her heart pumping adrenaline through her veins at breakneck speed. The clock read just after one in the morning. The sound was probably Luke coming home, but she wasn't taking any chances. She reached under her pillow and grumbled as her hand found nothing but bed sheets. She jumped up and grabbed the bedside trash can, holding it in the air as she crept down the hallway.

Luke turned toward the hallway as she crept into the living room. "Good lord, Aria. You almost gave me a heart attack." He held his hand on his chest and panted, his eyes wide.

She offered a sheepish shrug as she lowered the trash can. "Sorry."

"What are you doing up? Did I wake you? I was trying to be quiet, but this door sticks in the winter." Luke frowned as he jutted a thumb toward the front door.

Aria rocked her head from side to side. "Yes and no. The door opening woke me up, but it wasn't super loud or anything. I wake up easy. A self-preservation mechanism that came in handy back home. I guess my brain hasn't fully processed yet that we're safer here."

Luke's eyes landed on her hands. "Why are you holding the trash can?" At once, concern filled his face as he took a step forward. "Are you sick?"

Aria followed his eyes to the trash can, her cheeks getting hot. "No, I'm fine. I just..." She tucked her hair behind her ear, not wanting to admit the true reason. "I always carry something to protect myself. Someone took my baseball bat when all our stuff was out in the dirt, so I can't sleep with that anymore. I grabbed the closest hard thing I could find. Now that I'm more awake, I realize grabbing my Mace off the nightstand would've been a better choice."

The corners of Luke's mouth twitched. "You came in here ready to beat an intruder with a trash can?"

Aria was certain her ears blazed red. "Yeah, I know it's silly."

Luke cocked his head to the side. "Actually, I was thinking it's pretty badass." He walked to the refrigerator and pulled out a brown bottle. "Want one?"

Aria set down the trash can, feeling like a complete fool. "No, thanks."

Luke nodded, ran some water in a glass for her, and sat on the couch. "Honestly, silly is the last word I would ever associate with you."

Aria crossed her arms and pursed her lips. "Oh? But I thought I was just a silly kid."

Luke winced. "I was hoping you forgot about that."

Aria raised her chin, determined to keep her emotions in check and hold on to her hardened exterior. "No such luck."

"I should've known better. Your mind always was a steel trap." He ran his hand over his face. "Alcohol always made me stupid. That's why I don't touch the stuff anymore." When Aria's eyes traveled to the brown bottle in his hand, he rotated the label toward her and pointed to it. "Root beer. I still get the sensation of relaxing while drinking from a bottle, but none of the stupid effects."

Aria's mind traveled back to the bus. "You run a party bus, though. I saw the minibar at the back."

"I won't lie. It was hard at first to be around people drinking, but I'm on the clock. I never drank on the job. Any job. Even during my worst days. Plus, I don't supply the liquor, only the transportation and atmosphere. The minibar is stocked with glasses, water, fruits, sugar, and stuff like that. Additives for drinks but no alcohol. Saves me on liability and expense but also keeps temptation away."

Aria sat on the couch, tucking her legs under her so she could face him. "That all sounds very responsible. You know, I have to admit, I was always afraid your drinking would stop you from changing your life. I'm glad it didn't." She picked up the glass of water and ran her finger along the rim, bringing back more memories of that night. She stopped and raised her eyes to his. "So, what made you quit?"

Luke took a swig of root beer before answering. "Honestly?"

Aria nodded.

Luke stared at the bottle in his hand as if it held the answers. "That night in the bar was my last drink. I realized I didn't want to be the guy alcohol made me become. I didn't want to be the guy who hurt people I love. Who hurt my friends."

Aria took a sip of water, wondering which category she fell under, love or friends. Or maybe a gray area somewhere in between.

Luke rolled up his left sleeve, revealing a tattoo of a broken chain on his forearm. "I got this the next day to mark my sobriety. Breaking free of the chains of alcohol, so to speak. And I guess the chains of my past too. Every time I wanted a drink, I would look at it and remember there were better things in life. Things more important than a buzz. Things worth fighting for."

Aria studied Luke's face unabashedly, noting his strong features balanced by a softness in his eyes. A strong, caring man sat before her instead of the arrogant, carefree boy she'd once known. She had fallen head over heels in a teen crush for the Luke of her past and wondered how she would ever be able to control herself around this new and improved version. The truth and vulnerability clear in his dark eyes made her all but swoon. Every fiber of her being wanted nothing more than to run her finger along the contours of his face while his muscular arms held her against his body. Slight stubble covered his jawline and led down to his neck, so kissable her mouth watered.

"Want to join me for a movie?" Luke's soft, deep voice drew her out of her fantasy world. His eyes held hope and something else Aria decided not to interpret.

I'd better not if I know what's good for me, she thought, but her mouth had other ideas. "Sure. I'm awake, so might as well."

"Great. I hope you like cheesy sci-fi."

"I'll give anything a chance at least once." Aria realized the double meaning possible in her words, and the side-eye from Luke made her wonder if he caught it too. She had to get control of herself before she did something stupid. Still, she scooted a little closer as the movie began.

Luke

Luke's heart thundered so loudly in his ears he couldn't even hear the start of the movie. He could've sworn he saw desire in her eyes as she studied him. A smolder at the very least. Then she scooted closer to him. Perhaps she wanted him to make a move. Their roommate arrangement was still so new, so fragile, he didn't want to do anything to jeopardize that. He had to keep his distance yet again, as he had when they were teens, to protect her future, even if it meant protecting her from him. He'd had plenty of practice at keeping his pants on around her, and he would continue to do so. *How hard could it be?*

Halfway into the movie, Aria yawned, sinking back against the couch. Her eyelids blinked closed and open at an ever-slowing pace. Luke watched from the corner of his eye as her eyes slid closed. Her body leaned toward him, and he panicked, not sure what he should do. At the last second, he rested his arm on the back of the couch and allowed her to settle against his chest.

"Aria? Hey. Do you want to go to your bed? I can help you." He gave her shoulder a gentle shake.

Her eyes fluttered open for a second before easing closed again as she mumbled, "Hmm? I'm comfy, thanks."

"You want to stay here?"

She wrapped her arm around his chest and pressed farther against him. "Mm-hmm. So warm."

Luke's eyes traveled over her face, so peaceful. He couldn't recall ever seeing her so relaxed. He suspected she didn't realize she was clinging to him in her groggy state, but he also hated the thought of waking her again. It was only a snuggle anyway. He switched off the TV and shifted, swinging his legs up on the couch and leaning back on the pillows. Aria stirred but stayed curled against his side. He pulled the blanket from the back of the couch and draped it over them both. His body protested the uncomfortable setup, but his heart soared, the happiest it had ever been. Draping his arm over her, he drifted off to sleep.

Chapter 8

Aria

Aria rubbed her face against her pillow, breathing in the scent of Luke's shampoo. Wait. Her pillow wasn't firm. Or warm. A light snore came from above her head. Her pillow didn't snore either. Her eyes shot open, her pupils constricting in the bright living room. She eased her head upward, finding Luke's sleeping face. God, he was handsome. Her momentary swoon gave way to panic, and she scanned their bodies at a frantic pace. Still fully clothed. *Whew*. But she found her right leg draped over his and her right arm wrapped around his chest. She must've fallen asleep during the movie and used him like a body pillow. She laid her face in her hand with an inward groan. So much for keeping her distance.

The toilet flushed. Ben. He couldn't see them like this. She needed to get untangled from Luke pronto, ideally not waking him up in the process. Staring into his eyes while wrapped around him like a boa constrictor was the last thing she needed to do. She twisted, using the back of the couch to hoist her torso out of the pocket she'd been lying in. After managing to sit, she needed to get over his legs somehow. Surveying the situation again, she decided pulling herself up and over the back of the couch appeared to be the only option to get out of her predicament undetected. She hooked her foot and hand over the couch and tugged. Her shoulder and knee screamed as she hauled her weight awkwardly up toward the back of the couch. She'd almost made it when her hand slipped and sent her tumbling onto Luke.

Luke awoke with a startled grunt and a groan. "Hey, what are you doing? Trying to kill me?" He grabbed his crotch, the unfortunate recipient of her elbow, and curled into the fetal position.

Aria scrambled off him and jumped to her feet. "Oh my gosh. I'm so sorry. I didn't mean to hurt you. Especially not... there."

Luke flinched, his face red. "I tried to wake you up and take you to your room, but you hugged me and said you wanted to stay. You looked so peaceful, and I didn't want to bother you again. I swear I tried. It wasn't my fault." He struggled to sit up, still holding his groin.

Aria winced in sympathy. "I'm so sorry. I didn't mean to do that. I promise I wasn't attacking you. And I'm not mad at you."

"What the hell were you doing, then?" Sweat beaded on his forehead.

"I was... I was trying to get off the couch without waking you up." She stifled a giggle at her obvious fail.

Luke gave a pained bark of a laugh. "Well, I don't think it worked."

Ben padded down the hall, yawning and stretching his arms above his head. "I thought I heard you guys." He paused, frowning at Luke. "What's wrong?"

Luke straightened up, and Aria could tell he battled to hide the pain from his face. "I'm fine. Aria just startled me."

Aria snorted as Luke shot her a pointed look.

Ben, apparently satisfied with the answer, patted his stomach. "What's for breakfast? I'm starving."

"You're always starving," Aria said. She remembered it was Monday morning and glanced at the clock on the stove then sent a silent thanks to the universe that they hadn't overslept. There was still time to get Ben and herself ready and off to school. "Come on. I'll make you some breakfast. How does sausage, eggs, and toast sound?"

As Ben cheered his way to the kitchen, Aria glanced back to see Luke fall over onto the couch with a groan. "Sorry," she whispered, only to be met with a thumbs-up over the back of the couch.

Aria flipped the sizzling sausage as Luke waited at the table with Ben. She studied Luke from the corner of her eye. "Feeling better?"

He winced. "Mostly. Need any help with that?"

"Nope. I've got it." She swatted Ben's hand as he reached for the sausage she'd just taken from the skillet. "That's too hot. You'll have to wait a minute." She shook her head as Ben grumbled and plopped back down in his chair then turned her attention back to Luke. "So, how was the bus last night?"

Luke shrugged. "Nothing too crazy happened. It was a pretty mild night compared to some. I had a bachelorette party that almost deafened me with all the squeals. Pretty sure I ended up in at least a dozen selfies. I don't mind, though. Free advertising. Ironically enough, I also had a divorce party. I don't know the guy, but his ex-wife seemed pretty ecstatic to be rid of him. The best part of the night, though, was coming home. I've never slept better."

Heat crept up Aria's neck, a rather frequent occurrence over the past two days. "Sounds like an interesting job."

Luke gave a nod of agreement. "It is. I love getting to be a part of so many celebrations. You definitely meet some interesting characters in this business."

"What's the weirdest thing you've seen?" Ben asked, grabbing the plate of sausage as Aria started on the eggs.

Luke tapped his chin. "I think I'd have to say the weirdest thing was being booked for a funeral."

Ben's eyes grew wide. "No way. A funeral?"

Luke nodded as he got up and headed for the coffeepot. "Apparently, the person who died was a huge prankster and had put my number down as the 'ride service' they wanted their family to use. I guess whoever was fulfilling their wishes didn't notice me saying 'party bus' when I answered the phone. Imagine their surprise when I rolled up with the party lights on and upbeat music playing. We had a good laugh over that one." He pushed the brew button and went back to the table. "Honestly, the more I think about it, the more I love it. That person made their family laugh on one of the saddest days of their lives. That's kind of magical."

Aria pondered his words. "Yeah, that does sound pretty cool." Luke was pretty cool too. The more she caught tiny glimpses into his heart, the more she liked the man he'd become. Every time she talked to him and every time he came through for her, more of her walls chipped away.

Luke

Luke stood and began gathering dishes. "You cooked, so I'll wash today." He waited for Aria to protest, but she stared out the window instead. Maybe she was starting to accept the give-and-take of their arrangement. He hoped so.

"Um, can I use the computer for a bit?" Aria's voice held a hesitant edge.

"You live here now, remember? You can use the computer any time you want. No need to run it by me first. Okay?"

"Okay, if you say so."

After finishing the dishes, Luke walked over and noticed the map Aria had pulled up on the screen. "What are you looking for? I know the area really well. I can help."

Aria peeked back over her shoulder and teased, "Spying on me?"

"I have to make sure you're not looking up something naughty." He wiggled his eyebrows at her.

She gave a half-hearted laugh. "Yeah, right. I mapped out the shortest route to school for Ben and me yesterday, but I forgot to print the directions for him. My walk is going to be a little longer, but at least the neighborhoods will be nicer most of the way. For Ben, it'll be a lot longer. He's probably going to be late this morning even if he left right now."

Luke straightened, butterflies fluttering in his stomach as he sought the best words to explain what he'd done. Finding none, he slipped away in silence and went out the front door. He felt Aria's eyes trailing him, watching through the window as he got on the bus and came back in moments later.

Ignoring her questioning eyes, he strolled over to the computer desk. "You know, you two should take the bus. It's a lot easier. And faster. And warmer." Luke's fingers ran along the edges of the plastic cards in his back pocket.

Aria frowned. "That would be great, except I can't afford one bus pass, let alone two. Maybe in a couple months after I've been able to save up some money, but until then we'll have to make do."

"Then why don't you use these?" Luke brought his hand from his pocket, revealing the cards. He held his breath, bracing himself for the inevitable arguments and protests.

Narrowing her suspicious eyes at him, she took the cards. Her jaw dropped as she stared at the bus passes in her hands, and emotions waged war across her face in stunned silence. Without warning, she leapt up and threw her arms around his neck, making him stumble backward.

After steadying himself, he eased his arms around her. She clung to him, and he caressed her back as instinct took over. The weight and warmth of her in his arms was a natural fit, as if it was meant to be. He could hold her forever.

After a moment, she backed away, swiping at her face with her shoulder. "Thank you."

Luke laid his hand on her shoulder, craving to regain an ounce of their embrace. "You're very welcome."

Her eyes still swam with emotion. "You don't understand how much this means to me. To us. It takes so much worry and stress off my shoulders. I... I seriously don't know how I'll ever be able to thank you enough for all you've done for us."

Luke locked eyes with her and placed a hand on his chest. "I know how much it means, though. I went through a lot of the same. I get it. That's why I'm helping you. Besides, your reaction is proof enough how much it means to you."

Her eyes landed on his tear-soaked shoulder. "Sorry about that. I couldn't stop myself."

He rubbed at his wet shirt as if to dry it. "Nah, don't worry about that. It'll dry. Honestly, though, I'm shocked. I've got to admit I expected a fight. I figured a tackle was more likely than a hug when I saw you moving in on me."

Her eyes shimmered. "I actually wanted to fight it. Part of me was screaming to not accept it. That it was too much. But the other half of me knew how much I truly needed it, not just for me, but for Ben too. I guess you've worn down my defenses enough these past couple of days that my accepting and thankful side wins easier now. I'm very grateful. For everything."

The faint hum of attraction he'd tried his damnedest to ignore since the bus ride home buzzed through him like a bullet train. The gleam in her eyes hinted he might not be alone in this overwhelming feeling. Making her happy set his soul on fire in the best ways. If it wasn't for his aching back, thanks to sleeping on the couch, he would've sworn he was eighteen again, with his raging hormones crushing on the pretty girl next door. Only that girl had grown into a sexy woman… and only a bedroom door stood between them at night.

"What's wrong? Why are you crying?" Ben's unsteady voice called out.

Luke spun toward the kitchen and found Ben watching them, his face twisted in a worried frown.

"It's okay, Ben. They're happy tears," Aria said.

Ben cocked his head to the side. "You cry when you're happy too?"

Luke's heart dropped. Nothing had ever made either of them happy enough to cry before. Not that it shocked him, given their former reality, but it still drove a nail through his heart.

Aria held up the bus passes like they were winning lottery tickets. "Look. Luke got us bus passes so we won't have to walk to school anymore. Isn't that great?"

Ben snatched a pass and inspected it, his face filled with wonder. "Wow, I've never seen a bus pass before. I feel so fancy. Wait 'til my friends see this." Ben bounded toward his room, tossing a word of thanks over his shoulder as he went.

Aria shouted down the hall to Ben, "You still need to hurry up and get dressed, though, so you won't be late. And don't forget to put your homework in your backpack this time." Then she raised her eyes to Luke's. "Thank you."

Pride was still unfamiliar territory for Luke, often tainted by guilt or shame for even thinking about being proud of himself. But seeing the joy pouring from Aria for the first time in years, pride filled him from head to toe in the most intoxicating way.

Chapter 9

Aria

Aria inspected her reflection as she brushed her teeth before bed, unable to recall the last time she owned a full mirror. Her mom had broken theirs in a drug-induced rage one night, leaving Aria to tape together the largest pieces and make do with that.

How pathetic that seeing my full, uninterrupted reflection would be so meaningful, she mused as she studied the woman staring back at her. Aria's skin drank up her new moisturizer like a cactus in the desert soaking up rain as she smoothed the rich cream over her arms. She inhaled, filling her lungs with the sweet scent of jasmine floating from her hair. It was a welcome break from having Luke's scent surrounding her. Not that he smelled bad. Quite the opposite. He smelled good. Too good. Amazing. Tantalizing. She shook the thoughts from her head and zeroed in on her reflection. The face in the mirror glowed ten times healthier than the one that had stared back just days before. Her eyes sparkled with hope, and a warm glow replaced the dull paleness of her skin. Good food and rest must've worked miracles.

As she took in her transformation from what most considered basic self-care, the medley of emotions from the past few days hit her all at once like a punch to the gut. She gripped the sink as her soft features hardened. Rage toward her parents and her hard-knock life burned bright in her core. Anxiety and fear of an uncertain future and uprooted plans gnawed at her brain. The weight of caring for Ben shoved down hard on her hunched shoulders. She lowered herself to the edge of the tub, taking deep, panting breaths to stop the spiral. She closed her eyes, wrapping her arms around herself and rocking back and forth.

Through the dark storm of emotions, a singular ray of light broke through. Luke. Luke had swooped in when no one else would and pulled them from the depths of utter despair, lifting them from rock bottom. Because of Luke, they slept in soft, warm beds in a clean, safe house rather than on the cold, dirty streets. Thanks to Luke, hunger, pain, and cold were no longer staples in her daily life. She'd never felt so secure as she did with him, which was at once both exhilarating and terrifying.

The concept of being safe or happy felt foreign, her mind unaccustomed to processing such emotions. Through all the trials and upheavals, she'd become tough and independent. Guarded. Somewhere along the way, she had used the pieces of her broken home to build a fortress around her heart, the construction of every wall being fueled by trauma. With every act of selfless kindness from Luke, those walls chipped away, piece by piece. The most shocking aspect was that the breaking down of that fortress had a freeing effect. Healing. Perhaps she could use the broken pieces to build a new home, one not quite so broken. Maybe her life could be like one of those Japanese bowls her professor talked about, the broken pieces glued together with gold to celebrate the bowl's journey.

Invigorated, she climbed to her feet and gave herself a once-over in the mirror, fluffing her damp hair the best she could. It was high time to get out the gold glue and start celebrating her journey. Time to live.

Tiptoeing past Ben's door, she found Luke on the couch.

Luke set down the remote when he saw her, giving her his full attention, as always. "Hey. What's up?"

Aria shrugged, hoping he couldn't see past her façade to the changes happening within. "Nothing. Just need to relax a bit before bed. Mind if I join you?"

Luke's face flushed as his eyes flicked to the television. "As long as you don't give me a hard time about my movie selection."

Aria saw a classic romantic comedy cued and ready to play. "Are you kidding? That's one of my favorites."

"Well, isn't that some luck?"

Aria sauntered to the couch, but instead of aiming for her usual seat at the far end, she chose the cushion next to Luke. She smirked with self-satisfaction when his eyes flew open in obvious surprise. She stared ahead at the screen, pointedly ignoring him as he hesitated and eyed her before he pushed Play.

Luke

As the final credits began scrolling across the screen, panic seized Luke's chest. He'd squirmed during the love scenes as his body wanted to reenact them with the woman sitting inches away, but he hadn't thought about the awkwardness of saying goodnight afterward. If they were in the movie, they'd be holding hands and staring lovingly into each other's eyes. But this was reality. He snuck a glance at Aria, waiting for her to make a move. He resolved to let her control the situation because, left up to him, there would be no control.

"I guess I need to get to bed." Aria leaned forward as if to get up but stopped. "Luke... Can I ask you something?"

The trepidation in her eyes made his pulse quicken. "Of course."

"That night, in the bar... before Brandon came over. Was I hallucinating, or were you about to..." Her words trailed off, but her fingertips brushed her lips as her focus fell to the floor.

Luke swallowed hard. "You know the answer to that." He studied Aria's profile, pleading with the universe to grant him mind-reading powers.

Aria nodded almost imperceptibly before facing him, her eyes ablaze in a way he'd never seen. Luke's heart pounded wildly in his chest as she closed the distance between them. He had to be hallucinating.

Her lips caressed his, tender yet intentional, sending shivers throughout his body. His brain short-circuited as his teenage fantasy came to life, but his body switched into autopilot, his lips seeking hers. As his hand brushed her back, she pulled away, his mouth chasing hers and eager for more, needing more. Her warm breath caressed his ear with a whispered good night before she sprang to her feet and whisked herself away to the bedroom.

Luke sat with his mouth agape, staring at the empty hallway and trying to make sense of what just happened. Not wanting to take advantage of her situation or any misguided gratitude, he had tried to keep his attraction at bay. But with her lips on his, the long-smoldering embers erupted into flames, Aria's kiss like a jug of gasoline. He adjusted his pants and reached for his root beer, willing the cool liquid to douse the fire burning inside. The way she melted him, he knew not kissing her years ago had been the right decision. After a kiss like that, he never would've found the strength to leave and start his business. But they were both adults and out of that neighborhood, which meant the rules were different. They had to be. He needed more. Aria was his new drug of choice, and after that kiss, he was hooked.

Chapter 10

Aria

I'll pretend the kiss never happened, Aria thought as she chewed her turkey sandwich, her philosophy book lying unopened on the desk. Instead of taking advantage of the quiet student lounge and studying, her mind was preoccupied with replays of the night before. Kissing Luke in real life was a million times better than any of the kisses she'd played in her head over the years. The softness of Luke's lips and the fireworks exploding throughout her body. The way his eyes burned with desire as she pulled away. So good that stopping at only a little kiss had been much harder than she ever imagined. She'd managed, but it left her body craving him with an ache like none other. What she had thought would be a bit of harmless fun had shaken her to her core. But she had no room for romance in her life. No, she had to keep her wits about her if she was going to build a better future for herself and Ben. An independent future. And that meant not indulging in unrealistic fantasies with fairy-tale endings. She took another bite of her sandwich and picked up the book, determined to make herself forget about the kiss and anything it might have awakened.

Commotion behind her interrupted her thoughts as a group of students entered the lounge area, their rushed words jumbling together until one name sent chills down Aria's spine. She leapt from her seat and rushed over to the group. "Did you say Marion West? As in the middle school? What's going on?"

A tall guy with red hair gaped her way. "You haven't heard? There was a huge gang fight, and there's a ton of cops over there. The whole place is on lockdown until they get it under control. They're saying one kid got sent to the hospital."

He kept talking, but the blood pounding in Aria's ears drowned out his words. Her mind racing, she shoved her lunch and book in her backpack and bolted out of the door.

With the bus stuck in traffic, Aria jumped off before her stop and ran the remaining five blocks to Marion West Middle School. Ben's school. Elbowing her way through the crowd gathered outside, she fought to rein in her panic. Finally, she reached an officer. "I need to find my brother. Ben Sutton. How can I find him?"

"I'm sorry, ma'am, but no one is allowed in or out of the premises at the moment." The officer held up his hands as if he could hold back the pressing crowd.

"But I need to get my brother. I need to make sure he's okay." She craned her neck for a better view.

He set his mouth in a hard line. "I understand, ma'am, but I can't allow anyone onto the campus at this time. You'll have to be patient."

As she stepped back into the crowd, bits and pieces of conversations overwhelmed her as everyone waited for news.

What felt like an eternity later, the principal addressed the crowd. "An incident occurred today within a group of students, and the guardians of the students involved in the conflict have been notified. A lockdown was implemented as a precaution to prevent the situation from escalating, and it has now been lifted. There is no longer a threat to any of the remaining students, and school will proceed as normal. I understand some of you may wish to remove students early today. If so, I ask you to proceed to the office in an orderly fashion."

Aria's feet couldn't move fast enough as she claimed her spot in line. The minutes ticked by as kid after kid walked past with their guardians, and she inched closer to the office. Her heart lifted as she stepped up to the desk at last. "I'm here for Ben Sutton."

"And you are?" A woman with wavy brown hair eyed Aria over her glasses.

"I'm his sister, Aria Sutton."

The woman leafed through some papers and shook her head. "I'm sorry, but you're not on the list of approved people for pickup."

Aria froze. "But I'm his sister."

"I'm sorry, but unless you're his legal guardian or on the approved list, I can't let you take him."

This has to be a nightmare. Aria wished she could wake up from it. "Isn't there something I can do? How can I get on the approved list?"

A heavy sigh fluttered the woman's hair as she adjusted her papers. "I'm sorry, but only a legal guardian can add people to the list. I'm going to have to ask you to step aside."

With her heart plummeting to the floor and her head swimming, Aria backed away from the desk and fled out into the brisk air. Memories of her dragging Tasha to Ben's preschool registration and helping her fill out the paperwork flashed through her mind. Aria had tried to put herself as an emergency contact, but the school wouldn't allow anyone underage to be listed. Aria berated herself for not dragging Tasha back to the school once Aria had turned eighteen. Their mom was too far gone and too bitter to ask anymore. She was more likely to ban Aria altogether than to help her.

There has to be another way, she thought. And she needed to find it pronto.

By the time Ben got out of school, Aria had chewed her bottom lip raw. As soon as she saw his head bobbing in the crowd of students, she wove her way over to him and grabbed him in a hug. "I've been so worried about you. Are you okay?"

"I'm fine. What are you doing here?" Ben shrugged away from her embrace as he scanned the students around them, his cheeks coloring.

"I couldn't wait until you got home. I thought maybe we could ride home together and talk about what all happened. I know that had to be scary. It was for me."

Without a word, Ben headed for the bus stop. Aria trailed behind him, telling herself his attitude was probably a trauma response.

After a long, silent ride home, Aria shut the door behind them and watched as Ben grabbed a granola bar and plopped down at the table. She took the seat across from him and studied his strained features.

"What?" he asked with a mouthful of food.

"I need to talk to you about something. I think..." Her courage wavered, but she squared her shoulders and made herself carry on. "I think you should transfer schools. I've never liked Marion West anyway, and Luke's house is in a different school district. A better one with less crime and better student outcomes. It's also less than half the distance from here. How would you feel about that?"

Ben took another bite of the granola bar and chewed in silence for so long, Aria wondered if he'd even heard her.

Then he gave a slight nod. "Yeah, okay."

"Okay?"

"I mean, school can't get any worse than it is now. Might as well try a different one." His eyes darkened, hinting at his true feelings.

One topic down, one to go. She leaned forward, resting her elbows on the table. "There's something else that goes along with that. Only your legal guardian has the authority to enroll you in another school."

"But wouldn't Mom be my legal guardian?" Ben frowned and twisted his empty granola bar wrapper in his fingers. "She doesn't even have an address anymore."

"I know. But a guardian doesn't necessarily have to be a parent."

Ben shook his head, sending his curls bouncing. "Okay, so what does that mean? I don't get it."

"After I couldn't take you out of school today, I did some research about guardianship. I want to file paperwork to become your legal guardian." The words came rushing out with her breath, like ripping off a bandage.

"Sooo, you'd be like my mom?" Ben's words crawled out.

"Kind of. We would have to go to a hearing and get it approved, but afterward I could legally act like your mom. I'd be able to register you for school, take you to the doctor, get insurance for you, take you to get your permit, and all that other good stuff."

Ben's eyes traveled to the back door, focusing beyond the window. After several excruciating moments, he spoke. "Okay."

"That's it?" Aria searched his face for clues. "You're handling all of this better than I thought you would. It's kind of a big deal."

"Not really." He brought his eyes to hers. "You've always been the one doing everything for me and deciding stuff anyway. It won't be that different. You just won't have to ask Mom to sign stuff for you. Mom can't do any of that stuff you said, like take me to the doctor or get my permit, so someone has to."

"You're right about that, unfortunately." She let out a sigh of both sadness and relief. "Okay, so that settles it. I'll go ahead and start filing all the paperwork to get this going. Hopefully you'll start next semester in your new school."

Aria caught Luke's eye as he stuck his head into the hallway, and she nodded for him to join them. Relief flooded his face when she gave him a thumbs-up out of Ben's view.

"I thought I heard you guys in here. I was taking a nap so I can be rested for work tonight." Luke stretched, even though it was obvious he was lying, then joined them at the table. "So, what do we want for dinner?"

"I picked up some stuff for spaghetti and garlic bread." Aria got up and pulled ingredients from the cabinets, needing some physical movement to distract from the mental gymnastics that had given her a headache. "Anyone want a side salad?"

"Sure," Luke and Ben said in unison, eliciting a round of chuckles.

Ben leaned forward, resting his chin in his hand.

"Rough day, huh?" Luke asked.

A silent shrug was all he got from Ben.

"You know, I went through pretty much the same thing back when I was around your age," Luke said, getting up and grabbing a root beer from the refrigerator.

Aria watched him, trying to read whether he was telling the truth or fibbing so he could relate to Ben. She didn't remember anything like that happening when they were in school.

"Really?" Ben asked with a tone of disbelief.

"Yep." Luke sat back down and took a swig. "I was a freshman in high school, though, so a little bit older than you."

Aria nodded to herself. She hadn't thought about the fact that she and Luke weren't always in the same school due to their age difference.

"There were several different gangs, but two in particular downright hated each other," Luke continued. "Usually, they'd butt heads outside of school, and we'd all be talking about it the next day. Then, one day, I don't even know what started it, but a huge fight broke out in the cafeteria. I'm talking over a dozen kids duking it out and knocking over lunch tables. It was wild. And I was caught in the middle of it."

"What did you do?" Ben asked, his eyes almost bulging from his head.

"I took cover. The table next to me flipped over, and that was all the warning I needed. I scrambled over to one of the tables at the far side of the room, and me and this other guy flipped it on its side to use as a shield. Other students came and joined us, and we all hunkered there until the teachers and security guards got it all under control."

"You hid?"

"Heck, yeah, I hid. It was terrifying. I didn't want any part in that mess. That incident is why the school stopped using metal forks and switched to disposable. Plastic ones do less damage when used as a weapon. I was scared out of my mind."

Aria peeked over her shoulder to see Ben's face scrunch in thought and sent up a silent prayer that he would open up about his feelings.

As if he heard her plea, Ben spoke at last. "I was kind of scared today too."

"You'd be crazy if you weren't. Anyone in their right mind would be scared with that kind of violent chaos going on. And anyone that says they weren't is lying," Luke said with conviction.

"I really wanted to leave, but they said we had to go back to class. The whole rest of the day, I was nervous." Ben blinked several times as if blinking away tears.

"Well, hopefully you won't have to go to that school much longer. And if I know anything about your sister, it's that she'll find a way to make that happen for you." Luke cocked his head toward Aria.

"I hope so," Ben said.

Feeling it was safe to join the conversation without breaking the magic, Aria stopped washing lettuce and put her hand over her heart.

"I promise I will do everything I possibly can to get guardianship and get you transferred."

Ben's face brightened for the first time that day. "Thanks."

As Luke and Ben chatted about other things, Aria found her eyes wandering to Luke. Though she wished Ben would talk to her, she couldn't be more grateful that he had Luke in his life, and that gratitude chipped away another wall around her heart.

Chapter 11

Aria

The familiar beat of Aria's favorite song fueled the energy in her steps as she guided the vacuum over the carpet. She let go, allowing herself to get lost in the music and belting out the tune as the vacuum became her dance partner. Letting go of the vacuum, she twirled, a lightness in her spirit that breathed fresh air into her once-stagnant soul.

On her second spin, her gaze caught on a car pulling up to the curb in front of the house. Every cell in her body stopped in its tracks and stood at attention, fixating on the unfamiliar vehicle. She tiptoed to the window and peeked through the blinds.

They're probably looking for a different house, she chided herself.

A man wearing khakis and a blue dress shirt stepped out and began walking up their driveway.

A deafening ringing in her ears drowned out all other sounds. Her surroundings fell away, nothing left in her darkening world except the man approaching. This was it. Her worst nightmare was coming to fruition. After all these years, after all the hotline calls that fell on deaf ears, the Department of Family Services was there to rip her brother from her arms. Of course they would wait until she'd finally begun making her way in the world. The universe couldn't help her when she was a young child scrambling to take care of a baby brother she watched almost die. No, it waited until the help became a threat, until the light began shining at the end of the tunnel. She should've known the light would end up being a train. She knew life had become too good to be true.

The world moved in slow motion as the man's outstretched hand made contact with the door. The knocking reverberated in her bones until her stomach clenched and her teeth ground hard. She slid from the window, panting as she plastered her back to the wall, willing herself to sink into the drywall and escape the torment. Another knock ricocheted through her soul.

No, she couldn't let them take him. Not after all she and Ben had been through. Not when their path was bright for the first time in their lives. The doorknob rattled, squeezing the breath from her lungs. She braced herself for another knock. She flinched, anticipating the forceful announcement. Her panting breath deafened her as she waited for the inevitable.

A car door slammed. An engine revved to life. She scurried to peek out the window and blinked as she watched the car drive away, taking her nightmare with it. Her breathing slowed, not to normal but at least to a more sustainable rhythm. The cacophony of music and the vacuum assaulted her ears, and the room came back into view. She rushed to switch off the vacuum and radio, the once-energizing noise suddenly overwhelming her senses.

Her brain struggled to make sense of what had happened as her body clamored to return to equilibrium. She swept the area again for any signs of the car or man. Nothing. With the coast clear, she yanked open the door and found a bag hanging from the doorknob. She pulled it free and slammed the door shut. With her heart hammering, she dumped the contents on the counter.

Relief washed over her like a tidal wave as the emblem of a local church greeted her.

"Pamphlets," she breathed. "It's just pamphlets."

She sank to the floor, her body trembling from the rush of adrenaline.

"Ben is safe. Ben is safe," she said with a hand on her chest, willing her racing heart to calm. *I can't live like this,* she thought. Getting guardianship of Ben couldn't come fast enough.

Luke

Muffled sobs met Luke's ears as he opened the door, sending his senses into overdrive. His late-night exhaustion vanished, becoming an afterthought as he scanned for signs of distress in the dim light. Aria sat hunched in front of the computer, her face in her hands. Luke sprinted to her side and squatted, straining to see her face as a million questions raced through his brain. "What's wrong?"

"I... I can't find a good job." Aria dropped her hands to her lap.

Luke knelt beside her, his face twisted in confusion. "Why are you job hunting? I told you I don't need you to make more money. Especially now during the holiday season. I made around a thousand tonight alone, even after I take taxes out. We are fine with money. I promise."

She shook her head, taking in a gulp of air as her sorrow-filled eyes sought his. "It's not that. I got a call today about the guardianship. My income isn't enough to be considered a valid candidate. They don't think I can take care of Ben."

"But your mom has no income at all. And you live here rent free."

"They don't care. She can have him by default because she birthed him, but I have to prove my worth if I want to take him. If I don't somehow double my income in a couple of weeks, I can't be his guardian and he's stuck at that horrible school. I won't be able to keep my promises. And now that I started this process and brought attention to us, what if Family Services takes him away from me? What am I going to do?" Tears flooded her eyes again.

Luke's heart shattered for her and for Ben. It wasn't fair. There had to be some way he could help her. Something fast. An idea took root in his mind. Aria would think he was insane, but he couldn't think of another way to solve her problem. He blurted out the words before he could talk himself out of it. "Marry me."

Aria's tears halted. "What did you say?"

Luke swallowed, his mouth dry like he'd eaten cotton balls. He wondered if she could hear his heart banging against his ribs. "Marry me."

Aria put her hand on her forehead. "I'm sorry, but I think I hallucinated because I could swear I just heard you ask me to marry you."

Luke let out a nervous laugh and ran his hand through his hair. "Yeah, I did."

"Are you crazy?"

Luke recoiled a bit, his pride stinging even though he expected that reaction. "Hear me out. You need more income so you can get guardianship, and you need it pronto. I have a sizable income. If we get married, what's mine is yours. Boom. Problem solved. You get to claim the income, and it makes you staying here more legit too."

Aria chewed her lip, a nervous habit Luke had grown to love. "Well, that does make sense. I just... that's a lot for me to ask of you when you've already done so much. This is, well, it's a big deal."

"You're not asking. I'm offering. And I promise there are no strings attached."

Aria searched his face. "Either way, this is huge, Luke. Especially when it isn't even your problem to solve. How could you possibly be okay with it all?"

The idea of getting married terrified the hell out of him, but he'd never tell her that. Marriage wasn't something he'd ever envisioned for himself, though having Aria in the equation did make the idea more appealing. Regardless, she needed him, so his fears would have to wait. "I swear I'm okay with it, and I wouldn't offer if I wasn't. I don't really see any other way to satisfy the courts on such a short notice. Do you? And it doesn't have to change anything in our day-to-day lives. I promise."

Her eyes traveled to the computer screen then back to him. "I hate to admit it, but I don't see any alternative."

"So is that a yes?" Luke's eyes widened, a curious mix of excitement and nerves making his body hum.

Aria chewed her lip and then nodded. "As crazy as it sounds, I guess we're getting married. You can back out at any time, though. No hard feelings."

He resisted a sudden urge to sweep her into his arms, instead rising to his feet. "I won't back out. You know I wouldn't leave you high and dry like that." A silence hung between them, heavy with the gravity of their decision. So much for not changing things between them. He took a moment to steady his nerves before picking up the television remote. "Now how about you turn off the computer and pick out a movie for us to watch while I go change?"

Aria dried her face with her sleeve. "I think I can handle that. And I'll even pick the cheesiest sci-fi movie I can find, just for you."

"The cheesier, the better," he said then headed for the bedroom.

As Luke changed clothes, he let everything that had just happened sink in. If he had to get married, he couldn't think of a better person to do it with. And he would have to hope like hell it wouldn't ruin everything for them, like it did his parents. Being the one who brought joy and light into Aria's eyes was something he would never get tired of, and he couldn't let that change between them. Even though he knew their marriage would just be on paper, he couldn't help but think about what life would be like if it were real. If they could manage to stay happy and stand the test of time. And as he thought about a life together with Aria, he had a feeling a fake marriage was going to be harder than he thought.

Chapter 12

Aria

"Hey, Ben, can you wait a minute?" Aria put her hand out to stop Ben as he got up from the table.

Ben sat back down, annoyance and worry mixing on his face. "What's wrong?"

"Um, well, I need to tell you something." Aria's heart hammered against her chest. "You know how I'm trying to get guardianship, right?"

Ben nodded.

"Well, I found out that in order to do so, I need to make more money. A lot more. And fast."

"Why?"

"It's one of the requirements the courts look at to see if I'm able to provide for you," Aria said.

Ben frowned. "But Mom doesn't make any money at all."

Aria let out an exasperated sigh. "Yeah, I know, but she gets custody by default. I have to prove myself. It's not fair, but it is what it is. Anyway, I think I found a solution to the problem."

Luke left the breakfast dishes in the sink and took the seat beside Aria then gave her knee a squeeze under the table.

"I was talking it over with Luke last night, and he suggested I use his income." She inhaled through her nose and spoke on the exhale. "But in order for me to do that, we have to be married."

Ben sat back. "Wait, what?"

"If we get married, Aria can claim my income as hers on the paperwork. What's mine is hers, you know? Plus it gives her a stronger case for this being your new address for transferring schools," Luke said.

"It'll just be a marriage on paper for the guardianship process. It won't really change anything in our real lives." Aria's words flew out. "So what do you think?"

Ben's eyes traveled from Aria to Luke and then to his own lap, a silent war raging on his face. "I want you to be able to get guardianship so I can switch schools, so I guess do what you have to do."

Aria couldn't believe it was that easy. "Really? There's not really any other way if we want to go through with the guardianship hearing anytime soon, but I still want to make sure you're okay with it all."

"Yeah, I guess."

Aria's eyes darted to Luke. They were going to get married. She forced her thoughts back to Ben. "We were actually thinking about going to the courthouse today. I checked online, and we should be able to apply for a marriage license this morning and have it be ready in time for us to get married this afternoon. I'll need to stop by somewhere and get a dress since I don't have one."

Ben's mouth dropped open. "Today?"

Luke cleared his throat. "We figured the sooner the better as far as the courts are concerned. That way there's more time to file all the paperwork and get it processed. They might think we are trying to con them if we wait until right before the hearing."

"I want to go," Ben said.

Aria shook her head. "But you have school."

Ben leaned forward, elbows on the table. "But if you want it to look like it's real, I think I should be there. I can take Luke's camera and play photographer. It's more believable if it looks real. What if they ask for proof?"

Aria wondered when Ben had learned so much about crafting a convincing lie, but that was a topic for another discussion. "I guess you have a point."

"Of course I do. You're not the only smart one, you know." Ben crossed his arms over his chest, but his eyes held a teasing gleam.

"You're too smart for your own good sometimes," Aria said with a laugh. "Okay, I guess you can skip school just this once."

"I'll go finish up the dishes, and then we can head out," Luke said, pushing away from the table.

Aria's stomach fluttered as she slipped on the ivory dress, the soft chiffon cooling her skin. The V-neck and wraparound-style waistline enhanced the hourglass shape she hadn't realized she possessed. Bell sleeves and a flowing skirt gave the dress a timeless, ethereal feel. She clipped a silver rose in her hair by her right ear and slipped a silver chain over her head. Her fingers twirled the single white pearl pendant. Ben had insisted she needed jewelry to complete her ensemble, and she had to admit he wasn't wrong.

Seeing herself in the mirror, the reality of the day hit her with an intensity that made her stomach drop. She leaned a hand on the sink and focused on her breathing. She never planned to marry young, instead putting everything she had into her education, building her career, and getting as far away from her roots as possible. Now she was about to marry someone who was an integral part of those same roots. It all felt like she was failing at her dream. Her heart told her she wasn't, but her brain needed convincing.

"You're not giving up anything. Just adding extra steps," she told her reflection. Besides, they weren't getting married for real. It was all a show. A way to get what she needed to keep Ben safe. It wasn't forever. But when she looked in the mirror, it didn't feel fake. Maybe the idea of forever wasn't so bad. There were certainly worse things she could think of for her future than being married to Luke.

Get a grip, she thought as she closed her eyes and pushed all images of a fairy-tale future to the far recesses of her mind. The last thing she needed to do was fall in love with her soon-to-be fake husband. She needed a clear head if she was going to get through to the other side unscathed. Their marriage was merely a means to an end, and that was how she needed to approach it.

She flung open the bathroom door and strutted down the hallway with renewed resolve. As she entered the living room, Ben stopped midsentence and stared at her with his mouth agape.

Luke pivoted, his eyes opening wide when he saw her. Her heart fluttered as she watched his eyes travel over her body, seeming to drink in every inch of her. He took a step toward her. "Wow, you look... Wow."

"Well, thank you. You're not so bad yourself." It was Aria's turn to check out Luke. He wore a navy suit and tie with an ivory dress shirt that fit his muscular frame in a way that lit a fire inside Aria.

Ben rolled his eyes. "Are we going to go or just stand here all day?"

Luke gave a nervous laugh. "Right. Let's go."

Chapter 13

Luke

Driving to the courthouse, Luke drummed his fingers on the steering wheel, ready to burst from his own skin. Excitement buzzed through his veins more than he would ever admit to Aria. And that excitement terrified him. Growing up watching his parents fight, he'd never dared to imagine marriage as a part of his future. Not even a fake one. It felt both wrong and right at the same time. Deep down, his gut told him Aria was the right person, whether he wanted to listen or not, but the circumstances seemed so wrong. Of course, they had to do whatever they could to keep Ben safe, so there was no other choice. He would have to remind himself that he was marrying Aria so she could put his income on paperwork and leave his heart out of it.

Laughter trickled from the back of the bus, bringing him out of his spiraling negative thoughts. Seeing Aria and Ben giggling and bubbling with joy, he decided seeing them happy was worth the risk.

"We're here. Ready?" Luke could almost hear the hum of excited-yet-nervous energy coming from them all as he shut off the bus.

Aria's tight smile let him know her feelings mirrored his. She squared her shoulders and lifted her chin. "Ready."

Ben held up Luke's old camera. "I'm ready."

Luke's throat constricted as they walked into the courthouse, hand in hand. Instead of butterflies, he must've had a stampede of horses going wild in his stomach as they sat in silence, waiting to be called in for the judge.

"Luke Hardin. Aria Sutton," a clerk called from a doorway, beckoning them into the small room. The judge sat at a grand wooden desk, the only grandeur in the room. Aside from legal certificates and awards, the gray walls lacked any flair.

The ceremony was short and sweet, and as they said their vows, a twinge of regret plagued Luke, not for marrying Aria but for the lack of pomp and circumstance. She deserved better than a boring, musty room in a courthouse with Ben and the clerk as their only witnesses. He slipped the simple silver band on her finger. "I do."

"I now pronounce you husband and wife. You may kiss the bride," the judge proclaimed.

Luke struggled to tamp down the giddiness that bubbled up as he dipped his face toward hers. Ever aware of the audience and the need to appear believable, he brought his lips to hers for a gentle kiss, hoping the judge couldn't sense the mixed emotions. More than that, he hoped Aria couldn't sense how much he was having to restrain himself. When they parted, he caught a flicker of desire in her eyes before she looked away. He took her hand and escorted her to the door. "Come, wife, let's go celebrate." The word "wife," though foreign on his tongue, made his heart skip a beat in the best way.

Aria blushed. "Yes, husband, let's go."

As they stepped out into the sunlight, Luke had to remind himself, yet again, that he wasn't supposed to be this happy.

Aria

Sliding the cake-box lid closed, Aria stared through the cellophane at the purple buttercream roses and blue letters that used to spell out Congratulations before Ben ate the last half of the word. Her wedding cake. She licked her lips, still sweet from the icing, and was transported back to her wedding kiss with Luke. Though simple, that kiss had left her reeling. The entire drive home, her gaze kept being drawn to Luke as if pulled by a magnetic force. Paired with the way he'd ogled her, she would've sworn their wedding was real. It felt real. But it wasn't. It couldn't be.

She tore her eyes away from the cake and made a beeline for the bedroom. With the door shut behind her, she slipped off her wedding dress and hung it as far back in the closet as possible. She tucked her hair clip and necklace in a drawer under her socks. The farther she could get from reminders of a far-fetched fairy tale, the better. After slipping on some black sweatpants and a college T-shirt, she went back to the living room.

"There. Now I'm all back to normal, and we can go on like nothing ever happened," Aria said as she plopped onto the couch next to Ben.

Something strange flashed across Luke's face but then disappeared as he took a drink of his root beer.

"Do you have any homework you need to do tonight? It's almost bedtime," Aria asked Ben.

"Yeah, I guess I'll go finish it," Ben said, getting up and heading for his bedroom.

Though only a cushion separated her and Luke, she sensed his mind was a million miles away. If only the universe would grant her mind-reading powers. Maybe he was regretting marrying her. Or maybe he was as overwhelmed and confused by everything as she was. She decided to test the waters. "Whew. What a day, huh?"

"Yeah, pretty crazy," Luke said, lacking any readable emotion.

An awkward silence stretched between them. Credits rolled on the show Ben had been watching, so Aria picked up the remote. "Want to watch a movie? I'll let you pick."

The corners of Luke's mouth ticked upward, giving her a brief moment of hope, but he shook his head. "I was thinking about reading that new book I got about scaling up your business."

"Oh. Okay. Yeah, I have some homework I should probably get a head start on anyway." She stood to go to the computer but hesitated. "Are you okay? You seem a little off. Did I do something wrong?"

Luke got up and grabbed his book from the shelf. "I'm fine. I've been wanting to read this book for a while."

"Okay." She watched Luke stretch out on the couch and open his book before she took her seat at the computer. As much as she wanted press further, she would have to let the big, fat elephant stay in the room until Luke was ready to talk. A part of her was afraid to dig to the truth because if her instincts were right, the truth would change everything. She wasn't ready to find out that he didn't want to be married to her, and she sure as hell wasn't ready for him to say that he did.

Chapter 14

Aria

Aria slid her shirt on the hanger and hung it on the rod a week later, the sight of her clothes hanging next to Luke's still catching her off guard. The tension from their wedding night had dissipated, and they had settled back into their routine as if nothing had happened, like they'd planned. She hung up her last shirt then shut the closet. They moved through the small bedroom like a well-oiled machine. Or like an old married couple.

Behind her, Luke shut the dresser drawer and picked up his laundry basket. "That's the last of mine. I'll get out of your way now."

Before he could reach the door, Aria put a cautious hand on his arm. "Actually, can we talk for a second?"

Luke eyed the hand on his arm, his expression questioning. "Of course. What's on your mind?"

Aria slid her hand down his arm and brushed her fingertips along his hand, fighting the urge to grab it and never let go. "It's just that... I want to say thank you."

Luke's warm eyes crinkled in the corners. "You've thanked me a million times already. A million and one seems a little extreme."

She giggled and tucked her hair behind her ear. "I know, I know. But this time, I want to thank you specifically for how you are with Ben. For being a friend for him."

Luke waved a hand as if brushing her comment away. "No need to thank me. He's a great kid. The little brother I never had. It's fun."

"Obviously, I think he's a great kid too. Not everyone has treated him that way, though, so it means the world to me when you do.

And, well, he's never really had a male role model before, and I want you to know I appreciate you filling that void for him."

Luke rubbed his chest as a blush creeped up his neck. "Me, a role model? I don't know about all that. I'm hanging out with him. Nothing special."

"But it is special. He's never had that before. On the surface, it might look like you two just go do the laundry every weekend while I do homework, but it's so much more. I don't know what you two do or talk about during your guy time, but whatever it is, keep it up. Since Ben started spending time with you, he's more considerate, helping me with chores when I don't even ask him to. I can tell he has so much more confidence than he used to. He's happier..." She paused as she swallowed the lump of gratitude that rose in her throat. "It's amazing to see and makes my heart so full. I needed you to know how grateful I am."

Luke ran a hand over the back of his head and cleared his throat. "Wow, I, uh... I don't know what to say. I'm glad I could be a positive influence. But I also think you're giving me some of your credit. You laid all the groundwork over the last twelve years. I've only been in his life for a couple of weeks. Anything I've done is just the tip of the iceberg."

Aria took in the humble man before her, baffled that he'd somehow became even more amazing. Her lips tingled with the memory of their brief kisses. Other than their wedding, she'd kept her mouth to herself since that first kiss, despite their continued habit of late-night movies. Though she would never admit it out loud, she'd been testing Luke. There was no doubt he'd enjoyed the surprise kiss. She'd left him wanting more, his tented pants proving so, and she needed to see how he would handle that. He had let her leave instead of following her to the bedroom. Instead of coming on strong and trying to coax more from her, he'd respected her boundaries and followed her lead. Rather than becoming angry or cold, he'd continued to be a friend to both her and her brother. Even after they said vows, he still kept his distance. And at that moment, she stood before him, wanting nothing more than to fail her own test. She took a slow step forward, aware she'd been silent for far too long but too engrossed in her thoughts and the temptation to care.

Luke seemed to sense the shift in the mood as the air buzzed between them. He took a hesitant step toward her as his Adam's apple bobbed, but then he stopped short, pulling his eyes away. "I appreciate the compliment, but you really don't have to thank me. I better let you get back to your laundry." He resituated his empty laundry basket in front of him. "I'll be in the living room if you need anything." He paused in the doorway, locking eyes with her one last time before disappearing down the hallway.

Aria sank onto the bed, replaying the past few minutes over in her mind. She'd been ready to throw herself at him, to cross that line and go too far. And he stopped her. Maybe she'd stumbled upon a rare good guy with good intentions.

With the sigh of someone whose heart was healing, Aria moved to the dresser and reached into the basket for her underwear. Her face scrunched as unfamiliar panties greeted her. "What the...?"

She picked up a couple of pairs, the colorful lace dangling from her fingers as her cheeks blazed. There was only one explanation she could think of for how a stranger's underwear got in her basket, and it conjured the same images in her mind as the party patio. But she didn't have a legitimate claim on Luke and never would, so she would have to get over her unfounded jealousy. Even as her fake husband, Luke had the freedom to live his life as if nothing had changed. That was the deal.

With the unfamiliar underwear tucked in her hand behind her back, she made herself walk to the living room and face the impending awkwardness head-on.

"Uh, Luke, I, uh, think I found something of yours in my basket."

"Oh yeah? I thought we kept it all separate." When she didn't say anything, he frowned. "What was it? I didn't leave an ink pen in there or something, did I?"

"No, it wasn't that. It was, well…" She stepped forward and tossed the panties beside him on the couch like they were on fire. The floor opening up and swallowing her whole was much more appealing than talking about Luke's extramarital love life.

Luke stared down at the underwear, and an amused grin curled his lips. "I'm pretty sure those won't fit me. And even if they did, they're a little frilly for my taste."

"I know they're not actually yours, but I figured they belonged to someone you know." Her nostrils flared at his blank stare. He was going to make her say it out loud. "Like a girlfriend's or something."

Luke huffed. "What girlfriend? You know I'm not messing around with anyone. If I'm not home, I'm working."

She raised her hands to her hips. "Well, they're not mine."

"Are you sure?"

That kicked her temper up a notch. "Do you think I'm stupid enough to forget I bought underwear? I haven't bought any in a decade. I think I'd remember such a momentous occasion."

Luke's hands shot up in defense. "I don't think you're stupid. Maybe they were in the washer or dryer before we used it."

"I bought them." Ben's unsteady voice came from the hallway.

Aria pivoted on her heels, her anger taking a back seat to confusion. "What?"

Ben inched forward. "I had Luke take me to the store so I could surprise you. Every time I sorted your clothes, I felt sorry for you having that old underwear. You always bought me new ones, so I wanted to get some for you. I didn't think you'd mind. I didn't mean to make you mad or cause problems."

Luke faced Ben. "You were shopping for her? When you said you needed money for underwear, I thought you meant for you, man."

All of the tension left Aria, her face and heart softening. "I'm not mad. I didn't know where they came from and got, well, I guess I got a little confused and embarrassed when I thought I had some stranger's underwear. But I'm not mad at you. Thanks for thinking of me. It was a thoughtful gesture."

"Are you sure you're not mad?" Ben asked.

Aria offered a reassuring nod. "Yes, I'm sure. But next time, tell me about any surprises. Okay?"

"Okay." Ben's face filled with relief.

"And I'm sorry for all the confusion," Aria said to both Ben and Luke.

Luke gathered the underwear and held them out for Aria with a smirk. "At least I got to live out the rock-star fantasy with a pretty girl tossing her panties at me."

"Ha-ha. Really funny." Aria snatched them from his hand, her face burning hot, then rushed back to the bedroom.

Luke's voice tumbled down the hallway as his attention went to Ben. "Hey, man. Next time clue me in so we don't get in trouble, okay?"

Aria flopped onto the bed and buried her face in the pillow with a groan. Out of all the embarrassing moments in her life, tossing panties at her fake husband that she happened to have a crush on took the cake.

Luke

Luke yawned as he eased the door open, the familiar creak welcoming him home. He clicked on the lamp and pulled off his boots, a heavy sigh deflating his chest. As much as he loved his business, the nights with four parties left him drained. He grabbed his nightly root beer and shuffled toward the couch, stopping at the dark hallway. The late nights also meant Aria was fast asleep when he got home, which made for a boring time alone as he wound down. His thoughts wandered back to Aria assuming she'd ended up with another woman's panties. The hint of fire in her eyes had given him pause, making him wonder if she'd been disappointed or maybe even jealous at the thought of him with someone else. And that led him to wondering if she was more invested than she let on.

In the still silence of the night, with no distractions, he certainly couldn't hide from his growing feelings. His mind replayed their kisses again, as it had done a million times. Every time he relived those moments, his resolve to stay away from her melted bit by bit. And the look she gave him after calling him a role model for Ben would be burned into his brain forever. Thank goodness for laundry baskets because without his between them, he might not have kept his distance. Walking away from her almost used up every last ounce of his self-control.

He took a swig of root beer then tried to shake the thoughts. Dwelling on his inner turmoil wouldn't help matters any. With one last glimpse down the dark hallway, he walked around the couch, his heart leaping when he saw Aria lying against the pillow asleep. His eyes swept over her face, so peaceful and gorgeous, as he brushed her hair back with his fingertips.

"Aria?" he whispered.

Her eyes fluttered open. "Oh, you're home." She sat up, covering a yawn with her hand. "I tried to wait up, but apparently I didn't make it that far."

"Yeah, it's late. I'm pretty beat, so I won't stay up long." He sat down beside her in his usual spot. "Did you need something?"

Aria shifted toward him, pulling her legs under herself. "No, not really. I wanted to apologize for earlier. For losing my temper a little when you asked if the underwear was mine. Feeling as if someone is treating me like I'm stupid is always a huge trigger for me." When

Luke opened his mouth, she held up a finger. "It's okay. I know you don't think I'm stupid. And I'm sorry for making assumptions. That's not fair to you."

His spirit lifted despite his exhausted body. She'd been so worried about hurting his feelings, and she'd waited up for him. "Apology accepted."

Aria's mouth opened a crack, her eyes widening in surprise. "That's it? We're cool now?"

"We're cool."

Aria's features relaxed, and another yawn forced its way out.

"It's really late. We should probably skip the movie tonight and go to bed."

"Yeah, I think you're right." As she pushed herself off the couch, her hand brushed against his, and she recoiled with a shudder. "Your hand is like ice."

"Well, it's nearly zero out there even before the windchill." His body shivered right on cue.

She reached behind herself and retrieved the blanket off the back of the couch, tucking it around Luke before positioning herself against his side. "I don't give off much heat, but it's better than nothing."

He leaned in, relishing the weight of her against him. "Don't worry. I'll be warmed up in no time." For a variety of reasons, he added to himself.

Chapter 15

Luke

"**M**an, that was good. I haven't had fried chicken in forever." Luke patted his stomach as he leaned back in his chair.

Aria beamed. "Thanks. I'm trying to expand my cooking skill set now that I can actually buy stuff for recipes instead of whatever's the cheapest. Not bad for a first try, if you ask me."

"Not bad at all, apparently," Luke said, nodding at the empty platter.

Ring, ring.

Luke stood and retrieved his phone from the counter. "Hello?"

"How could you do this to your own flesh and blood?" his dad, Tom, yelled through the phone.

"What? Dad, what are you..." Luke strained to decipher the onslaught of slurred words being thrown his way. "I can't understand you."

"Connie wouldn't be in the hospital if it wasn't for your pansy ass running off," Tom said.

Luke's blood ran cold. "Hospital? Is she hurt? Which hospital? Hello?" The line went dead. He stared at the phone as if it might have answers.

Aria's hand rested on his shoulder. "What was that all about?"

Luke took a step back, still staring at the phone as his mind wrestled his dad's slurred and jumbled words into an order that made sense.

"Luke? What's wrong?"

He gave a slow shake of his head. "I'm not a hundred percent sure. That was my dad. He wasn't making sense and was obviously wasted, even more than normal, cussing me out for leaving and not being there for Mom. He said something about a hospital."

"Was she in an accident?"

Luke gripped his hair, his heart kicking into overdrive and his stomach threatening to spill its contents. "I don't know. I couldn't get him to answer me." His face twisted with panic. "What should I do? I don't know where she is or what's going on. I need to find her."

Aria took him by the shoulders. "It's okay. We'll find her. Let's take a breath and think about this. Obviously, we won't get anywhere with your dad." She chewed her lip as Ben came up beside her, and then she snapped her fingers. "If she's in the hospital, I'll bet she's at Midtown since that's the low-income hospital."

A burst of energy shot through Luke's body. "Of course. Why didn't I think of that?" He found the number for Midtown then punched it into the phone. After listening to a dozen prompts from the automated answering service, he hit zero for the help desk. "It just keeps ringing. No one is picking up."

Aria grabbed their coats from the rack. "Let's go there. Sometimes it's easier to get information when you're standing in front of someone."

"**D**amn it," Luke muttered, slapping the steering wheel as he stopped for yet another red light. The bright-white hospital sign shone up ahead, even in the afternoon sun, taunting him. His mom could be dying alone in a cold hospital room while he sat at a red light a couple of blocks away. The light changed to green, and he slammed his foot down on the accelerator, steering the bus toward the parking garage. One advantage to driving the party bus everywhere was getting to park in the bottom-level spots reserved for oversized vehicles.

He shoved the gearshift into park and yanked open the door but stopped as Aria and Ben stood to follow him. "Hey, uh... Do you guys mind staying here with the bus? I don't know what I'm going to find, if I even find anything, and... I think I need to do this alone."

Aria flinched, and he knew he'd wounded her. She took a breath and gave him an overly enthusiastic nod. "Yeah, sure. Of course. We'll be here if you need us."

He tossed the keys to her. "Thanks. I'll be back as soon as I can."

As he sprinted through the emergency room doors, he became lost in a sea of sick and injured people. No wonder nobody had answered the phone. He wove his way to the reception desk, cringing with every cough and moan from those he passed. He let out a rush of air when he reached the desk at last.

A young woman with cropped black hair and a sour expression greeted him. "What are you here for?"

"Oh, I'm not sick. I'm trying to find someone. Is there a Connie Hardin here?"

"And who are you?" the woman asked, her face deadpan.

"I'm Luke Hardin. Her son." He flinched as someone behind him yelled out in pain.

The woman typed on the keyboard for what had to be an eternity before shaking her head. "Sorry, I'm not seeing a Connie Hardin."

"She's not here?" Luke's face crumpled, and he dropped his head into his hands.

"You might try one of the other hospitals," she said, her voice an ounce less harsh than before.

Luke read her badge. "Please, Mary. Before I go driving all around town, is there any way you could find out where she might be? Is there some kind of database between hospitals or something?"

Mary's face softened with sympathy at last. "No, I'm sorry. I can't do that."

His eyes filled as desperation overwhelmed him.

"I'm sorry, but I need you to step aside so I can help the next person."

Luke nodded and squeezed his way toward the wall. He sank into a hard plastic chair, cradling his head in his hands.

A tap on his shoulder startled him. He bolted upright, and a woman he guessed to be in her late fifties greeted him. Her short gray waves shone in the fluorescent lights, and she gave him a concerned smile. "I'm Carol."

Luke blinked up at her. "Hi."

She showed him her badge. "I'm a nurse here. I overheard you asking about Connie Hardin."

Luke sprang to his feet. "Do you know where she is?"

Carol's eyes darted around, and then she motioned for him to follow her. She led him to a quieter hallway. "I know your mom, but I can't legally give you any information."

Luke's shoulders slumped.

"You know, I don't normally work in the emergency department. They were short-staffed and asked me to fill in," Carol continued.

Luke frowned, wondering why on earth she was wasting his time with useless information.

"I usually work in the chemotherapy room." She watched with expectant eyes. "I see your mom a lot. She's a sweet lady."

His eyes widened as his brain pieced together what she was saying. He took her hand and gave it a vigorous shake. "Thank you so much."

Luke bolted to the elevators, scanning the directory for the chemotherapy suite. He jabbed the button for the third floor and wrung his hands as he ascended. Bursting out of the elevator, he made a beeline for the reception desk.

"Is there any way I can see Connie Hardin? I think she's getting chemo right now," he said.

The receptionist blinked at him then typed on the keyboard. "Hold on a second."

She disappeared into a room, leaving Luke to shove his restless hands in his pockets to still them. She reappeared and motioned for him to follow her.

He swallowed as he stepped into the long room. A row of recliners lined the right wall, all facing the wall of windows on the opposite side of the room. Cabinets outfitted with machines and tubes sat next to each chair. He walked past an elderly man asleep in a chair, tubing running under his shirt and a nasal cannula giving him oxygen.

Luke reeled as he saw a sliver of a woman sitting in the last chair. His hand went to his stomach, willing its contents to stay inside. The nurse stopped short and motioned for him to continue.

"Thanks," he mumbled before taking those final strides. "Mom?"

Connie dragged her eyes from her magazine with a weary smile. "Hi, Luke. I'm surprised to see you here. What brings you by?"

Luke balked. A purple beanie covered her head, none of her long black hair in sight, and an emesis bag rested on her lap. "What brings me by? Gee, I don't know. Maybe finding out my mom is in the hospital. What's going on?"

She waved a hand. "Oh, stop being dramatic. It's not that big of a deal."

Luke gaped at her. "Not that big of a deal? You're getting chemo. That's an enormous deal. What is it? When were you diagnosed? What's the prognosis?"

She closed her magazine and set it aside. "Don't you worry yourself about all that. I'll be fine."

"Why didn't you tell me?" Luke's voice hitched at the pain stabbing his chest.

"Because I'll be fine. Worrying never did anyone any good."

Luke knelt beside her. "But you're my mom. I should know these things. I could've been here for you. Helped you somehow."

She took his hand in hers and laid her other on top, the frailty of her grip scaring him. "I was going to tell you soon. I only have two more treatments left, and then it'll be over."

"What's the prognosis?" he asked again. The fact that she kept avoiding his question left a bad feeling in the pit of his stomach.

"I have a scan in a few days, and we'll go from there."

More avoidance. "Can I come with you?"

She dropped his hand and retrieved her magazine. "Don't be silly. Those things take all day, and half the time you're sitting in waiting rooms for hours. Then more waiting for results. I'll be fine."

"I want to be there for you, Mom," he pleaded.

He watched her face shut down, a mask slipping on devoid of all emotion. "I'm not having you waste your days in here too. I'll call you when it's all over. Is your number still the same?"

"Yes." Luke felt as if he were in quicksand, all his grasping for a handhold only sending him into the depths faster. "Can I visit you at home, at least?"

She flipped the page with unneeded force and ignored the ripping sound. "I think we'll be moving again soon. Your dad doesn't like our current place much. I'll call you when we're settled."

He knew what that meant. Another eviction. Every time his dad drank the rent money too many months in a row, the apartment always seemed to grow issues overnight. Luke rose to his unsteady feet.

"So what do you want me to do, then? Can we at least talk about what's going on? I can stay until you finish your treatment."

Connie glanced up at the bag hanging on the IV pole. "I'm almost done. There's nothing to talk about. I'll call you when I'm better." She closed the magazine and faked a yawn as she cocked her head toward the other end of the room. "I think I'll follow his lead and take a nap while I finish up."

Luke's eyes scanned around the room, searching for something, anything, to help him get answers, but he came up empty. "So that's it? You want me to go?"

Connie pushed a button and made the chair recline. "I'm sorry. The treatments leave me pretty tired. I'll call you soon."

Luke stepped forward and took her cool, thin hand again. "I'm sorry I stayed away for so long. After what happened with Dad, I... I thought it was better that way. I'm sorry if I hurt you. Promise you'll call me. Please. I love you, Mom. I want to be there for you."

A soft smile brought a touch of light to her face as she gave his hand a weak squeeze. "I know. Love you too. Be safe."

Aria

Aria surveyed the area through the bus windows yet again and checked the time. Her body hummed with nervous energy as she paced inside the bus.

"He's been gone for an hour. Do you think he found her?" Ben asked.

Aria paused and bit her lip, wishing she had a cell phone so she could check on Luke. "I would think if he didn't, he would've been back by now. I wish he would've let us come with him." She checked the window again and sucked in her breath. "He's coming."

She pushed the door open and ran to meet Luke halfway, scanning his features for clues in the dull fluorescent lights of the parking garage. Her stomach plummeted as he neared, the anguish etched in his face as clear as day.

As soon as he came within reach, he wrapped his arms around her and buried his face in her neck. She blinked then slid her arms around him, her mind racing and heart breaking. She rubbed his back as she held him, waiting for him to form words. A passing siren blared, ricocheting off the concrete walls of the parking garage.

"Why don't we go on the bus?" She kept her voice soft as she spoke in his ear.

He let go and nodded, his eyes bloodshot and face slick with tears.

Ben's pale face and wide eyes greeted them as they stepped inside the bus.

Aria led Luke to a bench and sat beside him, keeping one arm on his back. Her heart ached. She longed to take away his pain as she watched him drop his face into his hands.

"Luke... what happened? Is she..." Aria couldn't bring herself to finish her sentence.

Luke scrubbed a hand over his face. "She's not in the emergency room. She's..." He paused, taking a ragged breath and blowing it out in a rush. "She's getting chemo."

Aria sucked in a breath. "Oh, I'm so sorry."

Luke stared at the floor, his elbows planted on his knees. "From the looks of it, she's been sick for a while. I don't think she wanted me to know."

"Why?" Ben asked.

Luke tossed his hands in the air. "I don't know. She wouldn't talk to me about it. I don't even know what she has, how long she's had it, or what her prognosis is. She kept brushing me off and trying to pretend nothing was wrong. I don't understand what I did wrong."

Aria rubbed at the knots in his shoulder muscles. "You did absolutely nothing wrong. Denial is a powerful thing. So is fear. She probably doesn't want to talk about it because then she'd have to admit it to herself. After Dad shot himself, Mom acted like he never existed. If someone said his name, she'd act like she didn't hear it."

She shook her head as her mind threatened to take her down memory lane.

"I wish she'd let me help her. She basically kicked me out of there and told me to never come back. She said she'll call me." Luke straightened and ran a hand over his face again.

Aria rested her hand on his arm. "It sounds to me like she's trying to protect you. Right or wrong, she doesn't want you to see her struggle."

"I know, but—" Luke's eyes misted as his voice caught. "I wish I could help."

"I know you do. Maybe she'll change her mind." Aria's heart buckled under the weight of Luke's pain. She pulled him in for a hug, allowing her own eyes to fill.

That night, instead of keeping her usual few inches of distance from Luke, Aria eased down next to him, their thighs touching. Then she laid her arm over his shoulders and gently brought his head to lean against hers in a hug. "You looked like you could use a friend after all that's happened today."

Luke's rigid muscles loosened under her arm, and his body melted against hers as he sighed. "Thanks. I guess I look as rough as I feel, huh?"

"I wish I could fix it for you or at least make it a little better, but I can't. All I can do is be here for you the way you've been here for Ben and me." Her mind fought hard to control her body's response to having Luke pressed against her. She settled for rubbing his shoulder.

"This helps more than you realize," he said, his voice thick.

Though his words piqued her curiosity, she stayed silent, pushing thoughts of what he might've meant from her mind. Instead, she grounded herself in the moment, relishing the fact that she could comfort him in his time of need. The intoxicating weight and warmth of him against her body wasn't bad either.

Chapter 16

Luke

Luke's phone rang as he finished tying off the trash bag, and he hurried to fish it from his pocket. "Hello?"

"I hope you're happy now," an angry voice slurred through the phone.

"Dad? What are you talking about?"

"Your mom, you dipshit. She's dead," Tom spat.

The blood drained from Luke's face, and his hand ached from gripping the phone. "What? It hasn't even been a week since I saw her. Are you sure?"

"Of course I'm sure. What kind of stupid question is that? She's already off getting cremated. She better be dead. If not, that's some zombie shit going on."

Luke sank to the floor, the room tilting underneath him. "What are you doing with her ashes? Do I need to organize something?"

"You did enough when you abandoned her. Just thought you should know you can't disappoint her anymore. Don't call me."

Click.

Luke gaped at the phone, his dad's words obliterating his already shattered heart. If he'd known the past six years would be his mom's last... He rushed to the bathroom as his stomach heaved with regret. He should've visited more and been less selfish.

He scrambled to his feet and rushed to the door, needing to leave but not knowing where to go. He yanked on his coat, shoved his feet in his boots, and grabbed his keys.

Steering the bus through lunch hour traffic, he gripped the wheel for dear life, his knuckles whitening. In shock and on autopilot, he didn't know where he was going until he got there. Slamming the bus into park, he stared through the windshield at the ramshackle liquor store. The neon lights sliced through the gray winter landscape, seducing him with their promises of blissful escape. He could almost feel the burning of the alcohol slipping down his throat, numbing his pain. He imagined his fingers wrapped around the door handle, his demons curling their bony fingers, beckoning for him to cross over the threshold to the dark side.

He let go, slamming his palms into the steering wheel and letting out a primal growl as the war within his mind raged. He dropped his forehead to the wheel and clutched the back of his head, gulping for air as his soul resurfaced, rising above the blackened waters of hell. As he raised his head, he pushed up his sleeve and ran a finger over his tattoo as he begged for strength.

Aria

"See you tomorrow." Aria waved goodbye to the librarian as she stepped out into the dreary day. She tugged the other strap of her backpack onto her shoulder and set out in a jog, already late for her philosophy class.

She rounded the building and froze when Luke's party bus came into view. Adrenaline kicking in, she bolted for the bus. Through the windshield, she could see Luke slumped over the steering wheel.

She knocked on the door, her mind racing with a million worst-case scenarios, all of them involving Ben.

After a second knock, Luke's head shot up, and he searched around, his face wild and frantic. As his eyes found Aria, visible relief washed over him, color returning to his face. He pushed open the door and pulled her in, clinging to her as if she were his only lifeline.

Aria's blood ran cold. "Luke? What's wrong?"

He inhaled deeply, as if he'd been suffocating. "My mom... She's... gone."

Tears filled Aria's eyes, and she tightened her arms around him. "Oh, Luke. I'm so sorry."

"I never should've left. I should've stuck around or visited more. I missed the last six years of her life." He choked back a sob.

"There's no way you could've known." Aria caressed his back, knowing words were useless but saying them anyway. "And there's nothing you could've done to stop it. Things like that just happen sometimes. She knew you loved her. And she understood why you left. You know she wanted the best for you. I think that's why she didn't ask for help. She didn't want you to get sucked back into that world."

He tightened his grip on her as if she might float away. "I know you're probably right. I just... It's hard. And my dad..." A bitter grunt escaped. "He always knows what to say to press my buttons."

Aria hardened at the mention of Luke's dad. "Don't you for even one second take to heart anything that poor excuse of a man said."

"Aria, I... I went to a liquor store," he whispered, the sound of a broken man.

Aria gasped, her heart ripping in two. She sniffed, searching for the haze of alcohol in the air but only detecting the cinnamon air freshener.

"I went, but I didn't go in. I wanted to so bad, but I stopped myself and drove here. But I came so close. I'm sorry."

The anguish in his voice shredded Aria's heart. She pulled back and grasped his tortured face in her hands. "You came close, but you didn't. You held strong." She took his hand and pointed to his forearm. "This still applies. You're still free. Breaking the chains of addiction doesn't mean you'll never be tempted. It means you won't give in, and you didn't. I'm so proud of you."

She kissed his tattoo and then pulled him back into her arms, clinging to him.

"I don't know what to do," he said, his voice raspy.

"Forgive yourself, first and foremost. Let yourself grieve. And ignore anything that hateful man told you." She raised her head, his sorrowful eyes wrenching her heart. "And most of all, keep going. Your mom loved you and would want you to hold your head high and keep going. The best way to honor her is to live your best life."

Luke dried his face on his sleeve and took a ragged breath. "Yeah, you're right. She would want that more than anything." His eyes zeroed in on her backpack. "I hope I didn't mess up your day. I didn't know where else to go."

Aria shrugged her backpack off and let it fall to the floor with a thud. "All I had left was philosophy, and I have a hundred percent in there. Missing one class won't hurt."

"Are you sure?"

Aria looked at him, really looked at him, taking in his bloodshot eyes and the sweat beaded on his face. He stood before her raw and vulnerable, having sought her out in his most dire time of need. He'd let her into the darkest parts of him and never judged her for hers. As much as she struggled to keep the door on her heart sealed shut, Luke had managed to find the key. For better or worse, she had a feeling the door was about to open wide enough for him to walk right on in. Married or not, there was no mistaking the bond forming between them.

"I'm one hundred percent sure I'm right where I need to be."

Chapter 17

Aria

Knock, knock, knock.

"I'm never going to get this kitchen painted." Aria laid the paint roller on the pan and wiped her hands on her sweatpants as she made her way to the front door. Checking through the peephole, she frowned as she watched a woman tug at her too-tight jeans.

She pulled the door open enough to show her face. "May I help you?"

The bleached-blond stranger blinked at Aria. "Who are you?"

Aria straightened her back and tightened her grip on the side of the door. "Since you're at my house, I'm afraid I'll have to ask you the same question."

The woman crossed her arms over her chest and popped her chewing gum. "I'm Christine, but everyone calls me Chrissy."

"Hello, Chrissy. I'm Aria. What brings you here?" She balked at the coolness in her tone, unable to keep her emotions from getting the better of her.

"Is this Luke Hardin's place?" Chrissy craned her neck to see into the house.

Aria held the door tighter to her body to limit the woman's view. "May I ask what business you have with him?"

Chrissy huffed, shoving her black purse farther up her shoulder. "That's between me and him. Is this where he lives or not?"

Aria jutted her chin forward. "Yes, he lives here, but he's not home at the moment. You can leave your name and number, and

I can have him call you." She reached beside her for the pen and notepad and handed it to Chrissy.

Chrissy narrowed her kohl-rimmed eyes before taking the pen and paper, her long neon-green nails scratching against Aria's skin. "Can you make sure he sees this? It's important."

Aria gaped as her eyes landed on the paper. "Wait. Your last name is Hardin too?"

Chrissy shifted her weight, her bravado appearing shaken. "Yeah, so?"

"Are you related to Luke?"

"That's kind of why I want to talk to him," Chrissy said.

"Well, I grew up next door to him, so I knew his family, and I don't remember a Chrissy," Aria said, her tone skeptical.

Chrissy's strong, defiant attitude left like air rushing from a balloon. "Well, that's because it's a long story. One I'd rather tell to Luke than some stranger."

Aria took a deep breath, trying to center herself. "Look, I think we might've gotten off on the wrong foot. I default toward the defensive sometimes. I'm Luke's... wife." The word felt foreign to her tongue but made butterflies dance in her stomach.

Understanding dawned in Chrissy's eyes. "Oh, that makes sense. I bet you took one glance at me and decided I'm some hussy coming to steal your man."

The heat of shame traveled up Aria's neck. "Yeah, kind of. Sorry."

Chrissy shivered and ran her hands along her arms. "I'm not trying to be pushy or anything, but can I come in for a bit? It's freezing out here."

"What? Oh. Uh, sure," Aria stammered before stepping back and opening the door wide against her better judgment.

Chrissy's black stiletto boots dropped snow on their welcome mat as she took off her black leather jacket.

She looks like a biker prostitute, Aria thought. Chrissy turned around, leaving Aria feeling like a teacher had caught her cheating on a test.

"This is a nice place. Remodeling?" Chrissy pointed to the paint supplies in the kitchen.

"Just a little painting to freshen it up." Aria walked over to the roller and wrapped it in a plastic bag to keep it from drying out.

"Did I interrupt?"

"I was about to pause for a break anyway," she lied then motioned to the kitchen table. "Please, have a seat. Would you like some water or something?"

Chrissy sat down, still surveying the room. "Water is fine. Thanks."

Aria handed Chrissy a glass of water and sat across from her. "So, how are you related to Luke? I don't remember him having any cousins or anything like that."

"Well, like I said, it's a long story, but the short version is—"

Just then, the door swung open. "Honey, I'm ho—" Luke froze, a frown creasing his face as he looked from Chrissy to Aria. "Who's this?"

Aria jumped to her feet. "I'm glad you're home. Perfect timing. This is Chrissy, and she says she's family of yours."

Luke opened his mouth to speak, but Ben swung the door into his back.

"Oh, sorry, Luke." Ben stepped around Luke and stopped in his tracks when he saw Chrissy. "Who's that?"

This time, Chrissy stood and closed the distance between her and Ben. "Hi, I'm Chrissy." Turning to Luke, she added, "I'm your sister."

Luke

Gasps filled the room. Luke's brows furrowed as he shook his head in disbelief. "Sorry, but you've got the wrong guy. I'm an only child."

Chrissy tilted her head to the side and placed a hand on her hip, making her jagged, bleached hair bounce. "Actually, you were only raised like one. My parents are Tom and Connie Hardin."

"Sorry if I seem skeptical. It's because I am." Luke brushed past her and began putting groceries away in the cabinets.

Chrissy huffed. "Well, I can see the sarcasm is genetic."

Luke grunted in reply, in no mood to entertain this delusional woman.

"Okay, okay. I figured you wouldn't believe me." She marched over to the table and pulled a large envelope from her purse. "That's why I brought proof."

Luke paused and eyed the envelope, frustrated with himself as curiosity won him over.

Chrissy thrust the envelope toward him. "Will you at least look at it?"

Luke sighed, setting the last can of beans in the cabinet. *A sister? How is that possible?* he thought, but kept his features stoic as he faced her. "Fine. I'll look at whatever you brought."

Aria started for her bedroom. "Come on, Ben. Let's go put away the laundry."

"But we already did," Ben protested.

Aria shot Ben a pointed look and tugged on his sleeve, but Luke put his arm out to stop her. "No, stay. Whatever she has to say, she can say to all of us." *And I need you with me,* he added to himself.

Aria's eyes darted from Chrissy to Luke, and then she caught the glance of a wide-eyed Ben. "Okay, if that's what you want."

Luke took her hand and pulled her into the chair beside him. "It is."

Ben grabbed a pack of granola bars and settled in the other seat.

Chrissy gulped as she opened the envelope, the paper quivering in her hands as she set it in front of Luke. "Here's my birth certificate. And the paper showing where the state took me from them. I have a set of papers showing some of my foster home placements. There were a lot more than this, but I couldn't print all of them. Some pictures of my time at the children's home." She reached for her purse. "Oh, and here's my license. So you can see it's my legal name."

Luke scanned the documents with a careful eye, desperate to find loopholes and mistakes in Chrissy's obvious scam. His heart pounded faster as each document passed his scrutiny. He shook his head again, trying but failing to clear his mind and make sense of it all. "I don't understand. How could I have a sister I never knew about?"

"Well, for starters, I was born five years before you. By the time you came along, they probably forgot about me." She gave a bitter snort, though her eyes betrayed a wistful melancholy.

His resistance weakened, and he couldn't deny her proof. "Okay, so what happened? What's the story?"

Chrissy studied her long fingernails as if gathering her courage. "Well, I was a baby when they lost custody, so for the first bit, I have to rely on other people's memories. I was born with drugs in my system, so the state took me away. A nurse fostered me as I went through withdrawals."

Luke raised a hand. "Whoa. Stop right there. Mom wasn't perfect, but she didn't do drugs. Dad was an alcoholic, but I never saw Mom touch anything."

Chrissy snarled. "Well, aren't you the lucky one? She must've sobered up between kids."

Luke sat up straight, a fire lighting in his chest. "I'm sorry, but I don't see Mom being a druggie."

Chrissy sat up straighter, too, meeting his challenge. "You want to see the paperwork? I made copies of that too. Didn't think I'd need my medical records to meet my brother."

Brother. All the fight left him at that word. "Okay, fine. I'm sorry. It's a shock to hear that about Mom. Go ahead with your story."

Chrissy leaned back in her chair, crossing her arms over her chest. "Anyway, they tried to give me back once I was healthy. Didn't last very long. A couple of welfare checks later, I was officially a ward of the state. When I was a baby, it was easy for them to find foster homes. I had some lingering issues from the drugs, so none of the families wanted to adopt me, but they were fine with short-term fostering. Around the time I started school, I had more frequent moves. In hindsight, I guess I realized I was different from the other kids, so I started having behavior issues. I started being the bully so I wouldn't be the victim anymore. Most families don't like the troubled kids."

"What did they bully you for?" Ben asked.

Chrissy gave him a once-over before answering. "Thanks to the drugs, I have a learning disability. I also had some growth problems that made me smaller than the other kids."

Ben's eyes widened. "I get bullied for being smaller too. And for not having a girlfriend."

"You didn't tell me that." Aria frowned, worry lines creasing her forehead.

Chrissy's eyes filled with sympathy as she patted Ben's hand. "I know what you mean. Without these heels, I'm only five feet tall." She paused, scanning him again. "You don't look that small to me. Are the other kids giants or something?"

Ben's cheeks flushed. "I've grown a lot since we moved in with Luke."

Chrissy cut her eyes to Aria, and Luke could almost see the wheels turning. He didn't want to explain anything to her, so he motioned for her to continue. "So, what happened then?"

Chrissy's eyes darted to him. "Huh? Oh. I ended up in the Sacred Heart Children's Home. Stayed there until I aged out of the system."

"So did you keep getting in trouble, or are you on the straight and narrow?" The lack of detail in her rushed ending left Luke uneasy.

Chrissy lowered her eyes and began picking at her fingernails again. "I almost got kicked out of the home a couple times, but Paulette—she's the director—is pretty forgiving. Thankfully."

"What did you do that almost got you kicked out?" Warning bells rang loud and clear in Luke's head.

Chrissy nodded in Ben's direction. "I, uh, I'm not sure I should say in front of the kid."

Ben raised his chin. "I'm twelve. I'm not sheltered. My mom did drugs, and I know about sex. I'm not stupid. Or a baby."

Aria nodded in agreement. "As long as it's nothing too crazy, it's fine to say it in front of Ben. He's right that he's seen a lot."

Chrissy shrugged. "All right, if you say so. I almost got kicked out for inappropriate relations with the boys in the home."

Aria recoiled. "You'd think they would keep you separate to prevent that."

"Oh, they do." Chrissy snickered. "Separate halls for the bedrooms. Night monitoring. That kind of stuff. But during the day, kids are coming and going. It's pretty easy for a boy and girl to duck into a bathroom for a quickie. One time, there was this boy, Ramone. Whew, he could—"

Luke cleared his throat. The last thing he wanted was to hear about his potential sister's irresponsible sex life. "All right, so we know your childhood. What's life like for you now? How did you find me? Why?"

A flush spread across Chrissy's prominently displayed chest and up her neck. "I get by all right. I, you know, do what I have to do to survive. Nothing fancy, but I'm fed and clothed. As far as finding you, I always knew my parents' names. It wasn't a secret. I would see the domestic battery charges and drunk driving pop up online. I didn't know about you, though, until I came across our mom's obituary." Her voice hitched as her eyes filled with tears. "I hadn't worked up the nerve to go meet them yet. I guess I waited a little too long, huh? She probably wouldn't have wanted to meet me anyway." She swiped at a tear rolling down her cheek and blinked the rest away. "Anyway, I saw your name in the obituary and figured I would find you before it was too late. It took some work for me to find you since you don't have a criminal record. How'd you manage that one?"

Luke laughed, dispelling some nervous energy. "Well, in my early years a lot of it was me being lucky and not getting caught, to tell you the truth. I didn't do anything too bad, though. Lots of underage drinking. Been sober for six years now, though, and I'm never going back."

Chrissy seemed to consider his words. "That's amazing, Luke. You should be proud of yourself."

Luke touched his tattoo. "Yeah, I am."

Aria's arms wrapped around Luke's shoulders, and she gave him a squeeze. "I'm proud of you too."

Luke placed his hand on her arm, finding all the support a man could ever want in her eyes.

"Excuse me. I need the girls' room." Chrissy shot to her feet, a strange look on her face that Luke couldn't quite decipher.

Luke pointed to the hall. "Second door on the right."

Hearing the door click shut, Luke leaned toward Aria and kept his voice low. "She seems legit, but I can't help feeling there's something off. Something keeps making red flags pop up."

Aria nodded. "I agree. I can't quite put my finger on it."

Ben shrugged. "I don't know. She seems nice enough."

"I hope her intentions are good. We don't need any more drama," Aria said.

The creak of the bathroom door opening halted the conversation, and they waited in silence as Chrissy came back into to the kitchen.

"That's better. Now where were we?" She rounded the corner and plopped down in her seat across from Luke, appearing much more relaxed than before.

Luke's eyes homed in on Chrissy's face. "What's that on your nose?"

Chrissy's eyes became wide as saucers, and she brushed the back of her hand over her nose. "What? I don't know what you're talking about."

Luke's blood boiled. "Did you go snort coke in our bathroom?"

Chrissy waved off the accusation. "Don't be ridiculous."

"Then open your purse," he said, certain his suspicions were correct.

"What? No. Are you crazy? This is ridiculous." Chrissy tossed a frenzied glance at Aria and Ben.

"No, what's ridiculous is you bringing drugs into my house. You couldn't wait another hour? Even ten minutes? Are you that bad off? Is that how you make your money?" Luke's voice boomed louder by the second, but he didn't care. He was too livid to care.

"You've got it all wrong, Luke," Chrissy said, her tone pleading as she clutched her purse tight to her chest.

"Then prove it. Open your purse." Luke balled his fists to keep from grabbing the purse and seeing for himself.

Chrissy's shoulders slumped as she hung her head, her eyes locked on the floor. "I can't."

"I'm sorry, but I'm going to have to ask you to leave. Drugs aren't allowed in this house." Luke jabbed his arm at the door.

"Does she really have to leave?" Ben asked, eyes wide.

Luke shot him a stern look then swiveled back to Chrissy. "Yes, I won't tolerate drugs in my house."

Chrissy brushed a tear from her cheek and bolted for the door, leaving all her papers scattered on the table. "I understand. Maybe I'll see you around."

"Chrissy, wait," Aria said as Chrissy pulled open the door.

Luke jerked his head toward Aria, his temper ready to flare. "What are you doing?"

Aria gathered the papers before crossing the room to Chrissy. He watched as Aria wrote on the notepad and added her note to the stack. "This number is a place you can call to get help. Whenever you're ready. There's still hope. You don't have to continue down this path. Like Luke said, there's no room for drugs in this house. We've both fought too hard and too long to get away from them. But if you sober up, you're welcome to stop by. I'd like to get to know you better. I'm sure Luke would too."

Chrissy avoided eye contact as she shoved the papers in her purse and mumbled her thanks before scurrying away.

Aria

Aria stood motionless for a few seconds after the door clicked shut. A wave of nausea crashed in her stomach as feelings of déjà vu coursed through her.

"What was that?" Luke's voice boomed behind her, making her flinch.

"What was what?" Aria spun around, greeted by Luke's red face.

"Why did you tell her she could stop by? If she's a druggie, I don't want anything to do with her," he said, fuming.

Aria walked up and rubbed his arms, hoping the gesture could defuse the bomb inside his heart. "I know how you must be feeling right now, Luke. It's perfectly reasonable to be angry. And confused. And disappointed. I am too."

"Then why are you trying to be friends with her?"

Aria inhaled, biting her tongue so she didn't respond with equal intensity. The last thing their conversation needed was more hostility. "I wanted to extend an olive branch. Give her some hope. That's all."

Luke's frown deepened as he took a step back. "She's not your mom, you know."

Aria recoiled from the sting of his words. "Yes, I know that. But she is your sister."

"Are you sure you're not helping her because you couldn't help your mom? You know it won't fix anything, right? You'll still have all that guilt and pain. It won't take any of that away."

Aria squared her shoulders, her defenses firing. The mental reminder that he was speaking from a place of pain fell flat. "Yes, I know all of that. I know nothing will ever take away my guilt and pain over Mom, and I get to carry that burden forever. But I also know that just because Mom couldn't ever change, it doesn't mean Chrissy won't. What about your mom? Chrissy was born with drugs in her system, yet you never saw your mom use."

"Yeah, but—" Luke began.

Aria cut him off, jabbing a finger into his chest. "What about you, Luke? Look at that tattoo on your arm. Your mom overcame it. You overcame it. Chrissy deserves a fighting chance to overcome it, too, don't you think?"

Luke deflated, the harsh lines melting from his face. He raked a hand through his hair with a sigh. "Yeah, okay."

Aria blinked, shocked by his concession. "Yeah, okay?"

Luke tossed his hands in the air. "You're right. Okay? You're always right."

Aria stepped forward, putting a hand on his shoulder. "I'm not always right, but in this case, I know in my heart that I am. She deserves a chance to make a better life, just like the rest of us."

"Yeah, I know. I guess I got a little defensive." Luke walked to the refrigerator and brought out a root beer, a signal loud and clear of how stressed he was.

She studied his face while he took a drink. "How are you feeling about it all? That was a lot to take in."

"It was a hell of a roller coaster, that's for sure. I don't even think my brain has processed it all yet." Luke stared ahead, his eyes blank. "I have a sister."

"It's not always that great," Ben quipped.

Aria gave him a playful swat then refocused her attention to Luke. "So you believe her?"

"I guess so." Luke settled into a chair with a thud. "I mean, all the proof was staring me in the face. I... I always saw my mom as a victim in everything. You know? I can't wrap my head around this new version of her that did drugs while pregnant."

Aria took the seat next to him. "Yeah, I can see where that would be hard. Like whenever my mom talks about the past before she started drugs, it doesn't seem like it's possible for it to be the same person."

They sat in silence, both lost in painful memories.

"So, what now?" Ben asked.

Luke stared at the door. "That's all up to Chrissy."

A hard frown crinkled Ben's face. "So just because she does drugs, you're going to ignore her?"

Aria swallowed as she watched Luke lock eyes with Ben, bracing herself for another round of drama.

Luke leaned forward, holding Ben's gaze. "I meant what I said, Ben. I won't tolerate drugs in my house. Our house. We've all worked too hard to get away from that world. If you let it back in, even a tiny bit, it can end up ruining your life. Got it?"

Ben gave a silent nod, his expression uncertain.

The tension in the air made the hair stand up on the back of Aria's neck. Her instincts told her something alarming might be behind Ben's comments and questions regarding Chrissy, but she couldn't quite pinpoint the issue. "If you need to talk to us about anything, Ben, we're always here. Both of us."

Panic flashed in Ben's eyes a second before being covered up by what appeared like forced indifference. "There's nothing to talk about. I just think it's a little overkill. I like her."

Luke's stern voice came out low and even. "It's not about whether we like her or not, it's about keeping the three of us safe."

"It's us three against the world, right, guys?" She gave them both a pointed look, which earned her a "yes" from each of them.

She clapped, as if the sound could snap everyone out of the funk left in Chrissy's wake. "All right, now. Since you two are home, how about we make it us three against the kitchen? I could use some help finishing up the paint."

Ben jumped up with surprising enthusiasm. "I'll help with the roller."

"Great. That means you get to do the edging." She grabbed a brush from the counter and held it out to Luke.

Aria could have finished painting the kitchen by herself with ease, but she knew Ben and Luke would benefit from something productive to take their minds off the tumultuous turn of events. The knot in her stomach loosened as she watched the two most important guys in her life work together in harmony.

Chapter 18

Aria

Aria rested her head against the frosty city-bus window, watching the world, which was gray and dreary aside from the occasional punctuation of neon lights, slip past. The droning hum of the tires over the pavement lulled her inward, her brain free from other demands and able to concentrate on whatever thoughts lay tangled and ignored. In the monotony of the bus ride home from college, she could sit with those thoughts, untangle them, and maybe even come up with an all-important plan.

Despite the vast improvements in her life, she hazarded a guess that she would never be completely free of the anxiety devil on her shoulder. Over the past few weeks, though, her once-daily stressors had become more of a hill than a mountain even as the world continued to pile on drama. She'd even experienced happiness at times, a feeling that had eluded her for most of her life. For the first time, she had a safe place for both Ben and herself—and maybe even her heart.

And yet, among all the positives, a nagging guilt sat like a brick in the pit of her stomach. A negative force she couldn't ignore, no matter how much she tried. And she needed a plan.

That night, after the low rumble of Ben's snore trickled into the hallway, she joined Luke on the couch. "I've been thinking."

"Uh oh. Should I be worried?" Luke asked, his tone teasing.

Aria's mouth tugged up at the corners, his playful attitude improving her gloomy mood a tad. With the news of his mom and the ordeal with Chrissy, it had been days since she'd seen him smile. He could tease her all day long if it brought light back to his eyes. "No, you're fine. But the whole thing with your mom got me thinking. It's been a month since I've seen or talked to my mom. It's almost Thanksgiving already, and I don't even know if she's in jail or where she's staying. She could be dead, for all I know." Unexpected emotions welled in her eyes, and she flicked a stray tear away with a brisk swipe of her finger.

Luke held his arm out to her, an invitation she accepted without a second thought. She slid against his side, welcoming the intoxicating comfort she found there.

"So what do you want to do? What's the plan?" he asked, his voice soft as he rubbed his thumb on her arm.

The way he knew her, how her mind worked, brought more comfort than she could explain. "I need to find her without Ben knowing. Just in case..." Her voice caught, unable to deliver the words in her mind. "Just in case there's bad news. Do you think you could distract him the day before Thanksgiving so I can go find her? I thought maybe I could invite her over for dinner. If it's okay with you." She peered up at him with caution in her eyes, but the objection she expected was nowhere to be found.

"Whatever you want to do, let me know. I can take Ben to do some last-minute grocery shopping or something. You know I'll help you however I can." Luke's face softened. "You have such a big heart. Do you know that? You're so worried about a woman who put you through hell. Most people wouldn't care."

"I guess I can't bring myself to completely abandon her the way she abandoned us. She's still technically my mother, even if she was never a good one. I'm done throwing my life away to help her, but I can't seem to make myself stop caring completely. No matter how much it hurts."

Luke hugged her closer. "That's what makes you different from them. That's what makes you a good person."

"I don't feel like such a good person, but thanks." She eased out of his hug, afraid to linger there for too long. Luke grabbed the remote, but Aria sensed his mood darkening. "What's wrong?"

He flipped through the channels for a moment before answering her. "Talking about Thanksgiving... It really hit me that I won't have any more holidays with my mom. It feels stupid to be upset about it because I haven't celebrated anything with her for years, but the finality of it all and knowing I never will again kind of feels like a punch in the gut."

Aria longed to wrap him in her arms and hold him until all his pain disappeared, and it took all of her willpower to settle for resting a hand on his leg. "The way you feel about something is never stupid, especially something as complicated as grief. It's perfectly normal for you to struggle with all of this. I'm sorry if I stirred up some bad feelings by talking about inviting my mom."

"No, it's okay. The feelings were going to come up at Thanksgiving this year anyway."

Aria nodded. "Okay, I'll invite her and see what happens. And I'm always here if you need to talk about stuff."

"I know. Thanks." He gave her hand a squeeze.

Her chest ached at seeing his half-hearted smile, and she would've given anything to make it reach his eyes.

Aria's heart pumped adrenaline through her veins as she waved goodbye to Luke and Ben. With the party bus out of sight, she grabbed her wallet and keys and jogged to the bus stop.

She shifted her weight from one foot to the other as she waited, her stomach clenching at the thought of being back in her old neighborhood. After stuffing her wallet in her pocket, she considered the key chain in her hand. She'd never used a purse, which a thief could rip off a person's shoulder in an instant before they even realized what was happening. With her wallet in her pocket, a thief had to work harder. Her keys always sat firmly between her fingers, a set of improvised brass knuckles. After she got her Mace key ring, she switched to clutching it in her hand, thumb on the trigger. *Maybe one day I'll carry a purse and not weaponize my hand, but today is not that day.* She squared her shoulders when the city bus came into view.

"You've got this," she said to herself, though her voice held no conviction.

Her knees bounced while the bus chugged along. As her old street came into view, her resolve all but evaporated. She took a deep, steadying breath and chewed her lip as she pulled the stop cord.

Her feet crunched onto the crumbling sidewalk, every bad memory slapping her in the face like her mother's bony hand. She ignored the heads turning in her direction and the hum of gossiping, instead keeping her posture confident and her eyes trained on her target.

The faded and chipped door creaked open before her trembling hand could finish knocking.

"Hey, baby girl. Haven't seen your face around here for a while. A long while." Vick's beady eyes scanned her up and down, making her skin crawl. "You's looking good, baby girl. You hooking? I always knew you'd rake in some dough that way."

Swallowing to keep from vomiting, she sneered at her old landlord. He was more disgusting than she remembered, a feat she didn't think was possible. "No, I'm not hooking."

"Too bad. I woulda paid ya double." Vick licked his chapped lips.

Aria's hand tightened around her Mace. "I'm trying to find my mom. Have you seen her?"

"Yeah, I saw her a few days ago. She came to give me some payment." He adjusted his pants as his eyes traveled over her body again.

"Ya know, she still owes me lots. If you wanna help her out, I'll cut a hell of a deal."

"Do you know where she's staying?" Aria held her face deadpan, refusing to let him see he was getting under her skin.

"She said something 'bout the old bridge. That's all I know, baby girl."

Aria sped away from Vick, a vulgar remark about her butt trailing after her.

She buried her hands in her coat pockets as she approached the abandoned railway bridge that served as a makeshift shelter for the homeless in the community. The icy dampness seeped into her bones while she scanned the dreary landscape. As she drew nearer, the acrid smell burned her nose and made her stomach flip. Good thing she'd had a light breakfast. She approached the first conscious person she saw, an elderly man with one eye swollen shut. "Do you know Tasha Sutton?"

He pointed a shaky finger to the far end of the bridge. With a nod of thanks, Aria tiptoed her way through the trash, at one point almost stepping on a person sleeping under some plastic bags. Her heart longed to reach out, to help each and every tortured soul she passed, but her brain pointed out the impossible odds against that scenario.

Aria stopped short as her eyes landed on those blond curls she could recognize anywhere, no matter how dirty or matted they might be. The same curls that bounced clean and joyful on Ben's head. "Mom?"

Tasha moved as if under water, but the shock still kicked Aria in the stomach, sucking the air from her lungs. The drugs had kept Tasha thin for as long as Aria could remember, but now it seemed that every bone and joint in her body jutted out and threatened to puncture the skin—a painful, visible testament to her rapid decline. Tasha's sunken blue eyes were glazed over, staring through Aria rather than at her. Despite the near-freezing temperatures, her mother had donned short sleeves, allowing a full view of the dark track marks that marred her bony arms.

Aria managed a disbelieving, heartbroken whisper. "Mom? What did you do to yourself?"

"What do you care? Traitor. You left me to die." Tasha spat the slurred words.

Aria clutched her chest, Tasha's words piercing her heart like a dagger. Somehow, her mom always crawled out of her stupor enough to hurt her. "What? How could you say that? I didn't leave you to die. I had to take care of Ben. In order to do that, I had to stop taking care of you. You made it impossible for me to do both. I had no choice."

"You abandoned me." Tasha's voice became a whine, much like that of a toddler wanting sympathy.

Aria began taking a deep breath, but the smell made her cough. "I did what I had to do. For Ben. Now, look, I didn't come here to fight. Okay? I was worried about you. I came here to invite you to our house for Thanksgiving."

"You mean Halloween?"

"No, Halloween was weeks ago. Tomorrow is Thanksgiving. So do you want to come?"

"Where's my Benny?" Tasha craned her neck to search past Aria.

Aria gritted her teeth as the words burned like salt in open wounds. Everything was always about Ben, forever the favorite child. Aria assumed, with her pale skin and dark hair, she resembled her dad too much for her mom's liking. "He's at home. You can see your Benny tomorrow if you come. You can have a shower if you want one too. And some warm food."

"Okay."

"Okay?" Aria blinked. "Okay, meet me at our old house at eleven tomorrow morning." Aria took the piece of paper she'd written the instructions on from her pocket, knowing she couldn't trust Tasha to remember, and handed it to her mother. "Don't forget, Mom. For your Benny."

Tasha shoved the paper in the pocket of her jeans without a second glance. "I won't. Stop treating me like a child. I'm your mom, you little brat."

Aria opened her mouth, ready to snap and unleash the torrent of opinions she held about her mother, but stopped. It was no use. All that would accomplish was igniting another pointless argument that would lead nowhere. Without a word, she spun on her heels and picked her way back through the mess, her tight chest loosening with every step she put between her and that real-life version of hell.

Aria inhaled a shuddering breath as she dried her icy tears. Holding herself together on the ride home had proved a challenge, but she'd somehow summoned enough strength to keep the bulging floodgates closed until she stepped off the bus and into her new safe zone at Luke's house. Though time seemed to stand still in her grief, her numbed backside claimed otherwise, long frozen by the frigid concrete front step serving as her refuge while she let her emotions take over. Shivering, she forced her stiff legs to climb the steps, steeling herself before opening the front door.

Luke and Ben, bent over a cookbook by the stove, shifted their attention to her as she shuffled inside. The jovial spirit fell from Luke's face when he saw her.

Ben's face crumpled with concern. "Everything okay? Why is your face all red?"

Unlike her frozen body, her mind moved at lightning speed to come up with a lie. "I missed the bus, so I walked instead of waiting for the next. Not the best decision. The cold made my eyes water."

She rushed to her bedroom before Ben could ask any more questions. Breathing a sigh of relief, she leaned against the closed door.

"You okay?" Luke whispered as he tapped on the door.

Aria eased the door open, searching past Luke for Ben.

"I left him stirring the dough. It's thick, so it should take a while."

Aria stepped aside and ushered Luke inside. The second the door shut, she flung her arms around Luke, desperate for his comforting touch.

"I knew the bit about the bus was a lie. What happened? Is she...?" He left the sentence unfinished as he rubbed her back, bringing warmth back to her skin.

Aria squeezed her eyes shut to stop more tears from flowing. "No, she's alive. Honestly, I think what I found is almost worse. She's like a zombie. She looks so bad. I invited her, but I almost don't want Ben to see her like this. But it might be the last time, and I don't want that regret. I don't know what to do."

"I think you did the right thing. The rest is up to her." Luke tightened his embrace, squeezing her close.

Aria relished the protective gesture, grateful to have someone to lean on. Grateful for Luke.

"Can I stop stirring now?" Ben yelled from the kitchen.

"I better get back in there." Luke let go, concern etched on his face. "Are you going to be okay?"

Aria nodded, though her muddled brain and aching heart disagreed. "Yeah, I just need a minute."

"All right." Luke squeezed her hand before heading to the kitchen.

Aria sank onto the bed, breathing deeply until her heart rate slowed to normal and her eyes stopped burning. She rubbed her sternum, a futile attempt to massage away the tightness in her chest. Hearing laughter erupt in the kitchen, she scrubbed her sleeve across her face and went to investigate.

"Hey, guys. What are you up to?" Aria forced her voice to a perkier octave than her mood dictated.

Ben raised his head, giddiness in his eyes. "We're making chocolate chip and peanut butter cookies for dessert tomorrow. Luke is teaching me how to follow a recipe."

Luke nudged Ben with his elbow and cocked his head toward the bowl. "Hercules here snapped the handle off the spoon while stirring the peanut butter dough. But you're in time to try one of the chocolate chip ones. Hot and fresh from the oven." He waved his hands with a flourish above the cooling rack like he was in an infomercial.

Aria couldn't help but giggle at the cheesy gesture. "Have either of you tried one, or am I the first guinea pig?"

"You're the very first," Ben said, watching her with expectant eyes.

She picked up a cookie and took a cautious bite, the warm sweetness melting in her mouth. She took another bite and moaned as she savored the taste. "Mmm. Wow, you guys, these are so good. Way better than the ones Mom used to make." The mention of her mom brought a fresh sting to her eyes.

"Mom used to make cookies?" Ben asked in wide-eyed shock.

Aria walked over to the table and took a seat, buying time to tamp down her emotions and steady her voice. "Yeah, I was really little, so I barely remember. It was back before she went off the deep end. Back when she still had some sober days here and there. She would actually do mom stuff on those days, like cook for me and braid my hair. The thing I remember most is baking cookies with her." Aria felt certain that her eyes were loaded with so many thoughts to convey that Luke wouldn't be able to decipher even half. "I think cooking with someone is one of the best memories to have as a kid."

Ben gasped, his eyes getting wide again. "Oh, I have an idea. Why don't we have Mom come for Thanksgiving tomorrow? I bet she'd love a cookie."

Aria bit her lip as her eyes darted to the floor, guilt making it impossible for her to look at Ben. "Um, yeah. About that. I have something I need to tell you." She motioned for Ben to join her at the table.

"What?" Ben sank down in a chair across from her, his face contorted in confusion.

A heavy sigh whooshed from Aria as she braced herself for Ben's reaction. "I didn't actually have an emergency at the library to take care of today. Instead, I found Mom and invited her for Thanksgiving. After seeing her... I don't know if she'll come. I'm sorry I didn't tell you before. I didn't want to get your hopes up."

"You went without me?" The quiver in his voice sliced through Aria's heart.

She reached for Ben's hand, but he yanked it away. Ignoring the sting of his rejection, she soldiered on. "Ben, I wanted to protect you. I didn't know what I would find or if I would even find her at all." Her heart shattered to see Ben's wounded face. "I'm supposed to meet her at the old house tomorrow at eleven. You can come with me if you want to."

Ben sat up straighter, his features brightening. "Really?"

Seeing how much it meant to him, she couldn't bring herself to say no even though she wanted to. "If it's what you want. But I'll warn you, it wasn't fun going back there."

Ben nodded. "Yes, definitely. I want to go pick up Mom."

"We can all go," Luke said, his gaze full of sympathy.

Aria hoped her eyes conveyed how grateful she was for his support. She had a feeling she would need it more than ever at Thanksgiving. Ben would undoubtedly be as shocked by their mom's appearance as Aria was, if not more so, but she couldn't let the chance slip by. Seeing how far Tasha had fallen in a matter of weeks, Aria knew she wouldn't get many more opportunities, if any. She needed Tasha to be sober enough to play nice for one day. For Ben's sake. And all Aria could do was prepare for the worst while she hoped for the best.

Chapter 19

Luke

Driving through their old neighborhood, Luke felt his stomach churn and tie into knots. "I haven't seen it in the daylight for six years." He grimaced at a dilapidated house that should've been condemned years ago but had bright toys on the porch. "It hasn't gotten any better."

Aria's lip curled in disgust. "No, it just gets worse and worse."

As they pulled in front of their old duplex, Ben scanned the area at a frantic pace. "I don't see her. Where is she? Do you see her?"

Dread settled in Luke's stomach like a brick. Tasha was a no-show, as he predicted. He found Aria's face stony, her jaw muscles twitching. Her clinched fist let him know how fiercely she was fighting to contain her emotions for her brother. Their mom had let them down, yet again.

"Maybe she's running behind," Luke said, knowing it was a lie but hoping it would buy Aria some time to rein in her emotions and come up with a plan.

"Let's go find her." Ben hopped out of his seat and bounded for the bus door.

Aria's arm shot out to stop him in his tracks. "Wait. Let me go get her."

"I want to go too," Ben said, his tone whiny.

Aria's face was stern. "Ben, it's better if you stay here. Please, trust me on this." The force behind her low, controlled voice convinced Ben to sit back down. "Stay here with Luke. I'll be back soon."

Luke's heart sank as he watched Aria head toward the old bridge. If that was where she found her mother, no wonder she was so upset. Growing up, they all joked that the old bridge was where drug addicts went to die. As they got older and reality set in, the joke lost its humor.

Ben paced and fidgeted like a caged animal, his eyes flicking to the windows every few seconds.

Luke sensed an urgency to defuse the pressure building inside the boy. "Hey, how about we listen to some music, huh?"

As Luke reached to adjust the radio, Ben rushed past him, slamming Luke's arm into the dash. Before Luke could react, Ben flew out the door of the party bus, sprinting after Aria.

Luke jumped out of the bus and raced after Ben. "Ben, stop! Come back here!" he shouted.

Aria

Aria found Tasha in the same spot as the day before, only this time she lay curled in a filthy blanket. Aria bent to kneel but decided better of it as she scanned the filthy ground. Instead, she crouched down to nudge Tasha's jutting shoulder.

"Mom? Hello? Can you hear me?"

A faint moan let Aria know Tasha was still alive.

Aria patted Tasha's sunken cheeks, attempting to bring her out of her stupor. "Mom, it's Thanksgiving. You were supposed to come to our house to eat, remember? You wanted to see your Benny." Aria swallowed the bitter taste left by her last words.

Tasha finally stirred, her eyes fluttering open as she attempted to sit. Aria grabbed her elbow to help her up, and Tasha leaned against the concrete pier.

"Is that Mom?" Ben's small voice made Aria's head whip around.

"Ben? What are you doing here? I told you to wait in the bus." Aria fought to keep the fury from her voice, but her shrill tone signaled her failure as several heads swiveled in their direction.

Luke raced into view behind Ben and came to a halt when he saw Aria. He panted as he bent to rest his hands on his knees. "I... tried to... stop him... but he's... so fast."

Oblivious to the others, Ben stared at his mom with wide eyes, his mouth gaping open in disbelief. "Mom?"

Aria's hand reached for Ben's, but she paused. From the looks of him, seeing Tasha's pathetic state had sent him into shock. A simple touch from her could be the final jolt that would send him over the edge. The horrified fear in his eyes squeezed her heart like a vise. Knowing she needed to be gentle with him, she took a moment of silence and leveled her voice. "Yes, Ben. This is Mom."

Ben's head moved side to side, his curls swinging and his face blanching. "No. No, that can't be Mom. I don't know who that person is, but it's not Mom."

"Benny?" Tasha raised her head in slow motion, much like a creaking old door, squinting even though clouds blocked out every ray of sun. "Come here, Benny. Give Momma a hug." She lifted her shaky arms toward him, fresh track marks red and angry on top of the old.

Ben took a halting step forward, his eyes betraying the fierce battle taking place in his mind.

Aria softened her voice as she did her best to stuff down the hatred for Tasha brewing at her core. "You don't have to do anything you don't want to, Ben. It's okay."

Ben blinked at Aria as if he'd forgotten she was there. In seconds, his attention shot back to Tasha. With another hesitant step forward, he eased to his knees in front of her. "Mom, I... What happened to you?"

"My kids abandoned me," Tasha said, the hateful words hissing through her teeth. "Threw me away like trash. I knew your sister hated me. But you, Benny? I thought you loved me." Tasha's head dipped forward as the drugs tried to lull her back into her stupor.

"I do love you, Mom. I just... I didn't know what to do." Ben's eyes filled with tears. "I'm just a kid."

Fire sprang to a full blaze in Aria's chest and spread as if her veins flowed with gasoline. Any pity Aria had felt before burned to ashes in her rage. "That's enough, Mom. Don't you dare talk to Ben that way. He's twelve. He's not responsible for you. It's supposed to be the other way around, remember? You brought this on yourself by loving drugs more than your kids. Blame me if you want to, but leave Ben out of this."

Tasha's eyes popped open, one after the other. "You can't talk to me like that. I'm your mom, you little bitch. You leave my Benny with me. He's my baby. He needs his mommy."

Aria's nostrils flared as she fought the urge to scream, the urge to slap. Instead, she rose to her feet and looked down her nose at the hollow shell of a woman who was supposed to be her mom. She steadied her breathing before she spoke, her voice firm and as icy as the winter air. "No, what Ben needs is a stable home. A home that's warm and clean and has food. The home I'm giving him because you failed to. The last thing he needs is to sleep in a trash bag in this rotten, stinking hellhole." She twisted around with a huff, tugging Ben up off his knees. "Come on, Ben. Let's go home."

Ben dug in his heels and tried to yank his arm free of Aria's grip. "We have to bring Mom. It's Thanksgiving. We should be together," he said, protesting with panic and tears in his eyes.

A frustrated growl rumbled in Aria's throat as she dropped Ben's arm. "Ben, look at her. She can't even stand up. She won't even know she's with us, and she won't remember any of it. There's nothing we can do about it. She's too high." Aria hung her head and gripped her hair, wishing she could reverse the clock and never step foot back in their old neighborhood.

Ben yelped and fell to the ground with a thud.

Aria's head shot up, and her brain struggled to process the image of Ben sprawled on the ground and Tasha's hands tugging on his ankle. "Mom, what are you doing? Let go of him." Aria's adrenaline kicked in, and she dove for Tasha's wrists, yanking her mother's hands away from Ben.

Before Ben could scramble away, Tasha grabbed his shirt and dragged him to her with surprising drug-induced strength. Just as Luke's arms joined the chaos, Aria saw the glint of the knife and froze. Luke stiffened beside her as the world came to a complete standstill.

"Mom? What are you doing?" Ben screeched as the knife pressed against his throat.

Tasha leered at Aria. "You'll help me one way or the other, you ungrateful little brat. If you love your brother as much as you say you do, prove it. Give me all your money."

The blood drained from Aria's face. "What the hell is wrong with you?"

"Fork it over, or he gets it," Tasha hissed, pressing the knife closer against Ben's skin.

"Mom, don't. Please," Ben cried.

Aria's mind raced, hunting for a solution. As much as giving in to Tasha's demands made her want to vomit, it was the only thing she could come up with to end the nightmare. With fury shooting from her eyes, she retrieved her wallet from her pocket and threw what little cash she had in Tasha's face. "Here, you pathetic excuse for a mother. Go get high."

As Tasha scrambled after the money, knife in hand, Luke lunged forward and ripped Ben free from her grip, lifting him out of harm's way. Ben collapsed into Luke's arms, sobbing as Tasha slashed wildly at the air and yelled incoherent obscenities. Luke hoisted Ben up and began carrying him to the bus, sneering over his shoulder at the still-shouting Tasha.

Aria fell in step alongside Luke, rubbing Ben's back to soothe him. "It's okay, bud. You're safe now. We've got you." She snuck a glance behind her only to see Tasha thumbing through her money with a hungry gleam in her eyes.

Inside the bus, Luke set Ben down on a bench and inspected him as Aria continued to soothe him. Luke's eyes zeroed in on Ben's neck. "Looks like a tiny cut that barely punctured the skin. She must've had a really dull knife. Thank God."

Ben collapsed into Aria's arms as fresh sobs wracked his body.

Luke's hardened features softened as he ran a hand over Ben's back. "Let's go home."

When Luke moved for the driver's seat, Aria's heart stopped as she noticed redness spreading from a slice in his jeans.

"Luke, you're bleeding!" she shrieked.

Luke followed her line of sight and gave his leg a quick inspection. He waved her off as he took his seat. "I'll be fine. I want to get Ben home." He snapped his seat belt on and started the bus.

They rode in silence as the bus rumbled home, all reeling from the trauma of what had transpired. Aria held tight to Ben, never wanting to let go again. The world was a much too horrible place for her kid brother to wander alone. With Ben's sobs quieting, Aria kept her eyes trained on the ever-growing red stain on the back of Luke's leg.

Once home, Aria guided Ben to the door, her arm around his shoulder in wordless support. Her shoulder ached from the odd angle required for her arm to drape across Ben's taller frame. Her little brother wasn't so little anymore, in so many ways.

"We're home," Aria said with a rush of air, her rigid muscles relaxing as all three of them kicked off their shoes.

"I'm going to take a shower," Ben said with surprising normalcy.

Aria scrutinized his face, wishing she had telepathic powers to see what was swirling inside that head of his. "Are you sure you don't need to talk first?"

Ben grimaced, his upper lip curling. "No, I stink like that place. I need to take a shower."

Aria nodded, understanding the need to wash away all the evidence of what had happened, at least as much as possible. "Okay, whatever you need. Just let me get the first aid kit from the bathroom before you go in."

Aria ushered Luke down the hall, the first aid kit in hand. "Okay, go take your pants off and lie down on the bed."

"Geez, don't I at least get dinner first?" Luke teased over his shoulder as she nudged him into the bedroom.

Aria rolled her eyes. "I need to doctor your leg, you goof. I'll step out while you put on some shorts." Standing just outside the door, she listened as he drew in a breath when he removed his jeans.

"Okay, I'm decent."

Aria's heart skipped a beat as she took in Luke sprawled on the bed, just like her fantasies, but the fantasy ended when he repositioned onto his stomach and she saw the gash on his calf. Blood—both dark, dry patches and bright, fresh smears—coated his lower leg. She blinked away the mist gathering in her eyes and set to work wiping the blood away with a damp cloth. Luke flinched as she cleaned near the cut, and Aria winced.

"Sorry, I'm trying to be gentle."

Luke rested his face on his hands. "I'll be all right. Do what you gotta do. Ignore it if I flinch."

"I can't ignore it, Luke. I can't ignore any of it." She bit her lip as she finished cleaning the blood, matching him flinch for flinch. "This is a pretty nasty cut. I think it might need stitches."

Luke raised himself onto his elbows, twisting around to see the back of his leg. "Nah, just use some butterfly bandages. I think I have some liquid bandage in there too. I don't care if it's pretty, as long as it heals." He resumed lying on his stomach. "Beauty contests require too much shaving for my liking anyway."

Once again, he wrestled a wry grin from her as she dug for the antibiotic ointment. "Whatever you say. It's your leg." She paused, concentrating on applying the ointment and bandages. She taped gauze over the wound and clapped. "All bandaged up."

Luke rolled over and eased himself to a sitting position, taking care not to rub his calf on the bed. "How much do I owe you, nurse?"

Aria closed the first aid kit and tossed the trash in the can. "Owe me? It's more like I owe you. I don't think I'll ever be able to thank you enough."

Luke diverted his eyes and shrugged a shoulder. "No need to thank me. I did what anyone else would've done."

Aria stepped in front of Luke and locked eyes with him. "No, Luke. That's not true, no matter how many times you say it. You're always downplaying the amazing things you do. You put yourself in danger to save Ben. No one else would've done that. No one in our lives, at least. A dozen people were there, and you were the only one who helped. It was our own mother, our flesh and blood, that you were protecting him from, for crying out loud. You were a hero today. I don't care how much you deny it. You were Ben's hero. And mine."

Her heart raced as she cupped the side of his face with her hand, caressing his cheek with her thumb. Right then, her heart, filled with gratitude for the man in front of her, took full control. She pressed her lips to his, pouring all her unspoken gratefulness into the kiss.

His hands pressed her into him, and his mouth moved with hers, emboldening her to probe further. For once, her brain remained silent. No thinking, just feeling. His firm arms wrapped around her, pulling her closer until not even air remained between them. She melted into the intoxicating security of his embrace, her body aflame with desire, craving him.

A loud clank of the bathroom doorknob echoed down the hallway, and Aria sprang away from Luke as if he would burn her.

Ben mumbled incoherently on the other side of the bathroom door before swinging it open, rubbing his elbow, his face contorted in pain. He paused when he saw them.

Aria's heart raced, afraid he could tell what they'd been doing, sure guilt oozed from every pore of her body. She braced herself for the inevitable accusations.

Instead, Ben scrunched his eyebrows as he sniffed the air. "Do you smell something burning?"

Luke gasped, and his eyes grew wide, his beet-red face draining of color. "The turkey." He pushed himself off the bed and attempted to run to the kitchen, only to come to a stop with a growl of pain. "Ah, dang it. Stupid leg."

"Take it easy. I'll get it." Aria ran to the kitchen and flung open the oven, coughing as she fanned the billowing smoke away with an oven mitt. Forcing her burning eyes to crack open, she reached in and retrieved the turkey pan.

Luke limped over to the blaring smoke alarm and began fanning it with a magazine. "Open the windows!" he shouted above the noise.

Ben raced through the house at a frantic pace, shoving the windows open. Back in the living room, he began using a pillow to fan the smoke outside.

Aria set the blackened turkey on the counter and watched the chaotic scene unfold. A slight giggle escaped her lips, then another, until she burst into laughter.

Luke's face twisted as he continued to fan the alarm, but as he watched her, she saw his frown melt away as her laughter triggered his own.

Ben gaped at them both with bewilderment in his eyes before bursting into laughter as well.

With the smoke clearing at last, the alarm quieted, leaving the house filled with the glorious sounds of joy.

"This is ridiculous." Aria giggled as she wiped a tear from her cheek, unsure if it resulted from the laughter or smoke. Probably a little of both.

Luke limped over and surveyed the turkey, his face dropping. "Hopefully it's salvageable. I should've turned the oven off before we left. I didn't think about how long we might be gone."

"I guess you wanted a smoked turkey," Aria joked, earning her a deadpan look from Luke. "Seriously, though, I think only the skin is burnt. If we peel that off, it should be okay. Maybe a little dry, but that's what gravy is for, right?"

"Still looks better than any turkey we've had before," Ben said, peeking around Luke's shoulder.

Aria raised her brow at him. "We've never had a turkey."

"I know. So it's definitely the best we've ever had." He flashed a cheesy grin, much like one of Luke's.

That grin meant everything to Aria. Even when the world came crashing down around her, as long as Ben was happy and healthy, she could breathe. "You know, you're exactly right. This is our best turkey ever. And even with all the crap that happened today, it's still going to be the best Thanksgiving we've ever had."

Chapter 20

Aria

Aria eased the bedroom door open enough to peek in. Ben lay motionless in bed, the light rumble of his snore letting her know he was fast asleep.

"He's a tough kid. He'll be fine," Luke said as she plunked down on the couch beside him.

Aria hugged her knees to her chest, willing herself to believe Luke's confidence. "I hate that he had to see Mom for what she really is. Especially like that. I know how scared I was, and it wasn't me being held at knifepoint. I can only imagine how terrified he must've been."

"It sucks. It truly does." Luke caressed her back, melting away the tension knotted there. "No one should ever have to go through that. But on the bright side, maybe he'll finally be able to move on. Maybe he can let go of the guilt surrounding everything. Maybe you can too."

Aria chewed her lip as the wheels in her brain clocked in at highway speeds with no sign of slowing down. "Yeah, maybe. But he won't talk about it. He needs to talk. He acts like he's fine, but I know he's not. It's impossible for him to be fine." She dropped her face to her knees, her jaw aching from grinding her teeth. "I wish he would talk to me about it."

Luke slid his arm around her, and she let him guide her into the nook against his side that always calmed her. His thumb trailed circles on her arm as he rested his cheek on her head. "He'll open up when he's ready. We guys don't usually like talking about our feelings much. It's a macho thing."

Aria scoffed and pursed her lips. "Well, most of the macho stuff I've seen isn't very healthy. It's pretty self-destructive."

Luke held up his hands in mock surrender. "Hey, I never said it was smart. It's what we're taught, basically from birth. If no one teaches us it's okay to be otherwise, acting macho is the default set by the world around us. Even if it is toxic."

"I tried to teach him better." Aria bristled, pulling away. "I tried to show him that emotions are okay. I never told him he couldn't cry or talk about feelings."

Luke took her hand in his, his eyes seeking hers. "And you've done a great job. You really have. The best you can. But you can only do so much. While you obviously have superpowers to do all you've done, there's one thing that'll always be in the way. You're not a man. Sometimes only a positive male role model can combat toxic masculinity. No matter what you tell him, he has a lot of conflicting info coming at him from the rest of the world. He's learning how to be a man. It's not a simple task."

Aria's eyes dropped to their joined hands before traveling back to his face to take a good long look at the man before her. The sharp lines of his jaw peppered with stubble lured her in, and the crease in his forehead showcased the sincerity in his heart. In his eyes, she found unfiltered emotions and vulnerability. "If he turns out like you, I can rest easy."

A tight smile graced his lips, though his eyes darkened. "Thanks, but I have my downfalls too."

Aria watched him, wishing she could see inside his brain and read his thoughts. "Everyone has their downfalls. That's part of being human."

Luke stared toward the window as if he could see beyond the drawn curtains. His grip on her hand loosened, but she clutched tighter. "There's stuff I'm not proud of in my past."

"Everyone has that too. I'm learning regrets are a part of life. And whatever it was, you obviously learned from it because look at you now. You rose above. That's what matters in the end."

"I'm glad you see me as a good guy. I figured I was more suited for the part of the villain in your story after how I left things."

She sat in silence, formulating the words to express her myriad of emotions. "It definitely stung for a while. But looking back at everything with fresh eyes, I can see why you did the things you did. And believe me, you've more than made amends. I've never had someone be there for me the way you are. It's... Well, it's wonderful, honestly. Amazing." Her eyes went to his bandaged leg. "And what you did today... It means the world to me. Every time I think about it..." Her eyes flicked back to his face as the hunger in her core flamed to life. "Every time I think about it, I want to kiss you."

The pain and regret drained from his eyes. "Is that so?"

Aria's gaze traveled along his tantalizing jawline and landed on his sensuous lips. "Very much so," she said, her voice breathy.

A mischievous glimmer came to Luke's eyes. "I'm okay with that."

Aria leaned in, brushing her lips against his, reining in her desires to better savor the delicious softness she found. Luke's mouth pushed forward to meet hers with a hunger that made every ounce of restraint flee her body. She pressed herself against him, her mouth thirsting for his like the desert needing rain. The electricity from earlier sparked to life in an instant, every cell in her body aching to be against his skin. Aria tugged at his shirt, their lips parting only for a second as she pulled the fabric over his head. She ran her hands along his chest and across his shoulders, relishing the sensations she'd longed for since day one. His muscular body lived up to the hype she'd built in her fantasies—and then some. A shiver rippled through him, and she smiled against his mouth, intoxicated by the ability to make him quiver under her touch.

Luke's hands slid under her T-shirt, setting her skin ablaze as they traveled up her torso. He tightened his grip and rose to his feet, bringing her with him.

Aria broke the kiss. "Wait. What about your leg?"

Luke kissed the side of her neck. "What leg?"

Aria stifled a laugh as Luke carried her down the hallway and into the bedroom. When he placed her on the bed, she caught him wincing as his calf muscle stretched.

Aria sprang to her feet. "That's it, mister. You lie down right now and rest that leg so it can heal. Doctor's orders." She jabbed a finger at the bed and put her other hand on her hip.

Luke gave her a mock salute before climbing onto the bed. "Yes, ma'am. I've always been a good patient and don't plan to stop now. Especially when my doctor is superhot."

Aria crawled on top of him and slipped her shirt over her head, tossing it to the floor. She whispered in his ear, softly kissing his neck between words. "Good. Because I have some more medicine for you, and I'm pretty sure you're going to like it."

Luke

Luke stared up at the ceiling, stopping short of pinching himself to make sure he wasn't dreaming. Sleep tugged at his eyelids, reminding him he was awake, indeed. The warmth and weight of Aria curled against him under the sheets was, in fact, his miraculous reality. The smoothness of her creamy skin and the smell of her jasmine shampoo were truly his to savor and not a conjured fantasy. She sighed and snuggled closer against him as she succumbed to sleep, and he pulled his arm tighter around her shoulders, smoothing her hair with his other hand. He kissed the top of her head before relaxing against his pillow, his eyes homing in on her hand lying upon his chest.

"Sweet dreams," he whispered. When she didn't stir, he added even more quietly, "I think I love you."

Chapter 21

Aria

Aria blinked against the sunlight streaming through the window. Luke's chest lifting her head in a gentle rhythm brought memories of last night rushing back. She cuddled farther against his chest, wishing she could stay there forever. The distant sound of the fridge closing made her eyes fly open and her heart stop. She bolted upright, pushing on Luke's chest.

Luke grunted and rubbed the sleep from his face. "What's wrong?"

Aria shoved her hand over Luke's mouth. "Shh. Ben is awake already." She flung the covers back and jumped out as if the bed had burst into flames. "Oh no. How could I be so stupid?"

"Gee, thanks." Luke sat up and carefully swung his legs over the side of the bed.

Aria yanked a T-shirt over her head and rummaged for some pants. "I don't mean you. I mean, I should've set an alarm or something. Who knows how long he's been awake. He has to know you're in here. And he'll know why. He's not stupid."

Luke plucked some shorts from the drawer before she closed it and slid them on as he spoke. "Slow down. Let's play it cool. Is it really that big of a deal?"

"It'll be a big deal to him. We told him this whole thing was fake, yet here we are. He's going to think we lied to him."

Luke cocked his head to the side in thought. "Yeah, okay. I can see where that might be a problem. How about this? You can go see how long he's been awake. If he just woke up, we can say I came in to get clothes."

Aria scanned his still-bare chest, the sight making her all but lick her lips. "Okay, but I need you to put a shirt on if I'm going to pull this off."

Luke gave her a mock salute. "Yes, ma'am."

She took another breath, pulled the door open, and stepped into the hallway. She gave Ben a too-casual wave as she found him eating cereal at the table. "Hey, bud. How long have you been up?"

Ben shrugged, shoveling a spoonful into his mouth and avoiding eye contact.

Aria snuck a sideways glance, attempting to study him without him knowing as she started the coffeepot then took the seat across from him. "How are you feeling this morning?"

Another silent shrug accompanying another spoonful shoved in his mouth.

Aria drummed her fingers on the smooth wood as the awkward silence stretched between them. Unable to take it any longer, she dove in headfirst. "Anything you want to talk about?"

Ben replied with a humph. "What's there to talk about?"

"There are a lot of things to talk about. Yesterday was insane. I know you're struggling with some things, whether you want to admit it or not. I wish you would say something. Anything. Reach out to me. I'm worried about you."

"Yeah, sure. I can tell." His eyes rolled so hard she was sure he saw his brain.

"What's that supposed to mean? I always worry about you. I always have and always will."

"Yeah, I guess you were so worried about me last night, huh? When you were busy shacking up with Luke?"

"What?" Aria held back a groan.

Ben swiveled his face away from her. "I've been awake for over an hour, so I know Luke slept in your room. I'm not stupid. Two adults don't sleep in a bed together for no reason."

Aria's eyes darted to Luke as he walked into the kitchen, his mouth twisting in a grimace when he saw Aria's face.

Ben followed her line of sight. "Oh, look. There's lover boy. Want me to leave and give you two some privacy?"

"Of course we don't want you to leave," Aria said. "Can we please talk about this?"

"There's nothing to talk about." Ben got up and put his bowl in the sink then headed for the couch.

Aria followed him and moved the remote beyond his reach as she sat down. "We have to talk about why you're so upset."

"Because I don't know what to believe anymore. You lied to me."

She shot Luke a look that said "I told you so" and sighed. "I can see where it might seem like that, but I promise we didn't lie to you. If we did, then we lied to ourselves too." She cringed inwardly, her statement hitting a little too close to the truth. "Yesterday was crazy, and last night just kind of happened."

"I... I don't want to be alone. I don't want you to leave me," Ben said, his shoulders slumping.

Aria leaned back with her hand on her chest, her mouth dropping open. "What? Why would you even think that?"

"Because it's not us against the world anymore. You have someone else now. You two will be a couple and have your own life, and I'll be all alone." Ben's eyes brimmed with tears.

"What? No, absolutely not. How could you possibly think that?" Aria rubbed his back, shaking her head in bewilderment. "Me and you will always be a team. It will always be us against the world. No matter what. I will never, ever leave you alone in the world."

"You went to see Mom without me. You lied about that too," he said.

"Because I wanted to protect you." Why can't he understand that? Aria thought. "You saw her. You saw that place. It's not pretty. It's bad, even compared to our old life. I didn't know what I was going to find when I went, so I wanted to see it first. Heck, I didn't know if she was even alive, and I wanted to take the brunt of the shock so I could shield you from the worst of it. Because I love you, Ben. And I've got your back. Always."

"You say that now. But what happens when you and Luke have your own kids? You'll forget about me." Ben sniffed and wiped a hand across his eyes.

Aria's hands flew up in front of her. "Whoa, there. You need to slow it down, bud. Way down. No one is talking about anything serious and especially not talking about having babies. That's definitely not happening for a long time, if ever. Trust me. I have to get my career going so I can make sure we never, ever end up back in the projects."

Ben stared at the floor. "What if you and Luke fight and get mad at each other? Will we be homeless again?"

Luke, who'd been watching from a safe distance, approached the back of the couch. "No, that will never happen. I promise you won't be homeless. No matter what. You both will always have a home here. I'm a better person than that." He extended his hand toward Ben, his face set in earnest. "We'll be roommates until you no longer want to be. My handshake is my contract. Even if Aria moves out, you can still stay if you want to. Deal?"

Ben gaped at Luke with disbelieving eyes. "Even if it's just me?"

Luke nodded and nudged his hand closer to Ben. "Yep. I promise. Deal?"

"Deal." Ben's face brightened as he shook Luke's hand.

Aria put her hand on Ben's knee and searched his face. "Are we cool?"

"I guess so," Ben said.

Aria caught her brother's eye, wanting him to see that every word she spoke came from her soul. "Nothing has changed. I promise I will always, *always* be here for you. I'm always in your corner."

Luke patted Ben on the back. "Actually, you have two people in your corner. I'm here whenever you need me. For both of you."

"Cool," Ben said, but he didn't sound convinced.

Aria gave Ben's knee a slight squeeze, bringing his attention back to her. "It's okay if you're not okay. Change can be rough, and we've had a lot of it lately. I promise I'll do everything in my power to make you happy and keep you safe. You've been my number one from the day you were born, and you still are. Okay?"

"Okay." Ben's voice held a touch more enthusiasm but not by much.

"Try not to worry so much. That's my job," Aria joked, hoping to lighten the somber mood.

It worked. The corners of Ben's mouth ticked upward. "You do a pretty good job."

"She sure does." Luke nudged Aria's shoulder and chuckled. He clapped, his face lit with excitement. "Hey, I have an idea. How about we go shopping for some Christmas decorations today? The only thing I've ever decorated is the bus, so I have absolutely nothing for the house. Not even a tree. I could use some help with decorating the bus later too. I have some jobs lined up tonight and need it to be festive."

Ben dried his face with his sleeve, some light coming to his eyes. "We've never had decorations before."

"Well, it's time to change that. Go get dressed. We can grab some lunch while we're out," Luke said.

"Oh, lunch?" Ben jumped up and rushed to his room.

Aria watched him go, her heart twisting in a million directions. After his door shut, she faced Luke, tucking some hair behind her ear. "Thank you so much for that."

Luke rubbed the back of his head, his face contorted with guilt. "I helped cause the problem. The least I could do is help fix it."

"I'm so shocked by his reaction. I knew he might be upset and think we lied, but I honestly never expected that. Can you believe he thought I would abandon him? How could he have such little faith in me?" Aria dropped her face in her hands, the weight of failure pushing down on her shoulders with the force of a thousand pounds.

Luke rounded the couch in an instant and squatted in front of her. His finger lifted her chin, bringing her eyes to meet his. "Listen to me. You've done absolutely nothing wrong. His view of the world is changing, and that's scary as hell. I know I sure remember the day I saw the world for what it really was. The day my childhood ended. I'm sure you remember yours too. Ben is lucky that it took so long for his rose-colored glasses of innocence to come off. You were such a fierce protector of him that his childhood lasted twice as long as ours. He doesn't see what all you've done for him because you did it so well. But he'll come to see that in time. I guarantee it. There's absolutely no reason for you to feel sad or guilty right now. You did nothing wrong."

"Then why does it feel so wrong?"

He reached up and brushed a stray strand of hair from her face. "I'm guessing it's because you've never allowed yourself anything. You gave up everything for Ben, never allowing yourself any happiness outside of his. Your circumstances taught you that if you did anything to make yourself happy, then you were being selfish and taking away happiness from Ben. There wasn't enough to go around. But you're not in that world anymore. I'm here to help you. Both of you. There's room for you to have some happiness too."

The tenderness with which he tucked her hair behind her ear created an ache inside her, a desire for more of those tender moments felt deep within her mind, body, and soul. "Maybe you're right."

"I know I am." Luke rose to his feet and pulled her up and into his arms.

Aria sank into his protective embrace, and her mind let go. She let go of all her preconceived notions of how things should be and what she should do, and she let her heart give itself to the man who set it free.

Luke

Luke took a deep breath of the cinnamon-infused air, his elated mood undampened by the chaotic hustle and bustle of the store. He rubbed his palms together. "What should we look at first?"

"A Christmas tree?" Ben asked.

"Yes, definitely. Priority number one. I'll grab a cart."

Meandering toward the Christmas tree display, Luke noticed a plastic light-up Santa. "So, Ben, have you thought about what you'll ask Santa for this year?"

Ben huffed, attitude cascading off him in waves. "Uh, I'm twelve. I don't believe in that stuff anymore. I haven't since I was, like, eight."

Luke held up one hand in surrender as he steered the cart into the Christmas tree forest with the other. "Sorry, man. No offense. I'm out of touch with when all that stops." He paused in front of a tall, slender tree. "Now that I think about it, though, I was around six when I realized Santa wasn't real. My dad drank all the Christmas money that year, and I got nothing. What about you, Aria? When did you stop believing?"

Aria pursed her lips for a moment. "I don't think I ever believed in Santa. At least not as long as I can remember. Maybe when I was two or something."

"Really?" Ben and Luke asked in unison.

Aria held her hands out to the sides as if the revelation was no big deal. "I never got anything for Christmas, no matter how good I tried to be. We never had any decorations or presents. Christmas was just another cold, miserable day. Then, when Ben came along and Dad killed himself, I took over all the household stuff, so I took on the role of Santa for Ben. I wanted him to have that even if I never did. Kind of hard to believe in magic when you've never experienced any. It's even harder when you're the one making it."

Luke's heart shattered for the little girl who never got a childhood and for the woman who still struggled to allow herself any happiness. He yearned to wrap Aria in his arms, to comfort her, to kiss away the trauma and heartache etched in her features. With people milling all around, he settled for draping his arm across her shoulders. "I'm sorry. That had to be tough."

Aria waved his comment away. "It is what it is. Can't change it no matter how much I might want to. That's life."

"I know what I want for Christmas," Ben said.

"Oh yeah? What's that?" Luke asked.

Ben hugged Aria, making her blink in surprise. "I want you to be happy."

Aria hugged him back. "Thanks, but I'm already happy."

"No, I mean really happy. Not just kind of happy. I want you to have things you want." Ben pulled away from her.

"Thanks, but I have to ask, what brought this on?"

Ben dropped his eyes, digging at the ground with the toe of his shoe. "I heard what you said earlier. I was listening to you guys talk when I was in my room. Luke is right. All these years, I guess I didn't pay enough attention, and I didn't realize everything you did for me. Instead of being a brat, I should say thank you. I'm sorry I didn't trust you. I should know you won't leave me alone on the streets."

Aria pulled him in and squeezed him tight. "I love you, Ben. Don't you ever forget it."

"I won't." Ben tugged himself free and took a step back, scanning the trees around them. "I didn't realize there were so many kinds of Christmas trees."

Aria gave the tree next to her a once-over. "I didn't either, but I definitely don't want this super skinny one. It has a sickly appearance to me. Don't you think?"

"It definitely looks like it's missed a few meals." Luke laughed and pushed the cart toward the fuller trees.

Even as joy filled him, the togetherness and familiarity of picking out decorations together triggered an odd sinking in his stomach. Decorations for a home they shared as a couple. Talk about zero to sixty in no time. Only it wasn't like that for them, in reality. They'd known each other their whole lives. But something was pushing the panic button during what should be a glorious occasion.

Then it hit him. His new world, though amazing, was foreign territory. He'd never had a peaceful home unless he was in it alone. Having not one but two people to share his world in such a positive way felt like learning a foreign language. Maybe he could learn. And maybe they could beat the odds and build a beautiful life together.

Watching Aria and Ben laugh and argue over white versus colored lights, he decided right then and there to shove the panic into the shadows where it belonged and embrace the new happy family dynamic he'd stumbled upon. Maybe it was finally his chance to live in a home filled with joy rather than a broken or empty one.

Chapter 22

Aria

Adjusting the strands of twinkling lights, Aria allowed herself to get lost in the joy of it all, the smile on her face making its way to her heart at last. *Who knew a tree with a few strands of lights and some ornaments could cause such a transformation in both a home and a soul?* Her heart swelled to near-bursting as she watched Ben and Luke joke and have fun together.

As a child, Luke had always been her best friend and neighbor. As a teen, she'd seen him in a new light, drawn to his handsome face and charm. But in that moment, she caught herself experiencing more than friendship and lust. Much more. In the quiet moments when she let her guard down, her mind and heart explored the new feeling that left her lightheaded. It kicked her pulse into overdrive, both thrilled and terrified her, and was something she'd only felt for her brother until Luke. Love.

Luke held out the golden angel and bowed. "All right, Ben. You get the honor of putting the star on top. Well, the angel, in our case."

Ben beamed as he took the angel and placed it on the treetop.

Aria noted the ease of Ben's movement with a pang of nostalgia. "Wow, Ben. You've grown so much. You barely had to reach to put the angel on. I'll bet you're going to need new clothes for Christmas."

Ben tugged at the hem of his shirt. "Nah, these are fine."

Luke switched off the overhead lights and stepped back to admire the tree.

Aria looped one arm behind Ben and the other behind Luke, pulling them close. Standing there, it was as if the warm glow of the

Christmas lights permeated through her. Her body relaxed as she soaked in the perfection of the moment. In one arm she held her not-so-little brother, who was safe, warm, fed, and loved. In the other she held the man she'd come to rely on, the man she dared to admit she loved. It was, hands down, the happiest experience of her life.

"It's perfect. All of it."

Luke

Luke plopped onto the couch, rubbing his bright-red hands together to warm them.

"Well, today was a whirlwind, huh?" Aria sighed as she sank into Luke's open arms and handed him his ritual post-work root beer.

"Yeah, it definitely was." He set the root beer down and wrapped his arms around Aria.

She curled against his side and closed her eyes, peace gracing her face.

Luke watched her, thanking his lucky stars for the little slice of heaven he'd stumbled upon. Knowing he was part of the reason for the peace on her face filled him with a pride he'd never known. "So does this mean I'm officially dating my wife?"

Aria giggled. "Yeah, I guess so."

Luke rested his cheek on the top of her head as he relished having her curled in his arms. "Can I tell you something?"

"Always."

"I've been wanting to do this since the night I picked you two up."

"Me too." Aria lifted her face and kissed his cheek.

He tucked her hair behind her ear and pressed his lips to her forehead. "Pretending to not want you was getting excruciating."

"I appreciate you doing it, though."

"I didn't have a choice."

She straightened and faced him. "That's just it, though. You did have a choice. There's always a choice. And you chose to respect me. I set a boundary, and you respected that. I've honestly never had that happen before in my life. It means a lot to me."

Luke let her words settle around them before responding. "As much as I wanted to be with you, I didn't want to make things harder for you. And I didn't want you to think you owed me anything for helping you."

Aria put her hand on the side of his face, rubbing his stubbly cheek with her thumb. "And that right there, that thoughtfulness, solidifies the fact that you're an amazing man." A mischievous twinkle crept across her face as she brought her mouth to his neck, brushing her lips along his skin. She nibbled his earlobe, sending shivers racing along his body. Her breath caressed his skin as she whispered, "Now, how about we make up for lost time?"

Luke gave a low, hungry growl as his hands found their way under her shirt, and he pressed her body against his. "Not going to hear any arguments from me."

Chapter 23

Luke

Three days later, Luke found himself pacing the floor, the clock glaring at him. Seven minutes until four. Ben should have been home already. He checked the schedule stuck on the refrigerator and shoved a hand through his hair when he scanned Monday. Aria's class had another thirty minutes left. Add in her commute home... He couldn't wait that long. Pulling on his boots, he made a mental note to have a discussion later about getting her and Ben cell phones. He scribbled on the magnetic notepad then grabbed his keys and bolted out the door. As he shifted the bus into reverse, Ben's head bobbed in the rearview mirror.

"Oh, thank God." Luke heaved a sigh of relief as he hopped out of the bus. "Hey, man. I was about to go looking for you."

Ben avoided eye contact as he brushed past Luke, making a beeline for the door. "Yeah, I had to stay late today."

Luke shut the door behind them, his relief evaporating as tension cascaded off Ben like a tidal wave. "What for?" Luke asked, careful to sound nonchalant.

Ben shrugged his backpack off his shoulder. "We've got a group project to work on."

Luke cringed. "Oh man, that sucks. I always hated group work. What's the project about?"

"Haven't decided for sure yet. I'm gonna go do my homework." Ben disappeared into his bedroom before Luke could say another word.

Well, that was weird. Luke sensed there was more to the story, but he needed to wait for Aria. No one knew Ben better than she did.

Aria

Aria hated the days when her classes ran late. She sighed at her watch as the bus slowed to a stop, noting she should've been home fifteen minutes ago. She chewed her lip, hoping Luke wasn't too worried about her.

When Luke pulled open the door as she walked up the steps, guilt coursed through her as she realized he'd been watching for her.

"Hey, I need to tell you something," he said, greeting her with a quick kiss. "It's about Ben."

Aria's face whipped toward his. "Is something wrong?"

Luke took her hand and led her to the table. "He's okay. He's in his room."

Aria melted into the chair, relief softening her muscles.

"But..."

"But what?"

"Well, he was about a half hour late getting home. He said he has a group project he was staying late for, but he seemed off. He was kind of moody and didn't want to talk to me. Went in his room and hasn't come out since. He didn't even grab a snack."

Aria's brows knit together as a frown overtook her face. "That's not like him. I better go talk to him."

As she stood to go, Ben entered the kitchen. "I'm hungry."

Aria stepped toward him. "Hey, I was going to come talk to you. I heard you had to stay late today. Everything okay?"

"If you're going to rat me out, why not tell all of it?" Ben glared at Luke.

Luke held up his hands defensively. "It's not like that, man. I didn't rat you out. I told her you had to stay late for a project. That's all. It's the truth. I won't lie to her."

Aria studied Ben's face. "What's going on, Ben? Why are you taking that tone with Luke? Is there a problem at school?"

"Nothing is wrong, okay? Geez. Lay off, will ya?" Ben stomped to the refrigerator and ripped the door open.

Aria exchanged a worried glance with Luke. Something was definitely wrong. "Ben, you can tell me anything. Whatever is going on, I can help you. We can figure something out together." No response. Aria swallowed, afraid to hear the answer to her next question. "Are you still upset about me and Luke?"

Ben slammed the refrigerator shut and turned on her. "No, I'm not upset. I don't care what you two do. I know adults have sex. Okay? I don't care. And I don't need you to be my mom."

Aria recoiled at his outburst. "I'm not trying to be your mom, Ben. I'm your sister and always will be. But as your sister, I care about you. I just want to make sure you're okay. Me and you against the world, remember?"

The hard edges of anger on Ben's face softened. His shoulders dropped as an exasperated sigh escaped his mouth. "I know. Sorry. I had a bad day. I just need some space."

Aria took a reluctant step back. "We all have bad days. It's okay. Want to talk about it?"

Ben shook his head, his eyes landing everywhere but on her face. "Not really."

"Okay, but I want you to know I'm here whenever you're ready." Aria bit her lip, wishing she could make him talk but knowing better than to push. Ben was on the cusp of that tumultuous time transitioning between a child and a young man. She had no clue how she was supposed to raise a teenager, especially a boy, when she was only twenty-three herself. Thank goodness she had Luke around for a man's perspective.

She put her hands on her hips and plastered on a cheery face, trying to lighten the mood. "How about I cook some dinner? Want some cheeseburgers? I can use the pepper jack cheese you like. Some food always makes you feel better."

Ben offered a weak smile. "Sure."

"**I**'m worried about Ben." Aria snuggled next to Luke on the couch and looked toward Ben's door, the thumps of music pounding their way out.

Luke followed her line of sight. "Yeah, he's a tough nut to crack sometimes."

"What do you think is going on with him?"

"It's hard to tell. At that age, it could be a number of things. Maybe he's still dealing with what happened with your mom. Or he's still dealing with us being together. Maybe he's having trouble at school or with a girl. Heck, it could be hormones going wild."

"I guess I'll have to wait until he wants to talk about whatever it is." Waiting sounded like pure torture.

Chapter 24

Luke

"Hey, how was your night?" Aria greeted Luke with a kiss before he could respond, her lips a welcome warmth against his icy skin.

Luke slipped off his snow-covered coat and wrapped his arms around her. "Cold and long. But better now that I'm holding you."

She shivered in his arms. "You go get under the blanket, and I'll get your root beer."

Luke kicked off his boots and headed for the bedroom. As he waited for Aria, he realized it had been over a week since he fell asleep to the glow of the television. These days, he spent his nights cuddling with Aria and talking about whatever came to mind. He didn't miss his old sci-fi movies in the least.

"Here you go." Aria handed him the root beer before joining him in bed.

"You know, I'm not sure I even need these anymore. Being here with you relaxes me better than anything else." Luke took a drink anyway. Waste not, want not, after all.

Aria nodded in agreement. "I feel like I sleep so much better with you in here. Though I'm still ready to beat someone with a trash can if I need to."

Luke chuckled at the reminder of that first night he came home from work.

Aria settled against him, her head on his shoulder. "So how was work? Anything weird?"

Luke cast a sidelong look over her face as he set down his root beer. "Actually, the funniest thing happened earlier."

She gave him her full attention. "Oh yeah?"

Luke nodded, his lips twitching with a suppressed smile. "I've noticed work has been a little busier this year. I mean, the holiday season is always busy, but I've had to turn down jobs for the first time in my life, due to not having openings. Lots of college kids are suddenly calling me up."

Aria began picking at the comforter. "Yeah, I've noticed you've been pretty busy."

"That's an understatement. If this keeps up, I might have to expand the business. Buy another bus. Hire a second driver. The works."

Aria's finger trailed along his knuckles. "That's a good thing, though. Right?"

"Oh, definitely. I have to make sure it's sustainable first, but having a lot of customers is always a good thing. The funny thing, though, happened when I was dropping off my last party. It was a bunch of college kids. One guy threw an arm around me and said he was a marketing major and that my ad in the college paper was genius." Luke looked down at Aria, whose hand stopped moving. "What's funny is, I don't remember ever putting an ad in the college paper." When Aria remained motionless, he put a finger under her chin and pulled her face to meet his. "Thank you."

Aria's cheeks flushed as she gave him a sheepish grin. "You weren't supposed to find out."

He gave her forehead a light kiss. "You didn't have to do that. I know it costs money for ads."

"I wanted to pay you back for all you've done for me. And for Ben. I knew you'd never take money from me, so I did what I could with what I have."

"Well, you're right. I won't take your money. The spike in business does make things a little trickier, though, with the phone call I got today." Luke's pulse beat in his ears.

"What phone call?" Aria asked, watching him with concern in her eyes.

"Well, I was going to wait until it was official, but I was talking with the city council. You know I've gotten awards from the city for the party bus. I guess they see me as a pretty good businessman because they contacted me and said there's an opening on the city tourism board. And they asked if I was interested."

Aria gasped. "You're going to serve on the tourism board? Is it a paid position? What about the party bus?"

"I haven't officially gotten the offer yet, since I just talked to them today, but I do know it's a paid position. I don't know how much yet. If I do get the offer and if I accept it, I wouldn't be able to do both that and the party bus. Well, I technically could since the hours don't overlap, but I wouldn't have much time at home." He placed his hand on her hip and tugged her a little closer. "That's an issue for me now that I have something to come home to. I've been thinking through the options ever since. The way I see it, I can either sell the business or I can hire a driver."

Aria placed her hand on his chest. "The party bus is your baby. You fought for that thing tooth and nail and used it to drag yourself, as well as me and Ben, out of hell. I'd hate to see you sell it. I think you should hire a driver. You were already thinking about doing that for a second bus anyway. It wouldn't be much more hiring two versus one, as long as the profit would still be there."

Luke tapped her temple. "That's why I run everything by you. I love that brain of yours. And you know me so well."

"So do you think you'll take the job?"

Luke thought for a moment. "I'm not completely sure, but I think so. It's definitely more predictable and steadier than the party bus. Safer too. But I wanted to hear your thoughts on it all."

She raised herself onto her elbow. "This is a great opportunity for you, but I also know how much you love the party bus. I'll support you in whatever you decide. I want you to be happy. Hopefully I didn't make the choice even harder for you with all the new business for the bus."

Luke stroked her hair, wondering how on earth he'd landed such a thoughtful woman. "A thriving business is never a problem. If anything, having the uptick in business makes it even easier to take a step back and hire a driver. By the way, you're also a genius. I can't believe I never thought to advertise in the college paper."

"Probably because you never thought about the paper until you rescued me."

"That's true," Luke said. "Though I wouldn't say I rescued you. Gave you a hand, sure, but you're more than capable of rescuing yourself. You don't need me."

Aria leaned closer and threaded her fingers through his. "Either way, I do know one thing."

"What's that?"

"No matter whether I need you or not, I want you." She raised his hand to her mouth, teasing him with her light-as-air kisses brushing against his skin.

He tugged her closer so her face met his, one hand burying itself in her hair as the other cupped her butt. With a hunger burning deep within, he brushed his lips against hers, teasing her the way she'd teased him. "Well, good, because I sure as hell want you."

Chapter 25

Aria

Aria's heart hammered as she walked up the steps to Luke's dark house. With only two days before the end of the semester, she'd gotten stuck at the library helping last-minute study groups. She double-checked her watch and confirmed she was only a half hour late. Flashbacks of the eviction sent shock waves jolting through her. She cursed under her breath as she fumbled for her keys then shoved open the door. Dropping her backpack on the floor, she clicked on the lamp beside the door and scanned the room.

"Hello?" Silence. Her heart plummeted to the floor as a wave of nausea crashed in her stomach. She went to leave but saw a note taped beside the door.

Aria,

I went to find Ben. Left at four. We're getting cell phones for you two ASAP.

Luke

Aria's chest tightened, and her breathing became shallow. Luke had been gone an hour already, which meant he hadn't found Ben with ease, if at all. *Where could he be?* Aria shook her head, trying to shake out the thoughts beginning to swarm. She raced out the door to the bus stop, praying she was wrong.

By the time she stepped off the bus, no trace of sunlight remained in the sky. Shivering in the darkness, she sprinted to her old house, keys between her knuckles. The action triggered more flashbacks to that night two months ago when her whole life changed.

She'd vowed that night to never come back, yet she had come back for the third time.

Luke's bus came into view in front of the duplex, and she fought the urge to vomit as her stomach tied in knots. Her nightmare was becoming real. She ran to the bus, her pulse racing when she found it locked and empty.

"Ben?" she shouted into the darkness, not caring if she drew attention to herself. All she cared about was Ben. "Ben? Are you here? Luke?" Squinting into the ever-increasing darkness, she cursed herself for not grabbing a flashlight.

Her mind grasped for solutions as her eyes darted around. The bus. Luke kept an emergency bag behind the driver's seat. She found her key to the bus. Success. Once inside, she groped around for the bag, her hand finally landing on the rough canvas. After placing the bag on a seat lit by the beam of a streetlight, she dug for the flashlight. Nothing. *Luke must've taken the flashlight with him.* Aria threw the bag against the seat and sank to the floor, shoulders hunched and tears burning behind her eyes.

"Hey there, baby girl." A sinister voice came from the darkness.

Aria sprang to her feet, her eyes searching for the source and landing on a silhouette at the front of the bus. She knew that voice, the one that always made her skin crawl. "I don't have time for games, Vick. I have to find Ben."

"Ah, yeah, Ben. I seen him. He's been coming around a lot lately." He took a menacing step toward her.

Aria took a step back, slipping her keys between her knuckles as her mind recounted all the days Ben had come home late. "What? Why was he coming here? Wait, that doesn't matter right now. Where is he? I need to find him."

"Information like that has a price, baby girl." He stepped into the beam of light, his lips a sinister curl and his greasy hair slicked down.

"Don't come any closer, Vick. Just tell me where Ben is." The keys dug into her palm as she tightened her grip.

"That mom of yours... she's getting desperate. Keeps coming around wanting money, but I don't want what she's trading no more. Even I have standards. Ben's stepping up to do what you won't. He's helping her." Vick stepped closer and ran his tongue across his teeth.

Aria tried to take another step back, but her heart dropped as the minibar pressed into her back. He had her cornered, trapped. She swallowed, trying to contain the panic that shot through her. "Ben is with Mom? But she tried to stab him. Why would he... Wait. How is he helping her?"

An evil sneer took over Vick's face. "If you ain't got money, there's only two ways to get what you want in this neighborhood, baby girl. Drugs and sex. You know that. You know what your mom did, and you know what Ben is doing. And you know exactly what you've got to do if you want to help them." Vick licked his lips as his eyes swept over her body.

"Never," Aria snarled as she raised her chin with bravado and hoped he couldn't see it quiver.

"You think you're better than all us, don't you? Well, I got news for you, sweetheart. You're nothing but the daughter of a crack whore."

"Well, you're nothing but an ugly, greasy pig," Aria said, her fists balled.

Lightning flashed before her eyes as her left cheek exploded under the strike of his hand, sending her crashing against the minibar.

"You're gonna learn your place in this world yet, girl. And I'm gonna teach you." Vick grabbed her shoulders and threw her to the floor.

Aria gripped her head, trying to stop the world from spinning. "No." She became suffocated by Vick's weight on top of her. "Stop!"

"Shut up," he hissed.

The sharp edges of her keys dug into her fingers, anchoring her, keeping her from succumbing to the darkness that beckoned. By instinct, she'd held on to them as she fell. Vick let go of her arm as he tugged at her pants. Fighting through the fog in her brain, she squeezed her keys and punched with all her strength. Flesh ripped as her hand made contact with Vick's face.

"Ahhh, you bitch!" Vick wailed as he fell back, clutching his cheek.

Aria scrambled to her feet and stumbled as fast as she could to the front of the bus, the floor swaying beneath her. She tumbled down the steps and out into the darkness. As she struggled to her feet, a hand gripped her arm. Self-preservation taking the reins, she slapped and kicked with wild abandon, landing several solid blows on whoever the hand belonged to. A man's voice reached her ears, but her panicked brain refused to pause long enough to listen.

"Aria! Aria, stop. It's me. Ouch! Stop! It's me, Luke. Ouch! Damn it. It's Luke!" Luke wrapped his arms around her in a bear hug, trapping her arms. "You're safe. It's me. Stop. It's Luke."

Aria's brain finally registered Luke's voice, and she froze. "Luke?" She searched for his face, but her cloudy vision hampered her efforts.

"Yes, it's me, Luke. What happened to you?" He loosened his grip and twisted so she could see his face better.

"You're gonna pay for this, you little—" Vick jumped off the bus but stopped at the sight of Luke holding Aria. "Hand her over. I'm not done with her."

Luke tightened his grip on Aria as she shivered. "No, you're done. Forever. Go back to your pathetic life, and don't you ever touch her again. Don't even think about it."

"Oh yeah? And what are you gonna do about it, mister hotshot? You think you're something else, don't you? You and that little tramp are perfect for each other. I need to teach you both a lesson." Vick started toward them but halted at the click of a gun cocking.

Aria gasped as the streetlight glinted off the gun at the end of Luke's outstretched arm.

"If you're smart, you'll walk away, Vick. And don't look back," Luke growled.

Vick let out a bark of laughter that held no humor. "You're not man enough to use that."

Luke's hand squeezed the dark metal. "You wanna test that?"

"You wouldn't want to stain that precious, clean record of yours." Vick took a challenging step forward.

Luke shot him a cocky smirk. "I own this gun legally and have a concealed carry permit. I'm a law-abiding citizen and a respected businessman. Hell, I even got an award from the city. You really think the cops will care if I shoot a lowlife, sleazy landlord in the hood? All I've got to say is self-defense. They'll take one glimpse of Aria and shake my hand. I might even get another award."

Vick's eyes traveled from Luke to Aria. "That little tramp ain't worth all this trouble." He waved a dismissive hand in the air as he stalked back to his house, leaving a string of cuss words in his wake.

Luke kept the gun trained on Vick until the slamming of his front door rang out through the darkness. He holstered his gun, switching on the safety lock first, and rubbed Aria's back. "Let's get you on the bus." He motioned behind him. "Come on, Ben."

Aria sucked in a breath and spun around, the movement sending her head into a whirl. She fell against Luke and let him support her. "Ben? Oh, Ben. Are you okay? I was so worried." She stumbled toward Ben and threw her arms around him, sobbing with relief.

"I'm okay. Are you okay? What happened with Vick?" Ben asked, eyes wide with terror.

Luke nodded at the silhouettes of the crowd in the surrounding darkness. "How about we all get safely on the bus?"

Aria nodded as Luke put a protective arm around her then Ben. She let him lead her to the bus and felt her fears subside as he locked the doors behind them. Aria fell into the seat beside Ben as Luke started the bus.

Aria blinked her right eye at the brightness of the bus coming to life, but her left eye wouldn't budge. The wide eyes and paleness on Ben and Luke's faces alarmed her.

"What? Is it that bad? You two look like you've seen a ghost." Her fingers trailed along the side of her face, her cold fingertips a welcome respite against the heat in the taut skin.

Luke

Luke blinked, hoping his eyes were deceiving him and when they opened, all would be well. No such luck. The woman he loved was sitting before him, seriously injured. His brain overcame his initial shock, and he rushed to her side in an instant, leaving the bus idling. He sucked in his breath as he inspected her face. "I think you need to go to the hospital and get checked out."

Aria moved to shake her head but winced. "No, I just want to go home. I need to lie down and sleep a little."

Luke grabbed a pillow and tucked it behind her head. "Here, you can rest your head against that while I drive to the hospital." He pivoted to Ben, whose eyes swam with tears. "You sit here and keep her from falling over, okay?"

Ben nodded with force, as if his life depended on it.

Luke leaned in to whisper. "Try to keep her awake. She doesn't need to fall asleep right now. But keep her calm. We'll tell her about you later."

Ben nodded again, putting a protective arm around Aria the way Luke had earlier.

Chapter 26

Luke

The sight of Aria's swollen face hit Luke like a punch in the gut every time. Helplessness consumed him as she lay on the exam table in pain she refused to admit she felt. Having to be separated for what felt like an eternity for the police interviews had been torture. Being in the same room but unable to touch her wasn't much better. He wished he could take it all away. If only it was his face covered in a red-and-purple bruise and his eye swollen solidly shut. He could take the pain of that any day, but watching Aria suffer was almost more than he could bear.

"There. Finished with the stitches." The doctor stood and patted Aria on the hand. "They'll be by to take you for the CT scan shortly."

"Thanks," Aria murmured. After the door clicked shut, she put her hands by her side, attempting to push herself to a sitting position.

Luke rushed to her, grabbing her shoulders to help her. "Whoa, take it easy."

"I want to sit up," she said, her tone snippy.

"I know, but you should've told me so I could help you."

"Will you stop fussing over me? I'm fine." Aria tried to smile but flinched instead.

"Of course. Having your eye swollen shut, six stitches in your eyebrow, and a face too sore to smile totally counts as fine." Luke gave her two thumbs-up and an exaggerated happy face.

"Okay, when you put it like that, maybe I'm not totally fine. But still, I'm not fragile. You don't have to fuss over me." She crossed her arms over her chest, her mouth set in a hard line.

Luke shook his head at her attitude. "Well, I'm sorry, but I care about you, and I'm going to 'fuss over' you because you're hurt. You were assaulted." He took her hand, his heart an open wound at the very thought of what she'd been through. "And believe me, I know you're not fragile. If I hadn't bear-hugged you, I think you would've put me in the hospital too. Maybe while we're here, I should have them check my arms, shins, and ribs for fractures."

Aria rewarded his tease with a curl of her lips. "Sorry about that. It was dark, and I panicked."

"No need to say sorry. I don't blame you one bit. I'm just glad you're safe." He planted a gentle kiss on the uninjured side of her head.

The door swung open. "Miss Sutton? Time for your scan." A nurse pushed a wheelchair to the bed and assisted Aria into the seat.

Luke's hands twitched as he resisted the urge to step in and do it himself.

The nurse gave him a curt nod. "We'll be back shortly."

Luke nodded, words caught in his constricting throat as Aria disappeared into the hallway.

"It's all my fault." Ben's meek whisper came from a chair in the corner of the room.

Luke froze, his mind racing, searching for what to say to comfort Ben without letting him off the hook. After all, Ben was the reason Aria was in the hospital. No one could deny that fact. He took a deep breath then spoke slowly and steadily, picking his words with care. "You're not responsible for Vick's actions. He's the bad guy here."

Ben bent with his elbows on his knees, his head resting in his hands. "But the only reason she was there was to look for me."

Luke pitied Ben for the harsh lessons he kept learning these past few months, but Ben needed to learn them. "Yeah, you're right."

Ben's face jerked toward Luke. "What?"

Luke held out his hands, palms up. "You're right. I can't argue with that. The only reason Aria was there was because she was looking for you. If you'd come home, none of this would've happened." He motioned around the hospital room.

Ben bolted upright, his brows scrunched and his mouth agape. "What? I can't believe you said that."

Luke locked eyes with him, ready to give the final, painful blow. "Why not? It's the truth."

Confusion filled Ben's eyes. "But you're the adult. Aren't you supposed to say something to make me feel better?"

Luke sat in the chair next to Ben and leaned in, hoping his face struck the perfect balance between tender and stern. "All right, Ben, I'm going to give you some tough love, so hear me out. I'm not here to always make you feel better. That's not my job. That's not Aria's job either, though she tries so hard. We aren't your parents, never will be, but they're not in the picture, so we have to fill in where we can to help you become a good man. Okay?"

Ben gaped at him, slack-jawed. "But—"

Luke held up a finger to stop him. "I'm not done. Part of growing up is taking responsibility for your actions. That means when you mess up, you own it, but most importantly, you learn from it too. You messed up tonight. Big time. In the end, everyone will be okay, but it could've easily ended very differently. You made a big mistake. But it's okay. We all make mistakes. We're human, and we're all constantly learning. What you have to ask yourself is what can you learn from it? What can you do differently the next time around?"

Ben sank back in his chair, his eyes wide and face pale.

Luke put a hand on Ben's shoulder and gave him a pat. "I know that's a lot to take in, but it's part of life. You're still a good kid. You're just a good kid who messed up. It happens to all of us. Lord knows I've had my fair share of screwups. I wouldn't have this tattoo if I hadn't screwed up. But I'm proud to say I learned from them all."

They sat in silence for a minute, letting the words settle.

Ben leaned forward and stared at the floor. "I learned how dangerous that place really is. I guess Aria did a crazy-good job of keeping me away from the worst stuff because I swear I didn't expect... all that."

"Yeah, she did a great job," Luke said. "That's how much she loves you, Ben. Shielding you from all that couldn't have been easy for her. Honestly, I don't see how in the world she ever managed. But I think you owe it to her to stay away from there. Once and for all."

Ben leaned back in his chair, gripping his blond curls in his fists. "How could I be so stupid?"

Luke gave him a pat on the knee. "Well, once we're out of here and we tell Aria what you were doing, I'm sure she'll help you figure that out."

Ben gave a half-hearted chuckle as he dropped his arms to his sides. "Yeah, she's not going to be too happy with me."

Luke gave a matter-of-fact shake of his head. "Nope, she's not. But that's part of the natural consequences of your actions. You always have to consider other people because every decision you make affects others. Hurting the people you love can be a huge motivator for change. Trust me, I know." He tapped his sobriety tattoo for emphasis.

Ben scoffed. "Not for my mom. Nothing motivates her but getting high."

A resigned sigh escaped Luke as he leaned back. "Yeah, unfortunately. But whenever drugs enter the picture, all the rules go flying out the window. Drugs ruin everything."

"Yeah, they do." Ben's eyes misted over.

"Hey, guys. Miss me?" Aria asked as the nurse wheeled her back in.

Luke sprang to his feet and jumped into action, taking Aria from the nurse and helping her back into bed himself. Once she was settled, he spoke to the nurse, a little embarrassed by his eagerness but unapologetic. "Is she okay?"

The nurse's mouth curled at one corner. "It will take a little while to get the results. The doctor will be in to let you know as soon as he can." She nodded at Aria. "You take care. If there's anything you need, don't hesitate to ask."

As soon as the door clicked shut, Aria frowned at Ben. "Okay, explain yourself, mister. Now."

Luke watched Ben's throat bob as he swallowed hard. He knew they needed to talk about everything, but his number-one priority remained Aria's health. "Are you sure you want to do this here? Now? You need your rest."

Aria crossed her arms over her chest and shot him a fiery glare. "Yes, here and now. We'll probably be here at least another hour, if not more. No matter how many times they say shortly or soon, we all know they don't mean it. When we finally get home, I plan to pass out for a few hours before I have to go turn in my final paper for my literature class. Plus, Ben has school tomorrow, which he can't skip because he has tests. I refuse to wait until tomorrow evening to find out what the hell is going on. So spill."

Luke grimaced at Ben and held his hands out by his sides in defeat. "She has a point. You're going to have to tell her sometime, man. Might as well get it over with."

Ben sighed as if the weight of the world rested on his shoulders, shame written all over his face. "I've been going there after school to see Mom."

Aria's jaw dropped. "This wasn't the first time?"

Ben gave the slightest shake of his head, staring at the white-and-blue speckled floor tile. "I never had group work or after-school projects. Every time I was late, I was going there."

Aria stared at Ben, speechless. "I... I can't believe you lied to me like that. And for so long. That hurts, Ben. It hurts a lot."

Ben raised his head, his eyes swimming with unshed tears. "I know, and I'm sorry, but I didn't know what to do. I knew you didn't want me going there, but... I guess I felt like I needed to help Mom, that maybe you didn't try hard enough. Maybe I could help."

Luke winced at Ben's words, knowing they would cut Aria deep.

Aria recoiled as if he had slapped her. "Seriously? How dare you. You have no idea how hard I tried."

"I know. It was stupid, and I don't know what I was thinking. I guess I didn't want it to be true, and I didn't want the kids at school to be right." He hung his head.

Aria sat up straighter, the anguish on her face giving way to concern like the flip of a switch. "What kids at school? What are they saying?"

Taking Aria's hand in his, Luke wished he could fast-forward through the shock Ben still had in store for her.

Ben shrugged and picked at his thumbnail. "They've been giving me crap about getting kicked out of our house. Then they started talking crap about Mom and saying I'm a loser like her. That's why I can't get a girlfriend. I look like Mom, and I'll end up like her. I thought—" His voice cracked, and he cleared his throat. "I thought that maybe if I helped her get better, then all the other kids would shut up."

"You are not a loser, Ben. You hear me? It doesn't matter where you start out in life, you can go wherever you want. You just have to believe in it and work hard." Aria lay back against the pillow, cradling her head in her hand. She opened her right eye and squinted at him. "How were you helping her, exactly?"

Luke hated seeing Aria in pain and knew the conversation wasn't helping her rest. As much as he wanted to put an end to the discussion, he also knew Aria well enough to know she wouldn't back down until she knew the entire story. She wouldn't rest until all her questions were answered. He couldn't help but be filled with pity for the boy sitting in front of him, knowing this next part was going to hurt. He patted Ben on the back. "You have to tell her."

Ben glanced at her with trepidation, as if eye contact would make him explode, and turned his face away in shame. "I was giving her money."

Aria's uninjured eyebrow shot up. "What money? Where did you get money?"

Ben took a ragged breath, his voice coming out strained. "I, uh… stole some from Luke."

Aria bolted upright too fast, making her sway and grip her head. "What? How could you do that? After everything he's done for us." She turned to Luke. "Did you know about this?"

Luke put an arm around Aria, both to steady and comfort her. "Well, I didn't notice it at first. I get tips most nights, so I don't know the exact amount I come home with until I count it the next day. Apparently, he was getting into my tips before I counted them. Yesterday, though, I had a twenty-dollar bill missing from my wallet that I definitely noticed."

Aria whipped her face toward Ben and winced, sucking a breath in through her teeth. "I'm so shocked and disappointed."

Ben's eyes begged Luke for comfort, and Luke nodded for him to continue as he crossed the room and put a hand on Ben's shoulder.

"Th-that's not all," Ben stammered. "I-I gave some of the money to Mom, but it wasn't enough. I figured out a way to triple my money and gain some street cred to get the guys at school off my back."

Aria's good eye narrowed. "Are you saying what I think you're saying?"

Ben nodded almost imperceptibly, his throat bobbing again. "I had Vick hook me up with a supplier."

Aria huffed and swung her legs off the bed, her face beet red. "Drugs? Really? After what they've done to Mom? How could you even begin to think that was a good idea?" She slid from the bed and planted her feet on the floor.

Luke bolted to her side, grabbing her arm to support her. "What are you doing? You need to rest. You're not supposed to be up and walking around."

"I can't just sit here. I need to move." Aria fidgeted and grumbled with every wobbly step. After a few attempts at pacing, her shoulders dropped in defeat. "Fine, I'll sit back down."

Luke eased her back onto the bed and covered her with the blanket. "I know you're used to being superwoman, but right now you need to rest."

Aria leaned back against the pillow, squeezing her right eye shut. "How can I rest when my little brother is ruining his life? Drugs have taken everything from me my whole life. They made Dad shoot himself, and they ruined Mom. Drugs stole my childhood. They screwed up Chrissy's life. Now they're taking Ben." A sob escaped her as she rolled onto her side and curled into a ball.

Luke leaned over her, draping his arm around her. He would've given anything in the world to take away her pain, but all he could do was wrap her in a comforting embrace. "Shh. It'll be okay. Ben isn't gone. He's right here." Luke jerked his head to the side, motioning for Ben to join them.

Aria's eye shot open as she gasped. "Wait, Chrissy didn't have anything to do with this, did she? Is that where you got the idea?"

Ben squatted to be eye level with Aria. "No, it wasn't Chrissy. I, uh, started before she showed up."

Aria groaned. "And seeing Luke kick her out for drugs didn't give you a wake-up call?"

Ben hung his head again. "No, I guess I figured it was different because I wasn't bringing them into the house." His eyes met hers. "But I'm done with all that now. I promise. After seeing what happened to you... I can't do that anymore. And Mom... well, I'm done with her too. After everything I did for her, she still doesn't care. The crap she pulled tonight—" He stopped, his lip curling in disgust.

Aria's tears halted. "What do you mean? What did she pull? There's more? What happened?"

"I guess the money I gave her wasn't enough. She..." Ben's voice hitched, and his pleading eyes sought Luke's.

Luke nodded. "It's okay, bud. I'll tell her the rest." He struggled to take a deep breath, his chest tight as his heart shattered for them both. He knew this news was going to devastate Aria, but he also knew he had to tell her. "When Ben didn't come home and I found money missing, I had my suspicions. I drove straight there and headed for the bridge. When I got close, I heard Ben shouting, so I ran as fast as I could. Tasha was standing there counting money, and this guy, this stranger, had a hold of Ben. I figured they were mugging him. I yelled for them to stop and give Ben his money back." He paused as Ben shot to his feet and walked away to stand facing the corner, as if trying to hide. "Tasha said it was her money. She earned it. I decided it wasn't worth it, so I told the guy to give me Ben and let me leave. He tightened his grip and..." Luke gritted his teeth, not wanting to finish the story. "He said he bought him fair and square."

Aria's hand flew to her mouth. "No, there's no way. She didn't... Are you serious?"

Luke winced and watched Ben's back as he answered. "Unfortunately, yeah, I'm serious."

"Oh, Ben, I'm so glad you're okay." She held her arms outstretched.

Ben sobbed and rushed to her, clinging on for dear life. "She sold me."

Aria rubbed his back, her tears flowing freely. "I'm so sorry that happened to you. I can't even imagine how scary that must've been. I'm so glad Luke got there when he did." She reached for Luke's hand and gave it a squeeze.

Luke winced before he could stop himself.

Aria's gaze flew to his hand, taking in the sight of his bruised knuckles. "Your hand…"

He tucked his hand behind his back, out of sight. "I had to convince the guy to let Ben go somehow."

"Am I interrupting?" The doctor's voice startled them all.

Luke scrubbed his eyes and cleared his throat. "No, it's… It's been a long, hard night."

The doctor raised a questioning eyebrow but regained his composure. "Well, then. I have some good news for you all. The CT scan came back clean. There's no bleeding or fluid on the brain and no fractures. It doesn't appear there will be any lasting damage to the eye. The swelling and bruising will take a while to go away, but once they do, you should be as good as new. You'll need the stitches out in five to seven days, but other than that, you are good to go. Take it easy in the next day or so. I'll have the nurse send in a script for some pain meds."

Aria held up a hand. "No, I don't want any drugs."

"We'll send the script in anyway. Just in case you change your mind. They'll be in soon with your discharge papers."

"Thank you," Aria said.

With the doctor gone, they sat in silence for some time, absorbing everything and collecting their thoughts.

"I don't know about you guys, but I'm ready to go home and go to sleep." Aria yawned, right on cue.

Luke plopped in the chair beside the bed, suddenly drained of all energy. "Yeah, I feel like I ran a marathon. Or got hit by a bus. Or both."

"Yeah, I'm beat." Ben took the seat across the room and peeked over at Luke and Aria. "I'm really sorry for everything."

Aria sighed, leaning back and closing her uninjured eye. "I know you are. I hope we can finally put this all behind us. Once and for all." She opened her eye, zeroing in on Ben. "And I hope from now on you'll talk to me about stuff."

Ben nodded. "Yeah, I definitely learned a lot from all this. I promise."

"Good." Aria closed her eye again.

"There's one more thing."

Aria groaned. "What now? I don't think I can take anything else."

"Can we stop and get food on the way home? I'm starving." Ben patted his stomach.

Luke chuckled, his spirits lifting at the sound of Ben and Aria's giggles. "Yeah, bud. We'll get some food."

Chapter 27

Aria

Aria pried open her good eye, the bright sunshine searing her retina. A night of fitful sleep, thanks to pain and nightmares, left her groggy. As her head throbbed, she groaned and patted the empty bed beside her.

"Luke?" she croaked, unable to muster the energy for much more.

Luke must've been on high alert because he burst through the door in an instant. "Aria? I thought I heard you. How are you feeling? Need anything?"

"Ibuprofen. Water." She closed her eye and gingerly put a hand on her forehead as Luke sped out of the room. He came back in the blink of an eye, handing her two pills and a glass.

She eased to her elbow and took the pills. "Ben?"

"I got him up and fed and off to school. I drove him so he didn't have to catch the bus. Figured it was good for him to sleep in. He was tired but seemed okay. I told him I'm going to pick him up this afternoon."

"Thanks." If her head wasn't ready to explode, she would've kissed him. Her heart swelled because she knew she could count on him in her moments of need. She struggled to sit up, and Luke rushed to her side, helping her the rest of the way.

"What do you need? I can get it for you so you don't have to get up."

Aria managed a snort. "I need to pee."

Luke gave a small chuckle. "Oh. Yeah, I'm no help with that, huh? Here. Let me help you get there."

"I'll be fine once my headache goes away and the room stops tilting under my feet." She grunted as she let him pull her up from the bed.

"I'll make you some pancakes. Getting some food will probably help. And I have good news. The police called this morning and said they arrested Vick. They'd been looking for him for some other charges, too, so he should be locked up for quite some time."

Aria swayed as relief flooded her, and she felt Luke tighten his grip. "I guess I was more worried about that than I thought."

"You don't have to worry anymore. I'll keep you safe." Luke held fast to her elbow as she shuffled to the bathroom.

Aria felt him hesitate at the door, not letting her go. "I promise I'll be okay. If I need you, I'll whisper-yell for help."

Luke let go with deliberate, slow movements, his hands ready to catch her if she wobbled. "You good?"

Aria tilted her face upward a bit, his attentiveness and concern touching her heart. "I'm great, actually. Lean down here and give me a kiss."

"As you wish." Luke bowed then lightly pressed his lips to hers. "I'll be in the kitchen if you need me."

Aria avoided her reflection at first, not yet ready to see the aftermath of the attack, but after washing her hands, curiosity got the best of her. Her eyes crept from the sink, up the wall, and to the mirror. A gasp escaped her lips, and she recoiled as her right eye took in the swollen mound where her left eye should have been. Stitches held together a jagged cut, sealed together with blackened blood. Mottled black, purple, and red skin replaced her usual pale peach. As she ran her fingers gingerly along the taut skin, her eyes burned hot with tears. She combed her chestnut hair in front of her face, attempting to cover some of the damage. With a sigh of defeat and her shoulders sagging, she turned her back on the stranger in the mirror.

In the living room, Aria's gaze caught on the gun case lying casually on the coffee table. Luke had insisted on sleeping by the door as the first line of defense against any retaliation from Vick or those loyal to him. Thankfully, it hadn't come to that, but if her childhood taught her anything, it was that a person could never be too careful.

As she shuffled into the kitchen, Luke rushed to help her sit at the table.

"I'm fine. I just have a horrendous headache, like a hangover. Well, what I assume a hangover is like. I haven't ever actually had one." She bent toward the table, resting her head on her arms.

"Well, I had my fair share in the past, and they suck. I'm betting yours is way worse, judging by the damage he did." Luke set a glass of orange juice and a cup of coffee on the table.

"Yeah, it's pretty bad." Her voice cracked, betraying the emotions she fought so hard to keep hidden.

Luke slid a second pancake onto a plate and set it in front of her. He sat beside her, draping his arm across her back. "What's wrong? Do you need something?"

Aria gave a tiny shake of her head as she straightened, not trusting her voice to be steady.

"Come on, you can tell me anything. I'll help you with anything I can." His eyes bore into her battered face.

Aria shied away from him, pulling her hair over her face as much as possible. Her voice came out in a faint whisper when she put words to the torment that cut her soul. "I'm ugly."

Luke recoiled. "What? No, no, no. You're not ugly." Luke brushed the hair off her face and tucked it behind her ear. "You're beautiful."

Her face whipped in his direction, immediate regret filling her as pain ricocheted through her head. "I look horrible. The left side of my face doesn't even resemble a human. I don't even see how you can stand to look at me. Let alone kiss me." She loathed the tears that filled her eyes.

Luke pulled her into a hug, caressing her back. "Shh. It's okay. It's temporary. In a week or two, you won't even be able to tell anything happened. It'll be okay. You're still beautiful. I promise. You're always beautiful to me, no matter what."

She pulled back, wishing she could believe his words. "How can you say that? I don't even look like me."

"Because I'm in love with all of you, not just your face." Luke's eyes widened, and his mouth dropped open, the realization of what he'd said written on his face. "I mean, uh, it's not... just... I—"

Butterflies sprang to life in Aria's stomach, lifting her sour mood with their wings. The words she'd held sequestered in her heart for weeks bubbled to the surface. "I love you, too, Luke."

Luke let out a rush of air in a short laugh. "Yeah? Really?"

Aria tried to nod but winced at the movement, so she grabbed his hand instead. "Yes, really. Heck, I've loved you since I was thirteen."

Luke's eyes brightened as a huge, goofy grin took over his face. "Well, that works out perfectly because I've loved you since I was sixteen." He pressed his lips to hers in a tender kiss.

Aria's stomach growled loudly and furiously, making them both giggle. "I guess I better eat."

Luke's eyes danced as they parted. "Yes, you should. I'll go get the syrup." Returning to the table, Luke eyed the clock. "So, what's your schedule today? I can drive you wherever you need to go. I only have one job tonight, but it's at seven for an office party."

"I wish I didn't have to go anywhere." Aria groaned. "Luckily, all I have is to turn in a final paper for one of my classes today, and then I'm done for the semester. Thankfully, I've had it done for a few days already."

"You? Plan ahead? Surely not," Luke teased. "When do you have to be there?"

"I'm supposed to go anytime between ten and noon. I think I'll get there early to avoid bumping into anyone." Her hand self-consciously went to her face. "Think I could borrow your sunglasses? Mine might be too tight."

Luke took her hand from her face and gave it a gentle squeeze. "You can have anything you need. There's absolutely nothing to be ashamed of, though. You know that, right? All this does is prove how much of a badass you are. If anyone says anything, tell them they should see the other guy."

"You always know what to say to make me feel better." Aria giggled.

"Good. That's my goal. Seriously, though, did you see Vick's face? I hope I never make you mad." An adorable half grin graced his face.

Aria laughed, bringing her hand to her cheek. "Ah, don't make me laugh. It squishes my eye."

"Sorry, I'll try to contain my copious amounts of humor. In fact, I'll start the dishes and let you finish eating. Then we can head over to the college."

Aria's heart pounded against her ribcage like a wild animal caught in a trap. She placed a hand on her chest, certain her shirt was fluttering from the movement. The blood rushing through her veins made her head throb. She took several slow, deep breaths, yet the throbbing remained.

"Okay, Aria. You can do this." Her muttered words of encouragement lacked any genuine conviction, but perhaps she could fake it until she felt it. The cold air stung her face, and the sunglasses dug in against her swollen temple, an ever-present reminder of her current predicament. With another deep breath, she stepped onto the sidewalk, forcing step after step toward the literature department offices.

Peeking through the tiny glass rectangle in the door, she saw Professor Lawson sitting at his massive old oak desk, giving the impression of a sophisticated mountain man. The juxtaposition of his gruff beard and weathered face against his posh attire had amused her from day one. She swallowed hard as her knuckles tapped against the door.

"Come in," he called, his attention remaining fixed on his computer screen.

"Hi, Professor Lawson. I'm here to turn in my final. I hope it's okay that I'm early." She lifted her hand to tuck her hair behind her ear but stopped, instead brushing it so it covered more of her face.

He swiveled in his chair. "Ah, yes, of course." He froze as he saw her, his eyes wide. Ever the professional, he regained his composure and motioned to the seat across from him. "Have a seat, Miss Sutton."

Aria chewed her lip as she took a seat. *Please don't ask about my face. Please don't ask about my face,* she chanted to herself.

"So, Miss Sutton, the assignment was to pick a subject that is difficult to discuss. Something that is uncomfortable to read and even more uncomfortable to write about. You were to discuss the topic factually, with sources but also with personal experiences to enhance your points. Do you believe you accomplished this?"

Aria nodded once, grinding her teeth to keep from wincing. "Yes, I think so."

He laced his fingers together on his desk and leaned forward. "And what topic did you pick?"

"How drugs ruin lives."

He studied her for a moment. "And you find this subject uncomfortable? I would think this topic would be common ground, that most people could agree on that sentiment."

Aria's pulse quickened, intensifying the throbbing yet again. "With all due respect, I disagree. I personally know many people who, unfortunately, don't see drugs as bad things, People who don't see how drugs ruin the lives of not only the users but those around them. The level of denial found in drug-filled areas is astronomical. I've also found that those unaffected by drugs are in denial that it could ever happen to them and hold certain prejudices against those who are affected. It's a very personal topic, and I find it extremely uncomfortable to talk about."

The professor sat back in his chair, considering her words. "I'll accept the topic. I look forward to reading it. Thank you."

"Thank you." Aria slid the fifteen-page paper on his desk and stood to leave.

"Oh, Miss Sutton?"

"Yes?"

"If there's ever anything you need to discuss, academically or otherwise, my office door is always open." He slid her paper into a folder and watched her over his gold-rimmed glasses.

Aria's face burned, but she appreciated the sentiment more than he'd ever know. In a perfect world, she imagined her dad to be someone like Professor Lawson, an intelligent and cultured man with a big heart hiding under a stern exterior. "Thanks. I'll keep that in mind."

"Good." He tapped the folder on the desk, and his serious face brightened. "All right, then. Have a good Christmas break."

"You too." She bolted out of the door, unable to contain her excitement to be out of his office and on her way home. He was her favorite professor by far, but she'd rather eat a shoe than talk to anyone with her face looking like a bruised tomato. She darted through the halls like a character in one of Ben's video games, avoiding the people trickling into the building.

Back on the bus, she collapsed on the seat, safe at last. "Whew. I got my paper turned in, and I managed to avoid everyone but Professor Lawson. I call that a success."

Luke gave her a high five. "Let's grab some lunch then some cupcakes from Gilded Lilly to celebrate."

Chapter 28

Aria

At the sound of footsteps on the porch, Aria lifted her head from the book on her lap. She tucked a bookmark in its pages and rose from the couch as the front door swung open. "Hey, Ben. How was school?"

Ben and Luke exchanged silent glances and avoided eye contact with her.

Alarm bells rang loud in Aria's brain. "What? Tell me what happened. Now."

Luke nodded at Ben, who sighed with resignation and stuck his hands out toward Aria.

Aria inspected the scrapes and bruises scattered along his knuckles, her face contorting into a deep frown. "What happened?"

"I got in a fight after school." Ben pulled his hands away and tucked them in his jeans pockets with a shrug.

Aria groaned and sat back down, nausea creeping into her stomach. "Seriously, Ben? Is it going to be one problem after another now?"

Luke held up a finger. "Hold on. I think you should let him explain."

Aria blinked at Luke with her mouth agape. "Oh... okay. Explain, please."

Ben dropped his backpack at the end of the couch and plopped down next to it. He leaned forward, elbows on his knees, and stared at his clasped hands. "Well, obviously everybody heard about last night. It's all over the school. They gave me crap about it all day. Saying we're traitors and crap like that. I tried to ignore everyone and keep my head down, like Luke said. Then, at lunch, some guys started saying stuff about you. Saying you deserved what happened for being a tease and thinking you're better than everyone else. One guy was saying…" He paused as he cut his eyes to Aria. "He said some nasty, vulgar stuff. I tried to let it slide, but it was getting hard to sit there and take it. After school, I was getting my stuff out of my locker, and the same guy pushed me and gave me crap about not dealing anymore, calling me a, uh, let's say he called me a pansy. Then he said he couldn't wait for you to come whoring around for drugs again so they could get in on it. I snapped." His pained eyes met Aria's. "I'm sorry. I tried all day to ignore it, but I couldn't take it anymore. When I yelled at him to shut up, he shoved me into the lockers and told me to make him." The corners of Ben's mouth twitched upward. "So I did."

Aria pursed her lips, pride and frustration battling with each other. Her forehead creased from the stress of Ben getting into trouble yet again, but her mouth ached to celebrate him defending her and himself. "I'm surprised they didn't call me."

Luke stepped forward. "That's because they told me about it all. They were still in the office when I got there. I didn't see Ben waiting, so I went in to look for him. He told them I was his brother, and I guess they were ready to be done with it all because they accepted it and gave him a note to show his mom. I think they assumed he'd called me or something."

"So, what's the damage?" she asked, not even trying to hold in her sigh.

Ben dug in his backpack and pulled out a crumpled paper. "Coach Wilems broke it up and took us to the principal. They tried to blame it all on me, but it turns out the security camera has a crystal-clear view of my locker. They filed a report for my record, but since it's the end of the semester, I didn't get a detention or anything."

Aria put a hand on her chest, her breath rushing out as the tension left her shoulders. "I'm so glad you didn't get in trouble. That's the last thing we need right now." She scanned the paper as she waited for her blood pressure to regulate itself. "Go wash your hands and come to the table. I'll get the antibiotic ointment for those scrapes."

"I'll go start dinner," Luke said.

Aria retrieved the first aid kit and flicked on the light over the table. Judging by Ben's hands, he definitely made the other kid shut up. "You must've really laid into this guy. I'm surprised you didn't get in trouble, even with it being self-defense." She scrutinized Ben's pristine face. "Did he even land a blow on you?"

Ben sat up straighter, squaring his shoulders as she watched him puff with pride. "I have a cut on the back of my head from the locker. He got me in the ribs once or twice, but that's it. I didn't want to fight, but he asked for it, so I went all in."

Aria forced her mouth into a frown, hoping to hide how impressed she was. Fighting wasn't something she wanted to encourage, but she was glad to know Ben could hold his own. "Lift your shirt so I can see your ribs."

No signs of bruising.

"Can you breathe fine with no pain?"

Ben nodded, breathing deep for evidence.

"All right, let me see your head next." She cleaned the small gash and applied some ointment. Stepping back, she gave him another once-over and nodded her approval. "Well, honestly, you came out of it pretty good."

"You should see the other guy." Ben smirked.

Aria cut her eyes sideways to a chuckling Luke. She crossed her arms over her chest, attempting to appear cross, but the curl of her lips betrayed her. "I think I've heard that before."

Luke set down his spatula and held his hands up in mock bewilderment. "I have no idea what you're talking about."

The ensuing chuckles provided a much-needed lift to the mood, but Ben's joy appeared short-lived as his face fell.

"What's wrong, Ben?" Aria asked.

"I don't want to go to school tomorrow. I got so much crap from people today, just wait until tomorrow. Beating up one of the cool kids doesn't exactly make you popular." Ben's face twisted in agony.

"What do you have tomorrow? Do you have any tests?"

"No, and I already turned in all my stuff. I think we are watching a documentary in one class, and then they're having the Christmas party thing where they let us play around in the gym."

She shrugged. "So don't go."

Ben's eyes shot up to her face, his mouth falling open. "What?"

"Nothing important is going to happen tomorrow, so don't go."

Ben's face lit up but fell again just as fast. "Wait. I have to. They say you have to be there on the last day, or your grades don't count. I don't know if it's true, but I don't want to fail a semester."

Aria's mouth twisted in thought. "Hmm, yeah, that won't work."

"Maybe he could go for the first class, and then we pull him out early," Luke said.

Aria considered that then nodded in agreement. "That sounds like a good plan. That way he can avoid the free-for-all, also known as the Christmas party, and after-school crowds."

"I'm pretty sure you have to be there the whole day," Ben said with a pout.

Aria drummed her fingers on the table as she thought. "Think you can survive the Christmas party by hiding out somewhere?"

Ben's upper lip curled. "I guess."

"I'll get there early to pick you up so we can make sure you don't have to wait around," Luke said.

Aria wished she could fix everything for Ben. She gasped as she remembered the news she'd been waiting to share. "Oh my gosh.

With all the ruckus of you getting into a fight, I completely forgot about the news I got earlier."

Luke left the pork chops on the stove and joined them at the table. "What news?"

"We officially have a court date for the guardianship hearing, and it's next week." She reached out and gripped Ben's hands. "That means that if all goes well, you could start your new school next semester."

"I think I can definitely survive tomorrow morning knowing I won't ever have to go back." Ben jumped up and wrapped his arms around Aria's shoulders. "Thank you."

Aria's throat tightened as a storm of emotions churned inside her. "I can't make any promises, but I'm hopeful. The paperwork looks great now, so the odds should be in our favor. Once it's official, I'll send in the paperwork to switch schools for you. This is the start of our new lives. It's going to be better from here on out, Ben."

Luke

"Well, that went better than expected." Luke climbed into bed as he watched Aria gingerly put lotion on her face. He noticed her teeth chomping away at her lip as she slipped into bed. "What's swirling in that wonderful, always-busy brain of yours?"

Aria gave a huff. "Who says there's anything swirling in my head?"

Luke shot her a deadpan look. "I think I know you well enough by now to tell when your wheels are turning at full speed."

She shied away from him. "It's nothing. It's silly."

Luke tugged on her shoulder to get her to face him. "You don't have to hide away from me. You know that. I'm always here to listen, and nothing that bothers you is silly."

She eased around to face him, her fingers trailing along her stitches. "I wonder if I'll have a scar."

Luke took her hand in his, the vulnerability in her voice squeezing his heart. "You might, but so what? You're beautiful and strong. Battle scars tell the story of what you've survived, like a badge of honor. Our scars are our golden glue, like those Japanese bowls you were telling me about. You'll still be stunning. I promise. It would take a lot more than a little scar to ruin your gorgeous face."

Her eyes misted over. "Thanks." A comfortable silence stretched on for a minute before she spoke again. "Can I ask you a personal question?"

"Of course." That seemed rather obvious to Luke given their level of intimacy, so the fact she asked made him uneasy.

"How'd you get that scar on your cheek?" Aria's finger brushed along his skin as she traced the scar.

Luke stiffened. The question was bound to come up at some point. It surprised him she'd taken so long to ask, but that didn't make him any more ready to discuss it.

"If you don't want to answer, that's fine," Aria said, her words rushing out.

"No, it's okay. It's just a tough memory." How he wished he could fast-forward through the story that lay ahead, or better yet, rewind and make it never happen. He took a deep breath and let it out. "I'm sure you remember, but I didn't have this scar that night in the bar. Well, dissing you wasn't the only stupid thing I did that night. After you left, I got mad at myself. Back then, getting mad at myself meant punishing myself with more alcohol. I pounded a handful of beers in no time. Stumbled my stupid, drunk ass home only to bump into my equally drunk dad. Me being mad at the world, I decided for some stupid reason that I should pick a fight with him. I started giving him a piece of my mind, telling him all the crap I'd wanted to say for years. It didn't take long for it to become physical. Never took very long." Luke sighed and shook his head. "I broke a bottle, so Dad broke a bottle too. My mom jumped in and tried to talk sense into us both, but we were way too far gone to listen. Dad took a swing at me and accidentally nicked Mom in the arm. In hindsight, it wasn't bad. Just a minor cut. But to me, that day, it was the last straw. I lunged at him, and he sliced my face. I'm not sure if he meant to or not, but it didn't matter. The way he was, I always assumed the worst. I still do. The pain snapped me out of my rage, though."

He paused for a moment as the memories threatened to overwhelm him. "I'm weirdly thankful for it happening because I don't know what would've happened if I'd kept going in my stupid drunken rage. It could've ruined my life in a matter of seconds, and I could've sent myself to prison with a remorse I'd never shake off. I left that night and didn't go back. Told Mom I was sorry and left." Luke took a deep breath and let it out in a rush, releasing the pain that still stung fresh. "Like I said, I quit drinking after that."

Aria wrapped her soft arms around his shoulders. "Oh, Luke. That had to be such an awful night."

"Yeah, it was. For a lot of reasons. But it led to the best decision I ever made." He held up his arm, staring at his sobriety tattoo. "It led to me breaking the chains holding me back. Now look where I am. Business is going great. I have a clean house in a safe neighborhood." He paused, utter gratitude clouding his vision. "I have a magnificent woman in my life who loves me, and I get to hang out with her cool kid brother."

Aria craned her neck for a quick kiss. "And you have a new knack for focusing on the positives. Something I'm slowly learning from you. Your mom would be proud."

Memories of his mom flooded his mind, the pain of losing her still so raw his heart felt like it had a gaping wound. Her loss weighed heavy, like an anvil on his chest.

Aria's eyes filled with remorse. "I'm sorry. I never should've asked." She lowered her head and moved to roll away.

Luke tightened his grip to hold her in place, needing her reassuring embrace more than ever. "No, it's okay. You don't have to feel guilty. It actually feels kind of good to have that out in the open. I've never talked to anyone about it before. Hell of a thing to keep bottled up inside forever. I wish I could've seen her one last time. If I was more persistent and tracked her down again instead of waiting for her to call me, then I could've told her I know she did her best to protect me from Dad. That I'm sorry for leaving like I did and I don't blame her for anything. That I love her."

Aria cupped his cheek with her hand, her thumb rubbing against his stubble. "She knew you loved her. You showed it when you tracked her down at the hospital."

Luke sighed, his heart heavy as if made from lead. "I guess." Maybe one day he would believe that. Maybe one day he could forgive himself.

Chapter 29

Luke

The party bus rolled to a stop, and Luke gaped at the run-down house beyond his windshield. As much as he hoped he had the wrong address, deep down he knew he was in the right place. Picturing his mom battling her disease in such a heap of junk set his blood ablaze. If only she'd told him. He could've helped her. If only he'd come back sooner. Tears burned his eyes as his mind painted a grim picture, and his resolve fizzled. As his hand gripped the shifter, ready to back out, the front door of the house swung open, and his dad filled the doorway.

I guess it's now or never. Luke took a moment to steady his breathing then hopped out of the bus and made his way to the rotting porch. The cool air soothed his nerves as he closed the distance.

Tom's arms crossed firmly over his chest. "I never expected to see you back here in these parts."

"That makes two of us." Luke inhaled, the familiar sting of alcohol greeting him as usual. The clarity in Tom's speech was a good sign, though. Luke must've caught him while he was baseline drunk rather than blackout drunk. Baseline drunk was as sober as Tom got. Encouraged, Luke pressed on. "Can I come in?"

Without a word, Tom moved aside and jerked his head toward the door.

Luke stepped inside, his heart sinking further than he knew possible. Dust and mildew tickled his nose while his eyes took in a year's worth of filth piled around. Luke's hands balled into fists. *No one fighting for their life should be in such unsanitary conditions.* The door shutting behind him made him flinch.

"So, how'd you find me?" Tom asked as he strolled to the refrigerator and pulled out a beer.

"I figured the folks at Tooley's Bar would know where you were. I was right." Bitterness oozed from Luke's voice, but he couldn't stop it even if he tried.

A grunt was Tom's only response.

Luke averted his eyes, his vision catching on a silver urn sitting on the kitchen counter.

Tom followed his line of sight and shook his head. "Too bad you didn't come while she was alive. You're too late. This might as well be in the trash for how you treated her." He picked up the urn and dropped it into the trash can by the door.

Luke's stomach twisted at the sickening thud of the metal hitting the bottom. He pressed his lips together to hold in his rage. "You know why I couldn't come back. And Mom deserves better than being thrown in the trash."

Tom's eyes shot back to Luke. "Yeah, you're right. She deserves a son who's not a coward."

"You'd know all about that, wouldn't you?" Luke's tone became icy. "You're the ultimate coward. A man so afraid of life he hides behind a bottle."

"If I'm such a coward, why'd you run and hide from me for all these years? Huh?" Tom grabbed another bottle of beer and put it to his lips, guzzling the contents in seconds.

"I left because I didn't want to be anything like you, not because I was scared of you. I didn't want to drink my life away, never amounting to anything more than a coward with anger problems. Hurting everyone around me wasn't how I wanted to live."

Tom took a menacing step forward. "Then why'd you even come back here?"

Luke ran a hand through his hair with a growl. "Because I thought maybe we could talk like civilized people. Hell, maybe even like father and son. I should've known better than to try to get some closure. I'd hoped we could bury the hatchet, but I can see now the only way it'll get buried is if it's in one of our backs."

"Well, here you go." Tom turned his back toward Luke. "Go ahead and sink it on in."

With Tom facing away, Luke's eyes darted to the trash can. Before he could think it through, he scooped up the urn and stuffed it in his puffy coat. Glancing down at himself, Luke hoped his dad was drunk enough to not notice the bulge of the urn. With reconciliation out of the picture, he cut his losses and headed for the door. Balancing the urn in one hand, he gripped the doorknob with the other and threw his words over his shoulder. "I think it's safe to say we'll never see eye to eye. But I should thank you for making me the man I am today. Because with every single thing you did, you taught me exactly what I didn't want to become."

Luke stepped out, and a bottle crashed against the door as he slammed it shut behind him. His pulse thundered in his ears, and he sprinted away before his dad could notice the urn was missing.

In the safety of the bus, he slipped the urn out of his coat and tucked it safely beside the driver's seat. As he held the shifter, a twinge of guilt plagued him. He'd stolen his mom's ashes. *Did I just stoop to his level*? With a heavy sigh, he closed his eyes and leaned his head back against the seat. Memories of his mom played through his mind along with images of what her final years must've been like, alone with that hateful man. The woman who shielded him from his dad's drunken rage all those years deserved so much more than to be thrown in the trash. Luke couldn't rescue her from Tom while she was alive, but at least maybe he could ensure her ashes could rest in peace.

Luke opened his eyes at sound coming from Tom's porch, and he watched as his dad stepped out with the trash can the ashes had been in. He's coming for the urn, Luke thought, his hand resting on the cool metal.

But instead of walking toward the party bus, Tom went to a dumpster and tossed the trash can inside. He brushed his hands together then locked eyes with Luke through the windshield and flipped him off. "Now your mom is a piece of trash, just like you treated her."

Luke's hand tightened on the urn while his eyes shot daggers at Tom's back as his father disappeared back into the house. Any ounce of guilt he might've felt vanished without a trace.

Chapter 30

Aria

Aria rubbed her right eye as she padded down the hall to the bathroom. She winced as she flicked on the bright light. *Wait.* The light was hurting her left eye. She rushed to the mirror, letting out a yelp when a sliver of her left eye stared back at her.

"Aria? Is everything okay?" Luke's voice boomed, rife with concern, through the bathroom door.

Aria flung the door open, bubbling with joy. "I can open my eye."

The tension visibly melted from Luke's shoulders. "That's awesome." He leaned close and studied her eye. "The swelling went down a lot since yesterday. Let's get the eye drops they gave you. Your eye is red and irritated."

"Okay." Aria stared at her reflection again, unable to wipe the joy from her face. Maybe she would look almost normal by Christmas.

Luke fished around in the cabinet and grabbed the eye drops. "Do you need help, or can you get it?"

"I'll try doing it myself first." Aria pouted as she took the bottle from him. Eye drops were not her friend.

"Okay, I have breakfast waiting when you're ready. Yell if you need help."

A few minutes and a lot of tears later, Aria made her way to the kitchen, dabbing her face with a washcloth.

Ben raised his eyes from his plate, his back stiffening upon seeing Aria. "You okay?"

Aria waved the rag in dismissal as she sat. "Oh, you know how I am about my eyes. I don't see how eye drops ever work since my eyes water so much afterward. You'd think the medicine would wash right back out."

"Whoever makes the eye drops probably takes that into consideration." Luke placed her plate on the table and bent to inspect her eye again. "It's already looking a lot less red, so the medicine must be working fine."

"Good. I'm glad I look a little more normal today for the hearing." Aria dabbed her eye again then focused her attention on Ben. "How are you feeling about everything? Today is the big day."

Ben stared down at his plate and picked at his scrambled eggs with his fork. "As ready as I'll ever be, I guess."

Aria nodded and patted his arm. "I'm nervous too."

Facing the courthouse steps for the second time, Aria gulped. She couldn't help noticing the difference in their moods this time. She tightened her grip on Luke's hand. Anxiety had her close to chewing her bottom lip off, and beside her, Ben was pale and seemed ready to faint. She patted his back, attempting to comfort him even though she needed comforting herself. "It's going to be okay. Deep breaths."

Ben gave a nervous chuckle, but his worried eyes stared ahead as they entered the courthouse. Following the signs, they entered the courtroom teeming with people. She snuck a sideways glance at Ben, who swallowed hard as he surveyed the room.

"Aria and Ben Sutton." The judge's voice boomed, calling them to the front.

Luke took a seat in the crowd as Aria and Ben took their places in front of the judge.

Ben's eyes locked on the floor as the judge spoke, leaving Aria wondering if he heard a single word.

The room tilted, and she reminded herself to not hold her breath through all the formalities and legal jargon.

"And what of your mother? Why should she not be the legal guardian?" the judge questioned.

Aria straightened her spine. "Your Honor, if you read through the case files, I included a list of our mother's arrests. I also included some non-documented incidents that have happened throughout the years related to violence and drug use. Currently, Tasha Sutton does not have a residence or any income, with no attempts to get either. I am seeking guardianship so I can switch Ben to a better school in the school district in which he currently lives. Also, for the future, so I can make sure he is taken care of until he is eighteen and can legally care for himself. In the time that we have been living at our current residence, our mother has made zero attempts to contact us. I invited her here today, but she is not present. I also included a signed statement from her in support of terminating her rights."

Aria tried to gauge Ben's reaction, but his eyes remained glued to the floor. If hearing about his mom giving up her rights bothered him, he had one hell of a poker face. Aria hadn't told anyone about her one last visit to the old bridge, not even Luke. She watched the judge read over the statement she'd convinced their stoned mother to sign. Sure, Tasha probably hadn't realized what she was signing, but that was exactly why Aria was filing for guardianship in the first place.

"Thank you." The judge gave a curt nod and zeroed in on Ben. "And what are your thoughts, young man?"

Ben raised his eyes to the judge, his face paling more than Aria thought possible. He swallowed as his eyes filled. Aria slipped her hand in his and gave it a reassuring squeeze. More than anything in the world, she wanted her brother to be happy.

He stared down at their linked hands and inhaled. Squaring his shoulders, he lifted his chin and spoke, his voice even. "My entire life, my sister has been the one taking care of me. She paid the bills and bought me clothes and fed me. She kept me safe. All my mom has ever done is scare me and hurt me."

The judge studied Ben for a minute and nodded. "Thank you. Very well. The court hereby grants guardianship of Ben Sutton to his sister, Aria Sutton. Good luck to you both."

As he banged the gavel, Aria threw her arms around Ben, squeezing him tight as laughter bubbled out and tears of joy streamed like a waterfall. Ben relaxed into her arms, his relieved laughter filling her ears. After a moment, Aria let go of Ben and scanned the room, self-conscious because of all the eyes meeting hers, some of them misty.

When they reached the back of the courtroom, Luke greeted them each with a giant hug. "I'm so happy for you both."

"Thanks. I'm so relieved." Aria swiped her sleeve over her face then took both Ben and Luke's hands as they walked out and into a new future.

Once outside, Aria took Ben by the shoulders. "I promise to take care of you until you can take care of yourself. Well, actually forever, if I'm being honest, but you know what I mean."

Ben beamed at her, his face bright for the first time that day. "I know you will. You're the best." He wrapped her in a robust hug.

Aria squeezed him and patted his back. "How about we go celebrate?"

Luke chimed in. "I bought a cake. It's from the Gilded Lilly."

Ben rubbed his palms together. "Oh, their cake is the best. Let's go."

Aria's fingers gently smoothed lotion over her bruised skin, but her eyes drifted toward Luke's reflection in the mirror. Behind her, he lounged in bed, staring at his wedding ring as he twirled it on his finger. Try as she might, she couldn't shake a sinking feeling that he was unhappy. And she wasn't sure she wanted to know why.

Climbing into bed, Aria curled against Luke's side and tried her best to appear casual. "What are you thinking about?"

"Huh? Oh, it's nothing."

It sure didn't sound like nothing. She decided to try a different approach and ran her finger across his wedding band. "It's still so weird to see a ring on your finger. And my finger." She held up her hand for inspection.

"Yeah, it is a little weird," he said. "But a good weird."

His last words came out fast, like he'd been caught revealing too much and needed to backtrack. She shied away from him, bracing herself for what she was about to ask and not wanting to see his face when he answered. "Hey, I was wondering... Do you regret any of this?"

Luke's muscles moved under her hand as he shifted toward her. "No, why? Do you?"

"No, it's just that you've seemed a little... I don't know... off a couple times today since the hearing. You didn't even seem too crazy about the cake, and I know how excited you get about anything from the Gilded Lilly." She tried to hide the hurt in her voice but failed miserably. "If... if you're having second thoughts, we can always take the rings off and pretend it never happened and like we're just dating. We don't have to try to convince anyone anymore now that I have guardianship. Once I get a good job, I won't need your income, and we can get a quickie divorce. It won't hurt my feelings." She closed her eyes against her heartache, the massive lie burning her tongue as the words rolled out.

"What? No, that's not what I want." Luke's hand nudged her chin. "Please look at me. I need you to know that's not what's going on. Please."

She faced him at last, her eyes brimming with tears.

Luke caressed her cheek with his thumb, leaning down to kiss her forehead. "No, no, no, don't be sad. Don't cry. Shit. Sorry. I promise I don't regret anything. I don't regret marrying you. Or helping you and Ben. Or any of it. The whole guardianship thing just got me thinking about everything."

"And?" she asked, needing to know his thoughts for better or worse.

His eyes fell away from hers. "I know the whole marriage thing started out as a fake, but I was thinking that maybe someday it could be real. And maybe we could have a real wedding."

"But we did have a real wedding. That's how we got these rings, remember?" Aria wiggled her ring finger, trying to lighten the mood.

Luke sighed, throwing his head back on the pillow with his hand on his forehead. "But your wedding day is supposed to be this perfect, magical day filled with flowers and glitter and champagne. Not some quickie ceremony at a courthouse followed by a steak dinner and last-minute cake. You're supposed to have your dream dress and dream ring and take a dream vacation honeymoon. Not a bought-the-morning-of department store dress, plain band, and a trip to the couch. You deserve all the good stuff, the best, but instead you got whatever we could scrounge up."

She rose on her elbow and caressed his face as he'd done hers. "I think the ceremony we had was nice. And I believe you've been watching too many romance movies." She laughed, hoping he would join her, but he didn't. "Would it be nice to have all that stuff you mentioned? Sure. It sounds fun. Is it a requirement? Not at all. I don't need all that stuff because in the end what matters is the people involved. The fanciest wedding in the world means nothing if there's no love. Every day you see all these celebrities having lavish weddings and divorcing a year later. Besides, I loved my dress. I felt like a goddess in it. And I love our matching silver bands. You know I'm not a frilly kind of girl. Never have been and probably never will be. I'm practical. My wedding dress is the only dress I own, and my wedding jewelry is my only jewelry. Anything fancier and it wouldn't have been me. I go for simple and understated, and that's exactly what I got."

She could tell he didn't quite believe her, so she continued. "Plus, who would we even invite if we had a big ceremony? My drug addict mother and your alcoholic father and drug addict sister? Imagine all the drama that would bring. No thanks. We don't have any real friends worth celebrating with either. Ben was there with us. That's all that matters. I'll take my small civic ceremony with a great guy over all that mess any day, thank you very much."

Luke tucked her hair behind her ear. "You're an amazing woman. You know that, right?"

Aria cocked an eyebrow and gave him a sly grin. "Then I guess you were pretty smart for marrying me."

"Best decision I ever made." He pulled her to him, bringing his lips up to meet hers. After a moment, he pulled away. "I still think you deserve better. I don't want you to regret having such a lackluster day. Especially since it wasn't real."

"I won't regret it. This is real now, and now is all that matters. There's no reason to go through all the grand gestures when we can just move forward."

"Yeah, I guess you're right." Though Luke nodded in agreement, his expression suggested he wasn't totally convinced.

Aria kissed his cheek, his stubble pricking her lips, and then trailed kisses along his jaw. She paused, letting herself get lost in his dark chocolate eyes. "What we have right now is magical. Let's focus on that."

"I think I can do that." His mouth curled into his sexy half grin.

Aria brought her lips to his with an intensity she hoped would convince him where her words couldn't. He buried one hand in her hair and pulled her close with the other, his mouth seeking hers with an urgency that set her heart on fire.

As much as she'd resisted, she'd fallen hard for Luke, and the last thing she wanted was for him to feel less than. The pieces of her broken life were finally falling into place, and with him by her side, she knew she could face anything the world threw at her.

Chapter 31

Aria

Aria pulled her legs to her chest as she stifled a yawn. Sleep had escaped her most of the night as her imagination ran wild with visions of a picturesque Christmas morning. She clutched her coffee mug, taking absent-minded sips as she watched Ben's bedroom door with the patience of a toddler. The sounds of Luke putting the finishing touches on breakfast came from the kitchen behind her. The warm glow of the Christmas tree illuminated the presents below. For the first time, she understood the magic of Christmas.

Knowing she was about to witness Ben's first real Christmas was enough to make her heart swell to bursting. She had worked hard all these years making sure he got a gift from Santa each Christmas, but that was all she could ever manage. No tree or additional gifts. No stockings or lights. Devoid of all magic. *Not this year.* They were doing Christmas the right way, like a normal family. She would do everything in her power to never have another depressing Christmas ever again.

Her ears perked at the sound of movement in Ben's room. "Luke, he's awake," she whispered. A small gasp escaped her as she watched his doorknob move.

Ben meandered into the living room, rubbing his face and yawning. As he took in the sight of the presents under the tree, his face lit up. "What's all that?"

Aria sprang to her feet, too excited to sit still. "It's our presents. And we have stockings too." She waved her finger toward the three red stockings hanging on the television stand.

Ben scanned the stockings and the tree, his face the brightest Aria had ever seen it. "Wow, it's like a movie Christmas."

Aria nodded, too overcome with emotion to speak.

Luke wrapped an arm around her shoulders and motioned to the stockings. "Go see what you got, bud."

Ben lunged at the stockings and grabbed the one with his name written in black marker. His eyes grew as wide as saucers as he pulled out a little box. "A cell phone? Wow, I can't believe it." He hopped to his feet and ran to Aria and Luke, slinging an arm around each of them.

Aria hugged him back, her eyes swimming. "I got one too. This way, we can always call each other if we need help."

Ben let go, his eyes darting to the tree as he shifted his weight from foot to foot. "Can I open my other presents?"

Luke laughed. "You bet. Dig in there."

Without a second of hesitation, Ben hurried toward the tree and tore the paper off the first present. He flipped open the box lid, and his eyes lit up as he pulled out black boots. "Hey, these are like Luke's."

"I know how much you liked mine, so I figured you needed a pair of your own," Luke said.

Aria blinked back tears and moved closer to the tree, picking up another present with Ben's name on it. "Here, open this one next."

"Okay." Ben grabbed the present and ripped the paper off, letting out a gasp. "You got me a camera?"

"You seemed to have a lot of fun with Luke's old one. Do you like it?" Aria asked.

He gently opened the box and ran his fingers over the camera. "I love it."

"The guy at the store helped me pick it out." Aria leaned over to inspect it with Ben.

"It's perfect." Ben picked it up and turned it over in his hands. "This is the best Christmas ever."

"And you're not even done yet," Luke said, gesturing to the rest of the presents.

Listening to the joyful laughter mixing with paper ripping warmed Aria from the inside. This is what family should feel like, she thought. Seeing the joy on Luke and Ben's faces washed away the years of painful longing for that perfect family Christmas. It was finally her reality. Relaxing against the couch and taking in the scene before her, she couldn't quite pinpoint the feeling that encompassed her soul. Watching Ben be carefree and cheerful for the first time in his life, the indescribable feeling shone stronger. Peace. In that moment, the crippling anxiety and depression she had battled for as long as she could remember lifted like fog in the sun's comforting rays. The weight of a thousand stresses fell from her shoulders. Her soul soared, unencumbered by years of trauma at last.

"Hang on. I forgot something in my room." Ben pushed aside his pile of new clothes, jumped up, and bolted for his bedroom.

Aria shot Luke a quizzical look, to which he replied with a shrug.

Ben returned, holding something behind his back. "I got you guys something."

Aria raised her brows, rejoicing internally that she could move her left one again. "What? How?"

Ben chuckled. "Don't worry. I didn't do anything illegal. Not again, at least. I actually had a little money hidden in my closet from back when I was, well, you know. I figured it was a good idea to get you something with it to say sorry."

"Ben, you don't have to apologize anymore. It's okay. It's in the past. My face is basically back to normal now. See?" She wiggled her eyebrows for emphasis.

"But I wanted to get this anyway." Ben turned to Luke. "You sit on the couch too. It's for both of you."

Luke joined Aria, and Ben set a thin package on each of their laps.

"Open them." Ben rocked on his heels and clasped his hands, his eyes dancing.

Aria gasped as she tore the paper away, and a picture of her and Luke kissing at their wedding met her eyes. "It's beautiful." She traced the image with her finger.

Ben beamed with pride.

Luke tore open his package, revealing a selfie the three of them had taken on their wedding day. Their smiling faces radiated love and joy. "Wow, man. These are amazing."

"Thanks. I hope it's okay, but I downloaded some free editing software on the computer. I used it to soften the background and add a warm tone to the pictures. That way, you can't tell it's a courthouse with fluorescent lighting. And I edited a person out of the background in the one with all of us." Ben stood tall, apparently quite pleased with himself.

"Thank you so much. They're perfect." Aria stood and pulled him in for a hug, the picture still in her hand. She drew away and admired the picture again. "And you're talented. I think you may have a career in photography. I'm glad I got you that camera."

Luke stood and clapped him on the back. "Thanks, man. These are amazing. And hey, maybe you can be the photographer for Aria's articles when she's a famous writer."

Aria's cheeks burned at the compliment. "I just want to write something. Anything. I'm not planning on becoming famous."

Luke kissed her head. "You're being modest. I've read your stuff for school. It's good. I know you'll make it big."

"We'll see. How about we hang these pictures up? Where do you think they should go?" Aria changed the subject, still unaccustomed to such praise.

Ben's stomach growled in angry protest.

Luke took the picture from Aria and headed for the kitchen. "How about we eat breakfast first then hang the pictures?"

Luke

"I'm gonna beat you this time," Ben said, scrunching his face as he maneuvered the joystick on his controller.

Luke leaned to the side like it would help him navigate his car better. "You're gonna have to catch me first."

Aria joined them on the couch in time to see Ben's flashy green race car ram into the side of Luke's sleek black car. Luke groaned as his car went careening off a cliff.

Ben sprang to his feet as he crossed the finish line and pumped his fist in the air. "Yes!"

"Such a gracious winner," Aria teased as she opened her book.

Knock, knock, knock.

Aria's eyes fixed on the door. "Are you expecting anyone?"

Luke shook his head with a frown. "No, it's the day after Christmas. Everyone is either home or shopping."

Aria went to the door, and a gasp escaped her when she checked the peephole.

"Who is it?" Luke asked.

Aria bit her lip as she pulled the door open. "Chrissy, what a surprise. Come in out of the cold." Aria stepped back to let Chrissy inside.

Luke rose to his feet and noted the change in Chrissy's appearance. Snow boots and a puffer coat replaced her thigh-high stilettos and thin leather jacket. Her jagged bleach-blond hair boasted a softer hue and cut. But her face showcased the biggest difference. Gone were the dark circles and gaunt features, a healthy glow in their place.

"Sorry to drop by unannounced." Chrissy's cheeks flushed bright pink.

"Here, let me take your coat," Aria said.

"What are you doing here?" The roughness in Luke's voice surprised even him.

"Oh, I, uh, it's Christmas, so..." Chrissy fumbled with her purse, pulling out three large envelopes. "I know it's technically the day after Christmas, but I didn't want to barge in on your holiday yesterday. I was hoping today would be okay." She held the envelopes out to Luke and took a step toward him, her eyes filled with trepidation.

Luke stared at the envelopes, unsure of whether he wanted Chrissy in his life. Just when things were pretty much perfect, he didn't want to risk rocking the boat. If he took whatever she was handing him, she might take it to mean he accepted her.

"Hey, that one has my name," Ben said, peeking around Luke's shoulder. He looked at Chrissy. "Can I have it?"

Chrissy's face filled with warmth. "Yes, of course."

Ben grabbed it, ripping it open without hesitation. "Wow, did you draw this?"

Chrissy's eyes shone bright and hopeful. "I sure did. Do you like it?"

Ben ran to Aria, holding it so she could see. "She drew a picture of me. Isn't it so cool?"

Aria scanned the picture and looked at Chrissy with slight alarm. "How did you do this? Did you get a picture of him somewhere?"

Chrissy held her hands up. "No, don't worry. I'm not stalking you guys or anything. I'm supergood with faces, so I drew them from memory."

"Them?"

Chrissy nodded and held out an envelope with Aria's name. "I drew one of each of you." She glanced at the remaining envelope and back at Luke then placed his envelope on the kitchen counter. "I noticed you guys didn't have any pictures hanging up, so I figured I would draw some." She scanned the walls, her gaze landing on the newly hung wedding pictures. "I see you have some now, though."

"Yeah, but we definitely could use a few more." Aria slid her picture from the envelope, her mouth agape. "Wow, this is so good. And you did all this from memory?"

Chrissy beamed. "Yep, I had a lot of time to perfect them. It was part of my therapy."

Luke's ears perked at that. "Therapy?"

Chrissy hugged herself. "Yeah, therapy. After I... After what happened here, I was devastated. I kind of, well, I went on a bender of sorts. I got in pretty rough shape that night and landed myself in the hospital. Of course, I went to jail afterward. When they went through my pockets, I saw them pull out the paper Aria gave me. I told myself when I got out of jail, I'd call that hotline for help. And I did. Ever since then, I've been in rehab. I actually get treatment for free. It's amazing. I've been clean for three weeks. I know that's not very long, but it's the longest stretch for me."

Aria appeared beside Chrissy with tears brimming. "Oh, Chrissy, I'm so proud of you."

"Thank you. For saying that and for giving me the number that made it possible." Chrissy's eyes shimmered as well.

Aria grabbed Chrissy in a hug as a tear rolled down her cheek. "You're welcome."

Luke cleared his throat as they let go of each other, and Chrissy's eyes filled with fear. Luke sighed, rubbing a hand over his face. He didn't want to be the type of guy Chrissy looked at with fear. As hard as he tried to protect his new little family and his heart, he refused to let himself become hardened.

Luke forced his mouth into a smile, even if he knew it didn't quite reach his eyes yet. "Good job, Chrissy. I'm so glad to hear you're sober. I hope you can stick with it."

Visible relief washed over Chrissy. "Thanks, Luke. I'm trying my best. I even quit... uh, my previous line of work. The rehab place helped me see I wasn't doing myself any favors with that either. They did free testing, and thankfully, I didn't catch anything."

Luke could tell by Aria's face that she also read between the lines. "It sounds like you're doing great."

Chrissy nodded and held out her arms to display herself. "This is the healthiest I've ever been. It feels good."

Aria moved to Luke's side and took his hand as she spoke to Chrissy. "Where are you living?"

Chrissy gave a wry, knowing chuckle. "Don't worry, I'm not looking to bunk here. That rehab place is great. They hooked me up with a halfway house while I get back on my feet. Legally, this time. I work at a gas station right now, but I'm trying to think more long-term than that. Like I said before, I'm not great at school, so it's a little tricky."

"I'm sure you'll figure something out." Luke's eyes wandered to the envelope with his name scribbled across the front. He walked over and pulled out his portrait, taking in the exquisite detail. "You drew this from memory?"

Chrissy joined him at the counter, peeking around his shoulder. "Yeah, I'm crap with words and numbers, but I've got a good photographic memory."

Luke scanned the pictures of Ben and Aria next. "Seriously, these are great. You have a real artistic talent."

Chrissy stood straighter, and her face lit up. "I've always liked art because there are no rules. I can't spell a painting wrong or add up two sketches wrong. If you mess up a picture, you can figure out a way to make it work."

Luke studied the portraits again, a light bulb going off in his head. "I think you should get a portfolio together and work as a freelance artist. There're lots of businesses that hire artists to help them rebrand or design their logos and stuff."

Chrissy's face filled with excitement and hope. "Really? You think anyone would hire me?"

That was how Luke wanted her to look at him, not with fear. Luke snapped his fingers, pointing at her. "You know what? I'll be the first. I've been wanting to give my business card some... pizzazz, I guess is the word I'm searching for. It's not a thorough use of your talent, but at least it's something for your resume."

Luke grabbed a notebook and pen and took a seat at the table, waving for Chrissy to follow. He took out his wallet, pulling out a business card and laying it on the table. "See? They're just black with white lettering. They need something else."

Chrissy took the pen, tapping it on her chin a couple times, then began scribbling.

Aria caught his eye as she brought glasses of water to the table and gave him a thumbs-up.

Ben plopped beside Chrissy to watch her sketch.

A warm, peaceful sensation came over Luke. Aria was right. Chrissy did have good in her. He just had to open his eyes and heart wider to see it. He was thankful for the opportunity to give her the second chance she deserved. She rolled up her sleeves and continued sketching, but something on her wrist caught Luke's attention. He reached over, stopping her hand to see it better.

Chrissy shied away. "I hope you're not mad, but I loved the idea of a tattoo reminder. I got one like yours so I could remember my inspiration. So I could remember that when I grow up, I want to be like my little brother."

Chapter 32

Luke

A couple weeks later, Luke watched Chrissy step out of the gas station's sliding doors and stuff her hands into her coat pockets as she scanned the lot. When she spotted the bus, Luke waved, and she headed his way. He straightened his spine and inhaled, second-guessing himself and what he was about to do. It was too late to back out, though. He opened the bus door, and Chrissy stepped on.

"Hey, is everything okay?" Chrissy asked.

"Yeah, everything's okay."

Chrissy let out a breath. "Whew. Good. When I got your text that you wanted to meet, I was afraid something was wrong."

"Sorry. I didn't mean to make you worry. I needed to talk to you about something. Please have a seat." Luke gestured toward one of the benches in the back.

"Okay, thanks." Chrissy slipped off her coat and sat down. "Man, this thing has a good heater."

Luke sat across from her. "I make sure the heater stays in tip-top shape so all the women in dresses don't freeze."

"That's really thoughtful," Chrissy said as she studied the interior of the bus. "You did a really good job with this thing, Luke. It's amazing."

"Thanks."

Silence stretched between them as Luke scrambled for a way to start the difficult conversation. *Might as well dive right in.* "Look, Chrissy, I'm not really good at this kind of thing, and I'm not really sure where to start, so I'm going to be honest with you. You didn't know our dad, but I've spent my whole life doing everything I can to not be like him. Then when I first met you, I found myself kind of acting like him. Closing myself off and being hardened and bitter. I'm truly sorry for the way I acted."

"You don't have to apologize. I barged into your life out of nowhere, and it was a shock. I get it. And after what happened..." She tucked her face down.

"Well, something I've learned lately is that in order to move forward, you have to let go of the past." He got up and pulled a box from behind the driver's seat, then sat back down across from Chrissy, resting the box in his lap. "With that in mind, I went to see Dad back before Christmas. I guess I was hoping for a miracle or something, but all I got was the usual angry drunk. Sidenote, if you ever go see him, please don't go alone. It's not safe. Let me know, and I'll go with you."

Chrissy's mouth ticked up in the corners, but her eyes were melancholy. "Thanks. I'm not sure if I'm ready to meet him or if I'll ever be ready. But if I do, I'll let you know."

"Good." His grip tightened on the box as his pulse sped up. "Anyway, while I was there, I ended up rescuing what's in this box from the trash. At the time, I didn't know what I was going to do with it. But I knew I had to take it. It's been sitting in my bedroom, waiting for me to sort through my thoughts. Then you came the day after Christmas, and now I finally figured out what I want to do with it." He inhaled and held the box out toward Chrissy. "I want to give this to you."

Chrissy stared at the box as she took it. "Me?"

Luke nodded and held his breath as she opened the lid.

A hand flew to her mouth as she gasped. "Is this...?"

"Yes." Luke blinked back tears and cleared his throat. "I know how upset you were that she died before you could reconnect with her. You never got any time with her, so I thought maybe having her ashes could help you grieve and maybe get some closure. I've realized how important closure can be for letting go of the past, especially the stuff that hurts."

Chrissy's eyes shimmered as she gently lifted the urn from the box and cradled it in her hands. "I don't know what to say. All these years, I've wondered if she ever thought about me. Why couldn't she sober up for me? Did we have anything in common? So many questions, but I was too afraid of the answers to ever really reach out and ask her. I never got to work through the anger and pain with her or find out why she didn't try to find me. Or if she even cared where I was or what my life was like. And now it's too late."

Luke put his hand on her shoulder. "You get to decide what we do with the ashes. You can keep them, or we can spread them somewhere, or have them buried. It's your choice. I get to have memories of her from when she was alive, so I think you should get to decide her final resting place. That way, you get to have something special with her too."

Chrissy's face crumpled as she let out a sob.

Luke grabbed a box of tissues from the front of the bus and sat down beside her.

She took a tissue and dabbed at her tears. "Thank you. I don't know what else to say, but thank you."

"You don't have to thank me."

She lowered her eyes to the urn, rubbing her thumb over the shiny metal, then dabbed at her tears again. "Can I hug you?"

"Of course you can. You're family."

Holding the urn in one arm, she hugged him with the other.

As Luke hugged her back, the hardness in his heart softened as another piece of him let go of past traumas and healed.

"See? I told you this place has the best pizza." Luke wiped sauce from his mouth and took a drink of his lemonade.

Chrissy held up a finger as she finished chewing. "I have to hand it to you. This is the best pizza I've ever tasted. I'm glad you brought me here."

"Me too. I've had fun. Plus, good food is a necessity after dealing with all that emotional stuff." He could get used to having lunch with his sister.

"Definitely."

"Driving a party bus, I have to stop at all kinds of places to pick up food, so I've learned about some hidden gems. That's how I discovered the Gilded Lilly bakery. Best cakes in all of Chicago."

"It sounds like such a fun job." She rested her chin on her hand and stared into the distance, a wistful longing on her face. "I hope one day I can enjoy a job as much as you do."

That was the segue he was waiting for. "Speaking of that, how is the art going?"

Chrissy picked at her nails, long and bedazzled as always. "I've been doing little things here and there. If I get a weekend off from the station, I go to the park and do sketch portraits next to the hot dog cart. The cold weather keeps the crowd down right now, but it's nice for a little extra cash."

"That sounds fun."

Chrissy leaned back in her chair. "Yeah, it is."

"Have you done any bigger jobs? Any commissions? Other than my business cards, of course, which look great, by the way. Customers love them."

Her face brightened. "Really? That's awesome. I've done a couple of little things here and there. A portrait of a tiny dog for this old lady who saw me sketching in the park. A menu logo for an Italian restaurant downtown. Not much else. It's hard to get your name out there so people will trust you with money."

"They will soon. Trust me." Try as he might, Luke couldn't contain his excitement as he fished his phone from his pocket. He pulled up a picture on his screen and laid it on the table in front of Chrissy. "You see that building?"

"It looks like a huge old warehouse."

Luke laughed. "That's exactly what it is. How would you like to paint it?"

Chrissy choked on the water she'd been sipping. "Excuse me?"

"It's the big warehouse down by the farmers market. That neighborhood has been deemed 'up and coming' by the city, so they're doing this whole beautification campaign. Making it more upscale-looking and whatnot. Part of that plan involves painting that warehouse so it's not quite so ugly."

"And they want me to paint it?"

"Well, not the whole thing. A mural on the side facing the farmers market. One that 'showcases the beauty of the city.'" He made quotation marks in the air for emphasis.

Chrissy held up her hand, and her words tumbled out. "Wait a minute. I'm confused. Who is 'they'? How did they hear about me? Did they actually say they want to hire me? Without seeing my work?"

"Well, have you heard of Liam Worthington?"

"*The* Liam Worthington?" Chrissy gaped. "Of course I've heard of him. Who hasn't? He's one of the richest guys in Chicago and is gorgeous, to top it off. He's been Chicago's most eligible bachelor for as long as I can remember." Her eyes opened even wider. "Is he the one hiring me? Will I get to meet him?"

Luke rolled his eyes in mock irritation. "What is it with women swooning over this guy all the time? Anyway, I was at City Hall for a meeting, and I may or may not have shown them the portraits you drew of us. The city is commissioning the project, and the job came up in conversation. Liam had the meeting after mine to discuss the development of that neighborhood. His company is the one controlling the warehouse, so he gets the final say in who they hire for the mural. I told them about you and a little of your story. Don't worry, I left out the nitty-gritty details. I know that was overstepping on my part, but I only told them because the city loves hiring underdogs to help them out. It's great publicity. Then I showed them the pictures of your work that I had on my phone. Liam loved the idea, so of course, the city went along with him. Nobody says no to the man with all the money. All you have to do is go to their office on Monday and sign some papers."

Chrissy shot toward him, hugging his neck as tight as a boa constrictor.

"Oh, and I'll see what I can do about meeting Liam. I'll warn you, though, there's a rumor he's dating someone."

With a laugh, Chrissy let go of him and sat down. "You've done more than enough. Thank you so much. I can't believe you did that for me."

"Why not? You're the most talented artist I know."

She waved off his compliment. "You must not know any other artists, then."

"Hey, now, don't sell yourself short. You're extremely talented, and you deserve this job." Luke locked eyes with her so she could tell he was sincere, but he saw nothing but insecurity on her face. "Seriously, I might've had my doubts about you in the beginning, but you proved me wrong. I've done a lot of soul searching lately, and I completely believe that you can do this. I wouldn't have told them about you if I didn't believe in you. Now, it's time for you to believe in yourself and prove me right. Okay?"

"Okay, I'll try my best."

"Good," Luke said. Seeing the ounce of confidence shining in her eyes as she looked across the table at him, he knew he'd made the right decision. And he finally felt like the kind of brother someone would be proud to have.

Chapter 33

Aria

Aria shivered as the bitter wind burned her cheeks and froze her eyes. She pulled her gloved hand from her coat pocket and tugged her scarf up to her nose, thankful for all the accessories she now had to protect her from the cold. January had proven to be one of the coldest months on record, with temperatures rarely out of the single digits.

Warmth enveloped her as she stepped into the house, her wind-burned face aching from the abrupt temperature change. As she peeled off her layers of clothing, her heart filled with gratitude yet again. For as long as she could remember, her house had always been at the mercy of the outside temperatures. In the summer, the sweltering heat had turned their house into an oven, forcing them outside in search of a breeze. In the winter, water had frozen in a glass while they slept fully clothed and bundled in whatever extra fabric they could scrounge up. The luxury of wearing a T-shirt in the winter was something most people took for granted but not her. A heated home served as a glorious reminder of how far she and Ben had already come.

The oven clock showed 3:04 p.m. Ben would be home soon and proclaiming utter starvation. Aria scoured the cabinets for inspiration, the fact that she had options furthering her gratitude.

"Hmm. A day like today calls for soup," she said aloud as she gathered ingredients.

A thunderous knock at the door made her jump and spill egg noodles all over the counter. "Ugh, what a mess," she grumbled then yelled, "Coming!"

Upon seeing a police officer through the peephole, she yanked the door open, recoiling as an icy wind slapped her in the face.

"Aria Sutton?" The officer's face was grim and his tone flat, making Aria's heart sink.

"Yes, that's me. Officer..." Aria searched for a badge, but she found nothing but a bulky coat.

"Hibbens."

"Officer Hibbens. Please tell me this isn't about my brother." The room tilted as she wrung her hands.

The officer shook his head, but his face remained grim. "No, ma'am. It's not your brother."

Aria's hand flew to her chest. "Oh, thank God."

"Do you know a Tasha Sutton?" Officer Hibbens asked.

In an instant, Aria's relief vanished. "Yes, she's my mother." Aria's heart pounded in her ears as her mind raced with thoughts of her mom trying to take Ben away. *But she can't.* I'm his guardian now, she reminded herself.

The officer cleared his throat. "Ma'am, there's no easy way to say this. We believe your mother is deceased."

A rush of air escaped Aria's mouth as if someone had punched her in the stomach. "What? How? When?"

The officer's hard eyes softened. "Last night. Presumed hypothermia."

Her arm reached out as her knees threatened to buckle, and she gripped the table beside the door. Guilt coursed through her, and the blood drained from her face. As she had slept safe and sound in her warm, happy home, her mother had been freezing to death on the streets.

"Ma'am, are you all right?" Officer Hibbens stepped through the doorway with his arm outstretched as if to catch her.

Aria stared at nothing in particular. "I... She... I would've... I tried to help her. I just... I had to protect my brother."

"These things happen every year, especially in that area. I'm sure you did all you could."

Aria nodded, his words not reaching beyond her ears. "Yeah, I guess."

He took off his hat and gripped it in his hands. "I'm sorry, ma'am, but I'm going to need you to come with me and positively identify the body. There was no identification in the immediate area, and they can't get usable fingerprints. Some bystanders at the scene told us her name was Tasha Sutton, but she needs to be formally identified."

Numb from shock, Aria nodded as she stared at the brilliant snow beyond the window. "Can I call someone first? My little brother will be home soon, and he's expecting me to be here."

"Yes, ma'am." The officer moved toward the door, giving her space.

Aria pulled her phone from her pocket and dialed Luke's number. "Hey, can you cut your grocery shopping short? Something has come up, and I don't want Ben coming home to an empty house."

"What's wrong?" Luke asked.

"It's about my mom. I'll explain later." Aria sent out a silent plea to the universe for Luke to accept that and not ask any more questions.

"I just got to the checkout. I'll be there as soon as I can."

"Okay, great. I have soup started on the stove. Love you. Bye." She stared at the phone for a couple of seconds. It was the first time she'd used her phone for an emergency.

Walking into the morgue, Aria noted the stark contrasts to the scenes on television shows. Instead of being led into a cold gray room with a wall of body drawers, they led her into a cozy little office, much like that of a college professor. Instead of the weird smells of autopsies and formaldehyde, a mixture of pine cleaner and old paper greeted her nose. She started to ask Officer Hibbens what would happen next, but he'd already clicked the door shut, leaving her alone with her thoughts. She chewed her lip and took a seat as she scanned the room for something of interest to occupy her racing mind. The door creaked open, and she inhaled sharply. A short, plump man with snow-white hair entered and sat across the table from her. His white lab coat announced him to be the coroner, but he appeared better suited as a mall Santa.

He placed a photograph on the table in front of her, face down. "Take as long as you need." His round face held a tight smile and weary eyes fit for a man who spent his days in such grim situations.

Aria inhaled and exhaled, preparing herself to rip off the proverbial bandage. With a quivering hand, she flipped over the picture. She stared motionless at the paper, her brain struggling to process the image. Tasha appeared to be asleep, her ashen skin the only giveaway that her life was now extinguished.

Aria gave a small nod. "That's my mom."

"Tasha Sutton?" The coroner clarified.

"Yes, sir."

"I'm sorry for your loss, ma'am. I can direct you to a grief counselor if you'd like." The coroner's knowing eyes filled with genuine sorrow and compassion.

"Thank you, but that won't be necessary. Is that all I have to do?" A powerful urge to be out of that small room overwhelmed her. All at once, the air became stale and heavy as the walls drew closer by the second.

The coroner nodded. "Yes, ma'am. Officer Hibbens has your mother's personal belongings."

Aria bolted from the room, colliding with Officer Hibbens in the hallway. "Oh. Excuse me. I'm sorry. I..." She paused, at a loss for words to describe her feelings.

"That's all right. I understand." The officer gave her a kind, knowing pat on the shoulder then held up a bag with his other hand. "Here are your mother's things." When Aria made no motion to take the bag, he frowned. "Are you sure you're all right? Would you like me to give you a ride home?"

Aria moved her head side to side in what felt like slow motion, dragging her leaden arm up to reach for the bag. "No, that's okay. I can take the bus."

Officer Hibbens placed a firm hand on her shoulder. "I'm sorry for your loss." His heavy footsteps echoed in the hallway as he walked away.

Her mind a muddled mess, Aria bundled herself up and stepped out into the bitter chill. She clutched the bag to her chest as she wrapped her arms around herself and began walking home.

By the time she stepped into their driveway, the frigid temperature had worked its way through the puffy layers and numbed her entire body. Her feet refused to walk faster than a snail's pace, and her eyes burned with every blink. Her hand fumbled at the doorknob, unable to get a grip.

The door swung open, and Luke gasped as he pulled her into the house. "I heard the doorknob rattling. What happened to you? You're like an icicle." He peeled off her layers of winter gear, setting the bag on the entryway table without a second thought.

"I walked home," Aria mumbled as she stared at the floor.

"What? From where? Why? I could've picked you up." Luke led her to the couch and threw a thick blanket around her shoulders. He sat and pulled her toward him, rubbing his hands along her arms.

Ben stopped in the hallway, his face white and eyes wide.

"She'll be okay, Ben. She just needs to warm up. Can you get her those big fuzzy slippers?"

Ben darted down the hall, coming back seconds later with the shoes. As he bent and slipped the shoes on her feet, Aria patted the couch on the other side of her. "Ben, I need to tell you something. Sit down."

"What's wrong?" Ben sat as instructed, fear etched on his features.

"I don't know how to tell you this, but... earlier a cop came by and..." Her voice stuck in her throat as she longed for a way out of making her kid brother face yet another harsh reality.

"Did Mom go to jail again?"

Aria dragged her eyes from her hands to make eye contact with Ben. Luke's arm tightened around her shoulder in silent support.

Ben must have read the pain in her eyes because his voice quivered. "Did something happen to her? Is she hurt?"

Aria took a shuddering breath. "Mom is gone."

Ben's face contorted. "She's missing?"

Her eyes burned hot as she forced her mouth to form the words. "No, Mom died last night."

Ben's eyes grew large as the color drained from his face. "What happened?"

Aria took his warm hands into hers, her skin still icy. "They found her down by the bridge. She fell asleep and never woke up. It was just too cold."

"I'm so sorry," Luke said, leaning closer as if he could shield her from grief.

Ben took his hands from hers and stood, cradling his head with his hands. "I can't believe she's dead."

"I know. It was a shock to me too. Do you want to talk about it?"

"No." Ben's shoulders slumped, and he dropped his arms to his sides. "I want some soup."

Aria blinked at him. She must've misheard him. "Soup?"

"Yeah, the soup you made. I've been smelling it for an hour, and I can't stand it anymore. I'm starving." Ben strolled to the kitchen and got bowls from the cabinet. "You guys coming?"

Aria searched Luke's face for answers, but he shrugged and helped her to her feet. She watched Ben, studying him as he brought bowls to the table for everyone. On the exterior, he appeared normal, not like someone who had only seconds ago found out his mom had died. Perhaps he needed time to process it all. Maybe he was experiencing shock.

The soup warmed Aria from the inside, chasing the chill out of her bones. "This is perfect for this crazy cold weather."

"Weather no one should ever walk home in." Luke cast a sidelong glance in her direction.

"I know, I know. I needed alone time, and I didn't want to ride the bus full of strangers and risk small talk." She saw Luke open his mouth to speak and raised her hand. "I know you would've picked me up, but I didn't want to explain anything right then. Honestly, I couldn't. I needed time to process it. Besides, I'm fine. See?" She held up her hands and wiggled her fingers, displaying how their color had returned.

"I wonder if it hurts." Ben spoke into his bowl, his voice low and soft.

"If what hurts?" Aria studied him, trying but failing to read his emotions. His poker face had become strong.

"Freezing to death." His voice caught, betraying his calm façade.

Aria's heart shattered for him. "Oh, Ben, I..." She stopped, unsure of the answer to his question.

"I actually watched a documentary about that once," Luke said. When both Aria and Ben swiveled in his direction, he continued.

"They said it's pretty painless. You know how when you first go outside, it feels like the cold is stabbing you, but once you've been out there a while, you kind of get numb? Well, that initial shock is the worst part. You get to the numb stage, and then you get more numb. You kind of go to sleep. They say right at the end it feels like you're surrounded by warmth, and it's supposedly peaceful. Some people say it's the warmth of heaven."

Ben dropped his eyes to his hands and nodded. "I like that. I'm glad it's not painful."

"Me, too, bud," Aria said, giving his hand a squeeze. An image of the belongings bag popped into her mind's eye. "Oh, I forgot. The cop gave me a bag with Mom's stuff. Do you want to go through it with me? I'm not sure what we'll find. We can wait until later, if you want, or I can look first. It's up to you."

Ben eyed the bag on the table by the door. "Yeah, we can go through it now."

"Are you sure?" Aria didn't want to overwhelm Ben. Even with all he'd been through in life, he was still a child.

Ben gave a confident nod. "Yeah, I'm sure. If not, I'll think about it all night."

"I'll get it." Luke retrieved the bag, placing it on the table in front of Aria.

Aria took a deep breath, steadying her nerves and bracing herself for whatever she was about to dump out of the bag.

At first glance, the items that tumbled onto the table appeared anticlimactic. A belt, flip-flops, and a small dingy-green purse stared back at her.

"Not much," Ben said, surveying the items.

"No, it's not. Ready to look in the purse?" Aria picked up the handbag, the acrid smell burning her nose as she pulled the zipper open and dumped out the contents. Some loose change, a couple of hair ties, and random pieces of paper spilled onto the table. She picked up a photograph that had fallen face down, sucking in a breath when she saw the picture on the other side. Staring back at her was a sleepy little baby with a patch of blond hair. She held the picture out to Ben, her hand shaking.

"Who is this?" Ben frowned, studying the picture.

"That's you. That's your hospital picture." She gaped at the image in disbelief. "I didn't even know she had it. I didn't think they bought any."

Ben stared at the picture with renewed interest. "I was a cute baby, wasn't I?" He held the picture for Aria to see, but concern filled his face. "Are you okay? You look like you're going to puke."

Aria forced as cheerful a face she could manage, unwilling to burden him with her torment. "Yeah, I'm okay. I'm worn out from the cold and everything that happened today. I think I'm going to go to bed early, or at least go lie down."

"Okay." Ben hesitated, studying the picture in his hand. "Can I keep this?"

"Of course. You can keep anything you want."

Ben eyed the rest of the bag's contents. "That's okay. I think I'll just keep the picture."

Aria held the plastic bag at the edge of the table and dropped everything else back into it with a swipe of her arm.

"Aren't you going to keep anything?" Ben asked.

Aria stood and made her way to the trash can, dropping the bag inside. "Nah, there's nothing in there for me."

Chapter 34

Luke

Luke eased the door open, peering into the bedroom and finding Aria sitting on the bed, wide awake. He slipped into the room and shut the door behind him. "I thought you were going to sleep."

Aria hung her head, her chestnut hair obscuring her face. "I can't. Every time I close my eyes, I see her. Every blink is her picture. Even though I knew this day would come, it somehow still shocked me. And I don't even know how I should feel."

Luke eased down beside her and draped an arm behind her back. "I think you should feel however you feel. There's no right or wrong here."

Aria sprang from the bed and began pacing the room like a caged animal. "She was wearing a T-shirt and capris. In this weather. How out-of-her-mind high was she to not see something wrong with that? To not feel the bitter cold?" She stopped, bewilderment in her eyes. "While I was walking home earlier, I could feel myself starting to freeze. And that's with a long puffer coat, fleece leggings under my jeans, thick gloves, a hat under my coat hood, snow boots, and a giant scarf."

Luke shook his head, the cruel power of drugs never ceasing to amaze him.

She brought a hand to her cheek, still bright red from windburn. "I imagined myself in her shoes. I started beating myself up with all the would've, should've, could've crap. If I'd known she didn't have the coat that I gave her before we got evicted, I could've given her another one. I should've checked on her. But then I remember she would've sold or traded anything I gave her for drugs, so what's the point?" She plopped back onto the bed, dropping her face into her hands.

Luke leaned forward and rubbed her back, his heart searching for the right thing to say to ease her pain, if such words existed. "You can't help someone unless they want to help themselves. I know that sounds cliché, but it's true. Like you said, any help you'd given her, she would've turned right around and undid it. You tried your best."

Aria heaved a sigh and pulled her knees to her chest, her eyes brimming with tears. "You want to know the worst part of the whole mess? The worst part is, when I first heard the news, after the shock wore off, the first feeling I had was..." Aria paused as she choked back a sob.

Luke caressed her back some more, the gesture feeling inadequate at best. If only there was something more he could do. "Shh, it's okay. You can tell me anything. I won't judge you. Or don't tell me. It's entirely up to you. I'm here whenever and however you need me."

Aria buried her face. "You'll think I'm a monster."

He smoothed her hair and kissed the top of her head as he pulled her into his arms. "There is absolutely nothing you could say that would ever make me think you're a monster. Nothing you say could make me love you less. I promise. You're safe with me. All of you. The good, the bad, and the ugly. I'll be here through it all."

She took in a shaky breath. "The first feeling I had after shock was... relief. Relief that I could finally stop waiting for the inevitable, and I could stop worrying about her trying to take Ben. That we can all stop worrying about her horrible life decisions and move on with our lives. Relief that I can stop feeling guilty for not helping her more and she can't hurt us anymore. So much relief." She broke down in shuddering sobs as she curled into Luke's embrace. "I'm a monster."

Luke tightened his hold on her, needing her to know he wasn't going anywhere. "That's a very valid feeling when someone is such a negative force in your life. There's nothing wrong with you. And you're definitely not a monster."

Her eyes flooded with sorrow. "I mean, I'm sad too. It's sad when anyone dies. But I'm honestly not much more sad than I am when a stranger dies. If I ranked my feelings, relief would be number one, not sadness. Shouldn't I feel more grief than this? You were heartbroken about your mom. Why am I not heartbroken about mine?"

Luke smoothed her hair as she laid her head back against his chest. "Whatever you feel is exactly the way you should feel. Grief is complicated, remember? That's what you told me. Our moms were different people and played different roles. My mom was a bright spot in my childhood. I knew she loved me. You didn't have that kind of positivity with your mom. Sure, she was technically your mom, but how many times did she actually act like a mom?"

"I remember one time after Ben was born, before Dad killed himself. She gave Ben a bottle and was singing to him while he drank it, and I remember thinking that she actually acted like a real mom."

"Yeah, so only one time you remember her acting like a mom twelve years ago. That's sad. Tragic, honestly. And totally explains why you're not heartbroken."

"It still feels so wrong, though," she said, her voice barely above a whisper.

Luke lifted her chin so she could see his face, so she could see his sincerity. "It might feel wrong, but it's not. It's a problem with her, not you. Her actions led to you feeling like that. If she'd thought about something other than drugs all these years, you might feel differently. And I suspect Ben feels very similar to how you feel. I know he hides his feelings pretty well sometimes, but he didn't seem all that torn up about it. Think about all the things he's been through lately because of her. Would you blame him for feeling something other than sad?"

Aria snorted. "Ha. At least Mom halfway cared about Ben. It was his baby picture that she bought and actually hung on to. Not mine. Ben is twelve. After over a decade of her always selling and losing stuff, the one thing she managed to keep was a picture of her 'precious Benny.'" Aria made quotation marks in the air with her fingers as her lip curled in disgust. "I've never seen a single picture of me from my childhood."

Luke threaded his fingers through hers. "Like you said before, maybe you reminded her too much of your dad. Maybe that's why she didn't have your picture. Or they couldn't afford it. No matter the reason, though, it's not fair to you. You did everything for that woman from the time you were eleven. Probably even before that." Luke paused as he collected his thoughts. "You know what I think? I think deep down she felt guilty for you having to do everything for her and Ben. Guilt can make people crazy. Maybe she had to ignore you so she could ignore the guilt."

Aria rubbed her sleeve across her face. "Huh. I never thought of it that way before. That actually makes a lot of sense."

"I can be smart sometimes," Luke said as he nudged her with his elbow, hoping the playful gesture would lighten the mood.

It worked, bringing a smidgen of light back to Aria's face. "You're smart a lot."

"You think so?"

"You married me, didn't you?" Her sly grin brightened her eyes.

He kissed her forehead, elated to see the darkness dissipate from her face. "That I did."

"Bet you didn't expect all this drama when you picked us up that night." A twinge of regret crossed her face.

"Meh. I grew up next door. I know full well the drama that happens there, and I knew most of the drama you grew up with. Hell, I created some of it. And I picked you up because of drama, remember? What you call drama is just life. I knew life would happen." He cupped her cheek, caressing her smooth skin with his thumb. "What I absolutely did not expect, though, was that I would end up with a smart, strong, sexy wife and a great little brother-in-law. If you ask me, I struck a hell of a deal. I'll gladly live through the drama of life with you two. It's us against the world, right?" He leaned in, bringing his lips to hers in a soft kiss.

Aria wrapped her arms around his neck and rested her forehead on his. "I'm glad I have you in my corner. I don't know how I could've handled this without you."

He pulled back, gazing into those blue eyes so full of emotion. In their depths, he found her wounded soul, healing, but he suspected she was still afraid to let go and live. "You're strong enough that you would've pulled through it all without me, just the same. But I'm glad I was here to help you. And now Tasha can't hurt either of you anymore. You don't have to constantly worry about protecting Ben from her, and you can put all your energy into moving on with your life."

"It's so weird to think about not having that threat looming over my head. I'm not sure I know how to leave that behind."

He pulled her back into his embrace and kissed the top of her head. "You'll figure it out eventually. Maybe the old 'fake it until you make it' trick would work. You could act like the threat was never there so you can trick your brain into relaxing a bit. Pretend none of it ever happened."

"Pretend it never happened..."

Aria's voice held an odd tone that set Luke on edge for reasons he couldn't explain. It's her grief, he told himself. What else could it be?

Aria

"No, stop. Get off me!"

Aria's eyes flew open as she leapt out of bed. Luke mumbled behind her as she dashed out into the hall. She burst into Ben's room, slamming the door against the wall, her eyes scanning the dark room as her heart thundered in her ears.

At the loud thud of the door banging on the wall, Ben bolted upright in his bed, panting.

Seeing Ben safe in bed, Aria exhaled with a hand flying to her chest. "Oh, thank God. I thought you were being attacked."

Ben burst into tears and buried his face in his hands.

Aria rushed to his side, sitting on the bed and placing an arm around his shoulders. The dampness alarmed her. "Ben, you're soaking wet. And clammy. Do you have a fever?" She placed the back of her hand against his forehead. "You don't feel hot. Do you feel sick? What's wrong?"

Luke's frame blocked the glow from the hallway night-light as he entered the doorway, casting a shadow across the room.

"Can you bring a glass of water?" Aria asked Luke.

Luke disappeared without a word, reappearing moments later with the water. "I'll be in the hall if you need anything."

Ben took a sip of the water as he leaned into Aria. "I was having a nightmare."

Aria rubbed his back, relieved he wasn't sick. "Want to talk about it?"

Ben lowered his head. "Not really."

Aria struggled to hide the disappointment in her voice. "Okay, that's fine. Just know I'm here if you want to talk."

Ben let out a heavy sigh, one Aria recognized as weighed down with guilt. "I don't want to talk about it."

"I know. I'm not going to push," she said.

"But I think I need to. Even if it hurts."

Aria sucked in a breath, caught by surprise. "Oh. Okay, I'm ready when you are."

Ben sat silent, as if mustering his strength. "I was having a nightmare about Mom. I have them a lot, actually, but I didn't tell you because I didn't want you to worry more than you already do."

Aria squeezed his shoulders in a hug, touched by his concern. "Oh, Ben. Don't you worry about that. I worry about everything all the time anyway. In reality, you talking to me helps me worry less, even if we're talking about problems."

Ben stared down at his hands as he picked at a fingernail. "I know, I guess... I guess I feel guilty because..." Ben's voice caught, and he took a sip of water before continuing. "I never have happy dreams about Mom. It's always nightmares. It's always about all the bad things that happened. I had a hard time falling asleep tonight because I kept thinking about her."

"I understand. I had trouble falling asleep, too, because I was thinking about Mom and wishing things could've been different. It will get better as time goes on. It's all so raw right now." Aria hoped her words would ring true someday.

"I was trying to remember the good times with Mom so I could maybe help balance out the nightmares. The problem is, I—" His voice broke again.

Aria rubbed his back again, wishing for a better way to comfort him. "Shh. It's okay. I'm here for you."

"I couldn't think of any good times. Every time I thought of a happy memory, it was me and you. I don't have any happy memories with Mom." He hiccupped, on the cusp of sobbing.

Aria laid her head against his, knowing his grief all too well. "Me either."

Ben peeked up at her with shimmering eyes. "Really?"

Aria nodded as she gathered her courage. "I was actually talking to Luke about that before I went to sleep. I don't have happy memories of Mom either. In fact, while I'm sad she's gone, I'm also a little relieved because now the bad stuff with her will stop."

Ben gasped as he sat up straight. "You mean I'm not evil?"

"What? Of course you're not. Why would you think that?" She heard a *humph* from the hallway as soon as the words left her mouth.

"I felt like I was evil because I'm kind of glad I don't have to worry about all the bad stuff anymore."

Aria wrapped him in a hug. "I'm so glad you opened up to me. I have those exact same feelings. But Luke reminded me that there's no right or wrong way to grieve. The emotions are messy, and that's okay." They hugged in silence before Aria pulled back to see his face. "I wish you would've told me about the nightmares. Maybe I could've helped. I never heard you have them before, or I would've come."

"I know. I'll talk to you more in the future. Promise. Tonight was the worst I've had. I guess since I was thinking about memories so much. It was like all the bad stuff rolled into one." Ben's body trembled as he spoke.

"You're shaking." She rubbed his arm and found it covered in goose bumps. "Why don't you change into some dry clothes? Being soaked with sweat is going to make you chilly. I'll step out in the hall for a minute."

As the door clicked behind her, Aria locked eyes with Luke, who sat in the hallway outside the door. "Poor Ben. Did you know about the nightmares?"

Luke shook his head as he climbed to his feet. "Nope. Never heard him have any, and he never told me."

Aria hugged her arms around herself. "I can't imagine how alone he must've felt."

Luke's arms encased her in a cocoon of comfort. "Sounds like he's finally ready to open up."

"Yes, thank goodness."

Ben's door creaked open. "I'm done changing," he said then headed back to bed.

Aria let go of Luke and followed Ben. "Did you want to talk some more? Or did you want to see if you can get some sleep? I'm game, either way."

Ben twisted his sheet in his hands, staring down at them. "I'm super sleepy."

"Okay, that's fine. We can talk in the morning." Aria took a step toward the door.

"I don't want to be alone," Ben whispered.

Aria froze. "Do you want me to stay in here with you?"

Ben gave a small nod.

Despite the circumstances, a soft smile spread across Aria's face. The unruly, brooding teen who loomed over her by an inch had disappeared. She now witnessed the sweet little boy in cartoon pajamas who still existed hidden inside that hardened exterior. Ben hadn't wanted her to stay with him for years, and nothing would make her miss what very well could be her last opportunity.

"Okay, scoot over." Aria slid under the covers and laid her hand on Ben's, figuring a small touch might bring him comfort, a constant reminder of her presence. "I'm right here, Ben. Nothing bad will get you. I promise."

A yawn forced itself from Ben's mouth. "Thanks."

"Anytime, bud. I'm always here for you," she said then nodded over her shoulder for Luke to pull the door shut.

Chapter 35

Aria

Snow glistened under the bright sunshine, a trickle of water running along the sidewalk. The wind coursed through the buildings and along the riverfront, whipping Aria's hair against her face. She inhaled, the earthy scent of the river filling her nose as her eyes watered from the assault of light and wind. As she neared the edge of the water, she paused, taking in the beauty of the deep blue water in stark contrast to the glistening, snowy backdrop. Her lip quivered—such a picturesque view was unable to lift her heavy heart.

"Mom... I hope you can hear me wherever you are. I've been thinking a lot about where you might be. Honestly, I'm not sure if I believe in the afterlife, but I hope there is one so you can finally be free of your demons. I hope you broke the chains of addiction you weren't able to break during your time here on Earth. And I hope you can look down on me and 'your Benny' and see that we're okay now. We're going to be okay. We're happy. I wasn't sure what to do as far as burial and all. I tried to think of what you would've wanted." Her throat squeezed as she fought back tears. A gust of wind swept away the white billows of her shaky breath. "I decided you wouldn't want to be stuck in the ground, trapped forever in one spot. I remember, once when I was little, you talked about how much you liked rivers. You loved how rivers are constantly flowing, always changing, always a new adventure. You said you never step in the same river twice. So, if you're out there somewhere, I hope you like what I decided."

She moved the chilled metal urn around in her aching hands, the weight of it still surprising her. Then she waved a hand at Luke and

Ben waiting at the top of the stairs, letting them know they could join her.

Luke's warm, solid arm brought a welcome comfort across her back.

"Thanks for giving me a moment."

"Of course. You can have all the time you need." Luke inched closer and kissed the top of her head.

"Do you want some time alone, Ben?" Aria asked.

Ben shook his head without a word, his eyes avoiding the urn, instead focusing on the river.

"Shall we, then?" Sunlight glinted off the silver urn as she held it toward Ben.

Ben inhaled, filling his chest, then let the air rush out through his lips. "Yeah, I guess so."

Aria knelt down, her black pants doing little to shield her from the frigid concrete. She unsealed the lid and paused, squinting against the sun as she raised her face to Ben. "Do you want to help me pour them in, Ben?"

Ben shifted his weight from one foot to the other as he wrung his hands. Without saying a word, he dropped to his knees in front of Aria and extended a hand.

As they locked eyes, Aria gave him a small nod of approval. She'd witnessed so many changes occur in Ben over the past few months, all adding up to growth for the better. She made a mental note to tell him later how proud she was of the man he was becoming. She returned to the task at hand, and her eyes dropped to the urn as Ben's hand joined hers. Together, they tilted the unassuming silver vessel carrying their history.

A hot tear slipped down Aria's icy cheek as she watched her mother's ashes spill into the dark-blue water. "Be free of your demons and break the chains, Mom. Be free."

As Aria secured the lid back on the emptied container, Ben shot to his feet, slamming into Luke.

"Hey, you okay, man?" A concerned frown creased Luke's face.

"Yeah, I'm fine. I'm just freezing out here by the water," Ben said then bounded up the steps toward the bus.

Aria looped one arm through Luke's as she cradled the urn in the crook of her other arm. Together, they ascended the steps, following Ben at a much more somber pace. "I hope he's handling all of this okay." She chewed her lip and pressed herself against Luke as a gust of wind tugged at her coat.

"He will be okay. He has us to lean on if he needs it. I think he's eager to leave it all in the past."

Aria dropped her gaze to the steps before them, hoping for Luke's prediction about Ben to ring true. She understood the urge to leave it all behind. That had been her plan for as long as she could remember. Luke's words from the day her mom died echoed in her head. *Pretend none of it ever happened.* One thing that had become crystal clear, however, was that no one could ever truly leave their past behind. Her past was as much a part of her as her heart. The past made a person who they were, and she would learn as much from hers as she could to ensure that history would never repeat itself.

Never again would she allow herself to feel trapped, as she had for so many years as she struggled to survive in her mother's cruel world. Trapped by her duty to protect Ben from Tasha's bad decisions. By the uphill battle she faced every day as she fought to overcome her obstacles. And she would never, ever let anyone else be trapped by her. Even if letting them go would break her heart.

Chapter 36

Aria

Stuffing a thick stack of papers into her sock drawer, Aria slammed it shut and made her way to the living room. "Hey, guys. Have a good workout?"

Ben nodded as he handed Luke a glass of water. "Yeah, Luke taught me how to use all of the machines. He's so strong. You should've seen how much weight he lifted. It was like almost two of me."

Luke brushed the compliment away. "It wasn't that much. Maybe two of you before your growth spurt. You'll be lifting that much in no time if you stick with it. You're already doing great, especially as a newbie."

It had been two weeks since they'd said their final goodbye to Tasha, and Aria marveled at how easily Ben had moved on.

Pride shone in Ben's eyes under Luke's praise. "Is it okay if I shower first?"

Luke motioned toward the hallway. "Go ahead."

Aria watched Ben disappear into the bathroom as images of the paperwork in her drawer plagued her mind. "Hey, Luke, can I talk to you for a minute?"

"Of course."

"Let's go in the bedroom." Aria walked down the hallway before Luke could read her face, and she heard his footsteps behind her.

"Should I be worried?" Luke asked with a chuckle.

Aria didn't laugh as she closed the door behind him. "I want to start by thanking you for all you've done for me and Ben. You've helped us more than I could ever repay you."

Luke's features switched from joking to serious. "We've been through all of this a hundred times. You don't have to keep thanking me. We can move on."

"It's funny you mention moving on." Aria walked to the dresser and paused. "In the weeks since Mom died, I've done a lot of thinking, and one thing I keep coming back to is how you said I don't have to protect Ben from her anymore. You said I can finally move on with my life and pretend none of this ever happened."

A deep frown etched itself onto Luke's face. "I meant the stuff with your mom. To pretend all the traumatic stuff with her didn't happen. I didn't mean—"

Aria interrupted him, afraid she would lose her courage. "Throughout all of my reflecting on everything, my biggest takeaway is how trapped I've felt for all these years. Everything Mom did trapped me in one way or another. I couldn't run away because I had to protect Ben. I couldn't save money to get us both out of there because she always caused some kind of mess that ate up every dime I could scrounge up. Being trapped is the worst feeling in the world."

"You're not trapped anymore." Luke stood with his arms outstretched for her, but she took a step back.

"But you are. And the last thing I want is to make someone else feel as trapped as I felt." She opened the drawer and pulled out the stack of papers she'd hidden there. "I want to set you free. Without the threat of Tasha looming over our heads anymore, there's no reason for you to be stuck in a situation you didn't ask for. You deserve the chance to choose your own life."

"Aria, you're scaring me. What are you talking about?" Luke closed the distance between them, his eyes pleading.

"The only reason you married me was to help me protect Ben. You don't have to do that anymore. You can pretend it never happened and move on with your life. Follow the plan you'd set for yourself before we came and blew it all to hell." She held the papers out for him to take.

"What?" Luke's face reddened as he scanned the papers. "Divorce papers? Are you serious?"

"I know you said you love me and that you want this, but that was when you thought you had no other choice. You don't have to make the best of the situation anymore. I don't want you to be with me because you feel it's your duty or out of obligation. We can get a quick, painless divorce. It'll be like it never happened." She blinked back the tears that burned her eyes. She couldn't back down now. She had to do the right thing.

"Painless for who? Did you ever think to ask me about any of this?" He threw the papers on the bed.

"I knew if I asked, you'd never admit it if you wanted out of our deal. You're too nice and too afraid you'd hurt my feelings." Her heart shattered at the pain in Luke's eyes. *It's for the best.*

"Our deal?" Luke jabbed his hand through his hair. "Is that what you think of this? Of us? Because to me it felt like a hell of a lot more than a business deal, Aria. It felt real. How can you stand there and thank me for everything and call me a nice guy and then hand me divorce papers?" He picked the papers back up and shook them. "This is how you thank me? Did you even mean it when you said you loved me? You know what, don't answer that."

Tossing the papers at her feet, he grabbed his work uniform from the closet and stormed out of the room.

Aria chased after him, but when she got to the hallway, he was already slamming the front door shut behind him.

The bathroom door creaked open, and Ben stuck his head out. "What's going on? I thought I heard yelling and a door slamming."

"I think I messed up big time." Aria sank to the floor, wishing she could go back in time.

What have I done?

Chapter 37

Aria

Another yawn and another minute ticking by without a word from Luke. Aria rolled onto her side and checked her phone again. It had been twelve hours since he'd stormed out, and it was the longest twelve hours of her life. After dozens of unanswered phone calls, Aria wondered if he even planned to come home after work. She prayed he was safe, wherever he was.

The click of the front door unlocking made her sit up, and she listened to the sounds of Luke coming home from work. Relief washed over her, and she waited for the familiar thud of his footsteps down the hall. Instead, silence met her ears. She climbed out of bed and tiptoed down the hall. Her heart sank when she found Luke curled up on the couch, his back to her.

She inched closer and kept her voice low. "Hey, can we talk?"

Nothing.

Luke never fell asleep that fast after work, so that meant he was ignoring her. *Ouch.* She tried again. "I was hoping you'd let me apologize, and we could talk about everything. I didn't mean to hurt you. I swear."

"It was a long night. I'm tired." Luke's words came out flat.

Her head hung in defeat. "Okay, maybe tomorrow."

Sliding back into their bed alone, Aria pulled Luke's pillow into her arms and buried her face in it. "How could I be so stupid?" She didn't need the pillow to answer because she'd been berating herself all day. She'd let her mind convince her that a divorce was the only way to give Luke the future he wanted. To give him freedom. In the end, all she'd managed was to break his heart.

Luke

Clutching a coffee cup in his hands, Luke shuffled back to the couch and sank down with a yawn. Waking up with the sun after not falling asleep until well after midnight wasn't at the top of his list of pleasant mornings, yet there he was. But as much as he longed for the darkness of the bedroom, he couldn't bring himself to go in. As tempting as it was to sleep for hours with Aria's soft body curled up against his, he couldn't shake off the hurt from what she'd done. *A divorce?* He thought she knew him better than that by now, and he thought he knew her better too. *I guess I was wrong.*

His stomach growled, and he peeked behind him at the clock on the oven. If he was going to be up so early, he might as well take advantage of the extra time. After downing the rest of his coffee, he made his way to the kitchen and gathered ingredients for French toast.

Like clockwork, as soon as the food was done, Ben's door opened. Luke set a plate at Ben's usual seat as he came into the kitchen.

"Thanks. I hope this tastes as good as it smells," Ben said before taking a forkful and shoving it in his mouth. He chewed then gave a thumbs-up.

"I'm glad you like it." Luke chuckled as he sat down with his own plate. Even one of his favorite breakfasts couldn't lift his spirits. He wondered how much Ben knew about what had happened the day before. And whether Aria had been as upset as Luke was. Before he could investigate, Aria came into the kitchen. Her black pencil skirt and deep-emerald blouse kicked his pulse up a notch, and he almost forgot he was mad at her. Almost.

"Hey, guys." Her eyes flicked over Luke as if eye contact with him would make her burst into flames, and then her sights settled on Ben. "Do you have all of your stuff ready for school?"

"Why are you so fancy?" Ben asked, his mouth full of food.

Aria crossed her arms over her chest. "First of all, don't talk with your mouth full. It's gross. Second, I have to interview the president of the college for the school paper. Remember? I have to leave early, so I won't be here when you leave for school."

Ben swallowed his food before talking. "I can get myself ready."

"I know, I know." Aria's hands went up in surrender. "You're not a baby. Just make sure you watch the clock so you don't miss the bus. And on that note, I better go before I miss mine."

On instinct, Luke stood, ready to give Aria her kiss goodbye, but then he froze. She made eye contact with him this time, her eyes full of sorrow and trepidation. Instead of giving in to routine, he cleared his throat and took his plate to the sink. "Good luck with your interview."

"Thanks."

The pain and hesitation in her voice squeezed his heart, but images of her handing him divorce papers replayed in his brain. She walked behind him to grab a bagel to go, and his body ached for the familiar comfort of her hand touching his back in passing. He pretended to scrub his plate as he listened to her put on her shoes and gather her things, his heart breaking with every sound. When the door shut behind her, he dropped his plate and poured himself another cup of coffee.

How am I going to survive this? His heart wanted to forgive and forget, to go back to the way things were. Back to when their marriage felt real and his heart hadn't been pulverized. If only he could get his brain on board.

Chapter 38

Aria

The soft chiffon glided over Aria's skin as she slipped into her wedding dress. Her hands shook as she secured the silver clip in her hair and draped the pearl pendant around her neck. Stepping back from the mirror, she took in the full view of herself and swallowed.

After a week of tension and few words between her and Luke, her imagination ran through a dozen scenarios for how he would react to what she'd done, each subsequent version worse than the one before. Her plan could very well end in complete disaster. She could end up in bed, curled in the fetal position and bawling her eyes out. But she had to try. Mother Nature had flipped the switch to spring at the exact moment when Aria needed it most, which she decided to take as a sign from the universe that she was on the right track. One good thing that had come from a week of torment was that she'd finally figured out what she truly wanted in life, what mattered most to her.

Love.

Love had served as the driving force behind all the changes that had occurred in her life and within her soul. Her love for Ben had kept her focused and determined all these years when it would've been so easy to give up. Her love for the written word kept her motivated in college, even though dropping out would've made her life much simpler. Luke's love helped heal her heart in ways she hadn't realized it needed. Love became the golden glue that allowed her to use the pieces of her broken home to build a safe, happy home. Love helped her overcome the obstacles in her life so far and allowed her to be confident in her future. And she didn't want a future without Luke.

The pain on Luke's face when she'd handed him the divorce papers flashed in her mind for the millionth time. As much as she had always felt unlovable, that man loved her. Her eyes—and heart—were finally open to the truth. He wanted a future with her. He had told her as much countless times, if only she'd had the courage to listen. All along she'd been unfairly projecting her insecurities onto Luke. But she'd realized over the past few days, after seeing him so despondent, that just as his love had lifted her from darkness, perhaps she had done the same for him. When she had tried to set him free from the trap she thought she'd created, he hadn't gone anywhere. Instead, she'd found the divorce papers ripped in half in the trash can. *Love isn't a trap.* And that gave her hope that her mistake could still be forgiven.

Aria gave her reflection a curt nod and squared her shoulders. Holding her head high, she stepped out of the bedroom and marched into the kitchen.

Luke looked up from his coffee and newspaper, and his mouth fell open. "What are you doing? Why are you wearing that?"

"Because we're going to get married." Her fake confidence faltered, and she clutched her skirt to keep her hands from trembling.

"What are you talking about?"

She closed the distance between them and took his hands in hers, bringing him to his feet. Her stomach clenched as his bewildered eyes met hers. "I generally like to think of myself as a smart person, but six days ago I made the stupidest mistake of my life. I let grief and fear take over and ruin the best, most serendipitous thing that's ever happened to me. You. The truth is, I wanted nothing more than to stay married to you. But I couldn't make myself believe that you'd want to be married to me. Even though we didn't set out for this to be real, you were right when you said it felt real. The love was real, and it was so beautiful it scared me. I'm so sorry for hurting you. I love you, Luke, and I mean that with everything I am. And this is me pleading for a chance to fix this mess I've created."

Aria's heartbeat thundered in her ears as she searched his eyes for something, anything, hinting at his feelings. His silence seemed to stretch on for hours, though the ticking of the clock signaled mere seconds passing.

Finally, Luke's mouth curved into his sexy lopsided grin, and his hand cupped her cheek. "This past week was nothing but pure torture. I couldn't stop loving you no matter how hard I tried."

Tears filled Aria's eyes and she let out a half sob, half laugh. "Really?"

Luke nodded and brought his mouth to hers in a tender kiss. Aria wrapped her arms around his neck, pulling him closer as she deepened the kiss, relishing the feel of his strong shoulders beneath her arms. It had been far too long since her body had pressed up against his, and she never wanted to be without it again.

After a moment, she pulled away, panting. "We better stop if we're going to make it on time."

"On time for what?"

"You'll see."

Luke

"Can I take off the blindfold yet?" Luke asked as the cab hit a pothole.

"Not yet." Aria's hands adjusted his tie as she spoke, then she leaned in and whispered in his ear, "Did I ever tell you how tantalizing you are in this suit?"

Luke grinned like a fool toward the sound of her voice. "No, I don't believe you have."

Before she could say another word, the car rolled to a stop.

"We're here," she said as a door opened. She took his hands and led him out of the cab.

Birds chirped overhead, and the scent of damp earth greeted Luke as he followed her off the concrete sidewalk and onto a gravel path crunching under their feet. The early-spring sunshine beat down, taking the bite out of the chilly breeze. They came to a stop, and Aria reached up and slipped the blindfold off.

Blinking against the sudden brightness, it took a moment for Luke's eyes to adjust. When they did, he saw a wooden trellis draped with ivory tulle nestled under a redbud tree with pink flowers starting to emerge. Chrissy stood to the left in a pale-blue-and-ivory dress while Ben stood to the right in a navy suit matching Luke's. A man Luke didn't know but who looked suspiciously the way Aria had described her beloved Professor Lawson stood just beyond the trellis.

"What is all of this?" Luke found Aria's eyes shimmering up at him.

"Our wedding. I know it's not a lavish celebrity-style wedding, but it's better than the musty courthouse. We have everyone who's important to us right here, and we will do it right this time."

"It's perfect." He swallowed against the lump of emotion forming in his throat. "You're perfect."

"Ben is taking pictures with his new camera, too, so we'll have real wedding pictures." She motioned to the camera on a tripod beside them, and Ben held up a remote clicker. Then she stepped in front of Luke and took both his hands in hers. "I ordered a custom cake from the Gilded Lilly for us to pick up after the ceremony, and then we are going on a real honeymoon."

"What?" He couldn't believe his ears.

"I booked a room at a bed-and-breakfast on a lake outside of the city. It's too cold for swimming, but the views are gorgeous. And very romantic." She gave him a wink that made his stomach flutter.

"What about Ben?"

She cocked her head toward Chrissy over her shoulder. "Chrissy is going to stay with him this weekend. Ben will always be important to me, but I think it's time I start listening to everyone around me and take some time to focus on what makes me happy. What I want in life." She threaded her arms around his waist. "And what I want in my life is to be with you."

"Aria, I don't know to say." She'd planned out not only a wedding but also a honeymoon. For him.

"Say you'll marry me."

"I'd love nothing more."

Aria stepped to Luke's side and slipped her arm through his then led him to the trellis. In that moment, it was as if every piece of his broken life slid into place. Years of fighting for more out of life had led him to this place with people he loved. Gazing down at the woman of his dreams, her wedding dress glowing in the spring sunshine, he knew a future with her was a future worth fighting for.

Epilogue
Ten Years Later

Aria's pulse thundered in her ears as she studied the program in front of her for the umpteenth time.

"And now, for the moment you've all been waiting for. The American Journalism Association is honored to present our Excellence in Journalism award to Dr. Aria Sutton-Hardin." The announcer and audience clapped as Aria stood, knees wobbly as a newborn calf, and began weaving her way to the stage.

Her heart and stomach fluttered at odds with each other, competing for attention. Her sleek black dress clung to her skin as she carefully ascended the stairs, lacking confidence in her ability to remain steady in heels. *Why did I decide to dust off my one pair of heels tonight, of all nights?* The continued applause answered her rhetorical question. Oh right, she wanted to be fancy for the biggest occasion of her career and possibly the greatest highlight of her life she'd ever have.

Safely on the stage, she took a deep breath, trying to return her heart to a normal rhythm and quell the storm of butterflies in her belly. *Please don't puke. Please don't puke,* she chanted to herself as she approached the podium.

The president of the American Journalism Association held out a plaque and extended his hand with a nod. She placed one hand on the plaque and shook his hand with the other. The president turned toward a photographer, and Aria mirrored his motions, smiling for the camera as she struggled to contain her panic. The dim, moody lighting helped shroud the sea of people a tiny bit, but she much preferred being behind the scenes to being in the spotlight. Instead of focusing on the photographer, her eyes wandered several feet past him, and in an instant, her panic quieted.

Luke beamed back at her, as handsome as ever in his tuxedo and his face bursting with pride. Even after ten years of marriage, the sight of him in a suit still took her breath away. Beside him, Ben held up a camera. No doubt he would make sure the magazine he worked for would run a story on her award. After a few pictures, he lowered the camera and reached for the hand of his partner, Richard. Richard wiggled the fingers on his other hand in a wave to Aria. Her heart swelled seeing her brother finally happy and at peace with his true self.

In fact, for once in her life, all her loved ones were at peace. Chrissy just landed her third gallery exhibit and had her name on murals all over the city. Above all else, she continued winning her battle against her demons, one day at a time.

Luke's position on the tourism board provided him with a predictable day-shift schedule, which was a blessing when little Emma came along. Their beautiful gift from heaven, with dark, bouncy curls and eyes like the spring sky, brought more joy and energy than Aria had ever thought possible. She suppressed a giggle at the mental image of an exhausted Aunt Chrissy after babysitting the toddler all evening, when she gave Luke and Aria the gift of a rare night out.

As Aria floated on cloud nine back to her seat, she realized no broken pieces remained around her joyful heart. Her painful past and once-broken home had become merely a small piece of the foundation for this new life built by love.

Acknowledgments

This book would not have been possible without the love and support of my wonderful husband, Dustin. Thank you for always supporting my dreams, no matter where they take me. In the moments when I felt like giving up, you refused to let me. When the "mom guilt" ate away at my soul, you assured me that our kids were perfectly fine and happy. Also, to my kids, Bella and Levi, thank you for being as understanding as possible when Mom suddenly had work outside of being your mom.

I must also thank my mom, Roberta, for fostering the love for reading that led me to this point. From the moment you bought that ChildCraft encyclopedia set, you set me on this path. You never said no when I asked for money for book fairs and never discouraged my endless circling of books in the book flyers. I also may or may not have snuck some of your romance books in my teens, which made me fall in love with happily ever afters.

Thank you to my best friend, Chelley, for always being my overly optimistic cheerleader. Your abundant confidence in me and my abilities buoyed my spirits time and time again. Thank you for reading all the things and always making me laugh. My perfectionism and self-doubt never stood a chance against you.

Several others helped me cross the finish line, and I appreciate you all. Thank you, Emily, for reading through the manuscript and discussing all things writing. The Moms Who Write Facebook group provided much support and advice. You ladies are amazing. Being part of such a wonderful community has been such a blessing. I wouldn't be where I am today without the encouragement and support of my fellow authors. I'm beyond grateful for the advice and friendship of Kerry Savage, Barbara Conrey, Katie Mettner, Laura Kemp, Michelle Morhaime, and Kerry Evelyn, just to name a few.

To those who helped shape my story, I am forever grateful. I'm indebted to my wonderful content editor, Rashida, who endured my type A personality like the true professional she is and helped shape this story into the best version of itself. I must thank my line editor, Darlene, for helping polish this manuscript until it shone. Many thanks to my mentor, Erica, for her patience and guidance throughout the publication process. And lastly, a huge thank-you to Lynn for believing in me and my writing. I'm honored to be part of the Red Adept Publishing family.

About the Author

Twila Mason has been writing her own stories since she learned how to read. She is a writer of romance, women's fiction, poetry, and short stories. Her work explores raw emotions and the complexities of life while finding hope within every obstacle.

She lives the rural, small-town life in Missouri with her husband, two kids, and menagerie of animals. After obtaining a PhD in Cell and Developmental Biology, she's switching gears to follow her life-long dream of putting her fictional stories out into the world. When she's not reading or writing, Twila can be found crafting, farming, doing home improvement projects, or going on adventures with her kids.

Read more at https://www.twilamason.com/.

About the Publisher

Dear Reader,

We hope you enjoyed this book. Please consider leaving a review on your favorite book site.

Visit https://RedAdeptPublishing.com to see our entire catalogue.

Check out our app for short stories, articles, and interviews. You'll also be notified of future releases and special sales.